Easy Tiger

PRICKLE ISLAND ZOO
BOOK TWO

ALI K. MULFORD

ISBN: 978-1-923184-03-9 (ebook)

ISBN: 978-1-923184-04-6 (Paperback)

Cover: Yummy Book Covers

Map: Holly Dunn Designs

Interior formatting: K. Elle Morrison

Easy Tiger

Ali K. Mulford

To all of the animals who've left their permanent mark on my heart (and the few that have left their permanent bite marks on my body… I'm looking at you Jasper)

Note for readers: This book contains themes of parent loss, injury, heart attack, and animal death (old age/ non-violent), as well as sexually explicit scenes

PRICKLE ISLAND
• ZOO •
KEY
TOILETS
FOOD
SHOPPING
FREE WIFI
GIFT SHOP + ENTRY
ENTRY
CAFÉ
VET HOSPITAL
PLAYGROUND
REPTILE HOUSE
THE PECKISH PEACOCK
SAVANNAH
AVIARY
BABOONS

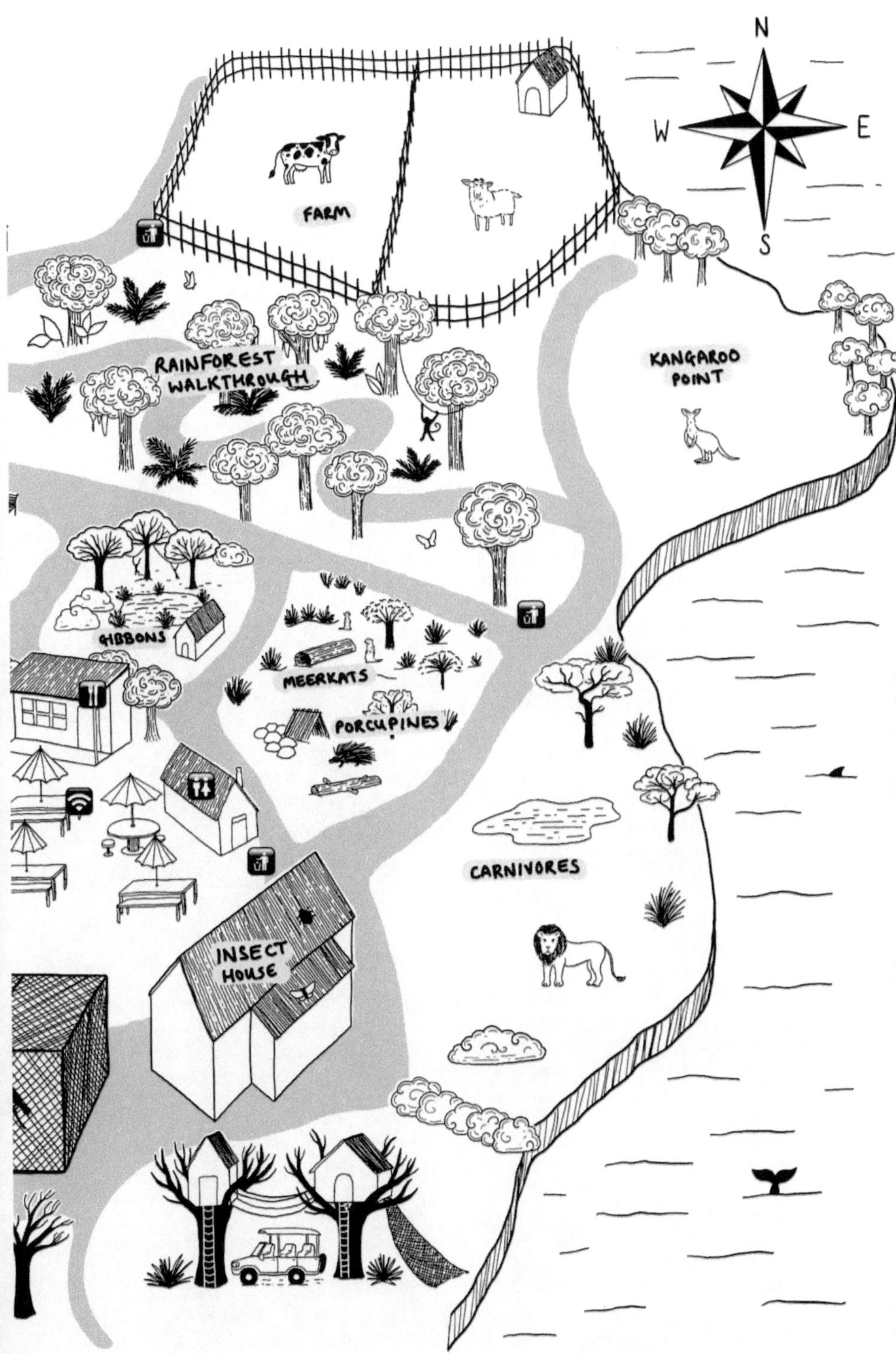

N
W
S
E
FARM
RAINFOREST WALKTHROUGH
KANGAROO POINT
GIBBONS
MEERKATS
PORCUPINES
CARNIVORES
INSECT HOUSE

MEET THE ZOO TEAM

Evelyn Lachlan (she/her) CEO of Prickle Island Zoo

Hawk Lachlan (he/him) Carnivore Keeper

Lark Lachlan (she/her) Primate Keeper

Finch Lachlan (she/her) Head Veterinarian

Dove Lachlan (she/her) Birds Keeper

Heron Lachlan (they/he) Hoofstock Keeper

Crane Lachlan (he/him) Reptiles and Inverts

Wren Lachlan (she/her) Farm Animals

Aya (she/her) Food Prep Manager

Mateo (he/him) Gift Shop Manager

HAWK'S JEEP
ISLAND ZOO

Chapter One

Hawk

I clanged my metal water bottle against the steel railing.

"Ladies! Let's go!" I called up the stairwell, shouting to be heard over the chorus of lemurs just beyond the window.

No amount of animal noise could wake one of us up.

I debated pouring a bucket of water on my sisters' faces to get them out of bed. After all, the floors in our house did have drains in them since this was once a capuchin monkey enclosure. Maybe I could just hose them out of bed . . .

The lions were already roaring for their breakfast, their early morning impatience matching my own. The gibbons had been whooping since four a.m., and at five a.m., I'd finally admitted to myself that I was too awake to sleep another half hour until my alarm rang.

Such was the life of a zookeeper, waking up before the

sun. But the hardest animals in the entire zoo to wrangle were my six younger siblings, well, five now that Lark had moved to New Zealand with her Kiwi boyfriend. Since Lark left, I'd taken up the mantle of most stressed-out sibling. We had one week until the first day of summer, and I was going to have a nervous breakdown if everything wasn't perfect.

"I hate you," Finch grumbled, stumbling down the grate stairs in a sports bra and baggy scrub pants. She rubbed the palm of her tattooed hand in her eye socket. "And if you call me *lady* again, Hawk, I'm going to swap Pippin's castration surgery today for yours."

"Good morning to you too," I said, taking another bracing sip of too-strong bean water. "Eggs are ready. Coffee's made."

Finch yanked on her Prickle Island Zoo-branded shirt, covering half of her tatted arms. She blinked at me, cocking her head like a curious lorikeet. "Eggs? Coffee? Who are you and what have you done with Hawk?"

I shrugged, ignoring the jab. "It's the first day of summer next week. The front-of-house staff will be arriving tomorrow and the volunteers soon after. I just want to make sure everything is right."

Finch folded her arms. "This is about the Westworths' ultimatum, isn't it?"

My gut plummeted even at their name. We had until the end of summer to prove that Prickle Island Zoo was financially successful enough to support itself without our long-time, wealthy benefactors. If we didn't, the Westworths would sell the zoo my ancestors built to another rich patron instead of giving it to us like they had promised my father before he died.

It all came down to these next three months.

"Everything hinges on this summer," I said, sculling back

another cup of black coffee before Finch reached out and yanked the mug from my shaking hands.

"I don't know," Dove said, stumbling down the stairwell. Her lavender-tipped brunette hair was tied up in a messy bun, her wire-rim glasses askew. "I think we need a miracle to make them leave the zoo to us now. We're nowhere near our target numbers."

"We can make it," I pushed. "We just need one good summer."

"One amazing, once-in-a-million-years summer," Finch pointed out, but then she softened slightly and added, "We'll do everything we can, Hawky Puck. Even if the Westworths sell the zoo to someone else, that doesn't mean our family can't buy it from them one day either."

Finch and Dove took their regular places at the kitchen island, grumbling morning greetings between each other. I perched on a barstool beside them, already in my khaki uniform. Even on my days off, I usually wore it. Saved me having to buy a wardrobe . . . not that I left the zoo for more than a trip to our local bar anyway.

I pulled out my phone and scrolled over one of the spreadsheets Lark insisted on sending me. It took me three cups of coffee to make heads or tails of it though.

"Please tell me you're not becoming the new Lark?" Dove asked, eyeing the spreadsheets. "You already have barely any chill."

"We don't need *chill* this summer," I countered.

"Aww. . ." Finch grabbed me by the shoulder and jostled me to and fro. "You're making me miss Lars." She pulled out her phone. "I wonder if she's up. What time is it in New Zealand?"

Lark was the third-born in our family after me and Finch. It had taken a lot to convince her to build the life she wanted elsewhere, but I was proud of her for doing so. This was only the sort of job you did if every cell in your body told you there was nothing else. And this was my legacy, realizing my father's dream to keep this zoo running for generations to come.

"I need you to come check on Guava today." Dove snatched a piece of toast off Finch's plate. Finch let out a little snarl and snapped at her hand like a hungry Tasmanian devil, but Dove extracted the toast with all digits intact. "Her shed is all weird and she might need help. I think we need to change her diet."

"I've got that dental on Loki this morning, but I'll come in the afternoon," Finch said, swigging back her coffee. "And Pippin's castration. Write it on the whiteboard in the prep kitchens so I don't forget. Email it to me too, just to be safe."

With scrawling animal tattoos from just below her jaw all the way down to her knuckles, Finch looked more like she should be at a tattoo and piercing convention than the operating table of a zoo. Though, at only twenty-nine, Finch was one of the most preeminent wildlife veterinarians in the state. The zoo's owners (and our de facto bosses), however, had feelings about the tattoos. Lately, I'd been making Finch wear long sleeves and surgical gloves whenever they visited. The last thing we needed was for them to give the zoo to someone else just because of my sister's tattoos that Mrs. Westworth had once called "unsavory."

"I just don't get it. If they were going to leave the zoo to Dad, why won't they just leave it to Mom instead?" Dove frowned into her coffee mug. "This is *our* family's zoo. *Our* great-great-grandfather founded it."

"*Founded* it is one way to say he introduced a bunch of porcupines to a private island," Finch muttered.

"It turned into a respectable zoo in the end." Dove huffed.

"With the money from the Westworth family," I reminded from across the table, tucking my pen behind my ear. "They own this zoo. And if they want to level this place and turn it into a tennis club tomorrow, they can."

"All of our family is buried here." Dove gestured wildly out the window and up the hill to where our family home sat. Mom and the rest of my younger siblings still lived up there in the old country house, our father's grave the freshest amongst the family plot that sat beside a willow tree twisted sideways by the ocean winds. "What will happen to them if someone else owns the zoo?"

"Well," I said with a sigh, turning and draping my elbow over the back of the chair. "They might let us stay and run the place . . . or they might make us leave and turn this place into a parking lot for their sailboats, in which case we could exhume the coffins and organize them to be reburied in a plot on the mainland, which in and of itself would be very expensive."

Finch yawned and refilled her mug. "Please tell me you don't already have a quote for that."

"I'm just trying to be prepared," I said lightly. "And it was Lark who already found a quote."

Dove snorted. "Of course she did."

"We *will* keep this place," I insisted. "We just have to prove to the Westworths that we are the best and most capable owners of the zoo. Maybe build another statue to them, play up their importance and all that."

Just as the words came out of my mouth, Crane and Heron rumbled in through the back door, a squawk ringing out as their pet macaw, Viago, flew into the room and perched on the back of the bar chair. Matilda, our resident boa constrictor, circled Crane's neck.

"You were saying something about us being capable?" Finch smirked around the rim of her coffee mug.

"I was *saying*," I growled, "that we need to be on our *best* behavior this summer."

I eyed my siblings—identical twins that I thought looked nothing alike and yet everyone outside of our family ended up confusing them. I should lock them in with the monkeys for the remainder of the summer. They'd just turned twenty a couple weeks ago and still acted more like they were thirteen when they were together. I was eleven years older than them, had practically raised them, and they'd always be kids to me.

"No messing around. Understand? It's important."

Heron held a piece of toast in their mouth, bending down for Viago to reach up and nibble at it. "Duh," they said through the mouthful.

Finch chuckled. "What you're doing right now would be considered *messing around*, Ronny."

"I am feeding the animals," Heron said, rolling their eyes. "That's what a good keeper does."

Finch gave them a light smack on the back of their head. "Most keepers don't feed their pets with their own fucking mouths."

"It's enrichment," Heron said.

Finch smacked a hand to her forehead. "You can't just do whatever you want and call it enrichment."

Heron shrugged. "That's what I'll say when the Westworths arrive."

"When the Westworths arrive, you two"—I cut off my bickering siblings and pointed between the twins—"will be helping Aya in the prep kitchens and will stay there for the remainder of their visit." They opened their mouths to protest, and I held up a hand. "Before opening hours and after closing, you can go wherever you like, but you are to stay behind the scenes during visitor hours. The Westworths will be watching us closely this summer."

The line of radios behind us crackled to life, and we all instinctively dropped our hands to our hips even though none were on our belts yet.

"I can see the ferry boat," Mom's voice called. "Is Hawk on his way down to pick up the fruit crates?"

Finch was the first to grab her radio. "If you're making this call, Mom, you already know he isn't."

"I sent the twins down to tell him," she said.

All eyes turned to Heron and Crane.

"Oh right," Crane said with a smug smile. "Uh. The ferry's here."

"Great, thanks for the warning." I reached for Finch's refilled coffee and swiped it before she could swat my hand away. Lifting it in cheers to her, I grabbed the truck keys off the magnetic hooks by the boot rack and headed out the door.

Today was going to be a five-coffee type of morning. We had work to do and a zoo to save.

Whale hello there
PRICKLE ISLAND ZOO

Chapter Two

Hannah

Mom frowned down at the skillet as she turned up the burner. "What if you ever need to move back in?"

"I won't, Mom," I sang as I fiddled with a strand of hair. How many times had we had this same argument? It always seemed to transpire in the kitchen during Pancake Friday. "I'm twenty-eight. I've had my own place for a long time now."

"And?" Mom balked.

"And I will find a way to make it work," I insisted.

"But you're going to quit the *Gazette* still, aren't you?" Mom's eyebrows pinched together. If worrying were an Olympic sport, Rebecca Murphy would win gold every time. "You've got to leave that job, Hannah. It's sucking out your soul."

"*Mom.*" We'd had this conversation so many times before. "It's not sucking out my soul. Dramatic much? But yes, I'm quitting."

Mom flopped a dish towel over her shoulder and returned to flipping pancakes in her cast-iron skillet. She wore her regular uniform of linen overalls, a black turtleneck, and enough jewelry to add twenty pounds to her lean frame. Her hair was messily collected atop her head in a silver bun, and she blew a stray lock off her face every few minutes rather than sweeping it back. "When?" she called over her shoulder.

"Soon."

"*Hannah.*" Mom parroted back my own mocking tone. Great, neither one of us was going to be an adult about this.

"Soon, Mom." I rubbed an exasperated hand down my face. "It's time for you to get that apartment in town. I won't be moving back, I promise."

"Fine," Mom said, fishing for another pot from under the stove. "The day you show me you can keep more than three figures in your savings account is the day I'll put this house up for sale."

"You just told me to quit my job!" I blustered.

"And find one that doesn't crush your soul. And pays better than just per article," she added with a wink. "Maybe something with benefits?"

"Not all of us can make it as professional artists, Mom," I said. "Maybe switching jobs every three months is the best I can do."

Thanks, ADHD.

When I got bored of something, I got "can't summon the will to get out of bed, would rather gnaw off my arms than do one more day at work" kind of bored. And then I'd hop to the next harebrained idea of what I should do for a career. I'd fallen into this job like the dozen others I had before it: bartender, receptionist, cashier, dog walker . . . Data entry was probably the worst. The one thing my dopamine-seeking brain loathed was monotony. It was on a whim that I'd submitted a few articles to the *Shoreline Gazette,* and honestly part of it was imagining myself cosplaying as Lois Lane while some sexy news reporter turned superhero swept me off my feet. Instead, I got picked up by a gossip column pretending to be a legitimate newspaper.

I'd been at the *Gazette* for three months and already my mom saw it coming: the boredom.

"You'll find the right job one day, honey," she insisted. "One that keeps you interested. One with lots of novelty and excitement. Until then, I'll keep this house as a backup plan. I don't want to blow all my retirement money in case you need it."

I hated the way she acted like spending her retirement the way she'd always dreamed was selfish. I hated even more that I was the only thing holding her back.

"Seriously?" I groused.

"Seriously." My mother set the skillet back on the burner with a louder clang than was necessary. Her many bracelets and bangles jangled around with it, her chunky turquoise and silver earrings tinkling like wind chimes with every turn of her head.

"Fine."

"Fine."

Just in case I needed any more reminders that my mother and I were cut from the same cloth . . . there it was. Chronically stubborn.

The houses all around ours were being torn down and beautiful, expensive houses rebuilt as the area gentrified. Mom had flyers in her mailbox every other day asking if she wanted to sell. This house would pay for her to have a very nice retirement apartment downtown.

Mom had me when she was forty-five, but she was the youngest seventy-three-year-old that I knew. Still, at some point, she knew she'd have to shut down her studio. I knew as long as she could hold a brush, she'd never stop painting, but the running of a whole shop—classes, auctions, events—it had just become too much. Luckily, there was a downtown café that had offered to sell Mom's paintings for a little income boost if she closed her studio. All the more reason for Mom to live in town. We'd get her a cute little artist's loft that she could splatter with paint, and she'd enjoy her retirement like the whacky creative she was. It was the life she'd always dreamed of. She was an artist for crying out loud, not a white-picket-fence sort of gal. But I knew she held onto the house for me, always putting my needs first, just in case her only child ever needed a house to move back into.

I hopped off the kitchen stool, snatching a steaming hot pancake off the plate beside Mom.

She waved her spatula at me. "You know I'm so proud of you, don't you?"

I hid my grimace. There was nothing to be proud of. I had no money, fair-weather friends, a job I hated, no love interests despite being pansexual and having a dating pool of literally every single adult in town, *and* my rent was astronomical. I lived in an apartment that Stuart Little would call *cozy*, and I was on the precipice of needing to move back into the very home I was trying to convince my mother to sell.

"Get ready for that bank account statement, Mom," I said to her pointedly, all bravado with no plan on how I would piece together that money. "Goodbye house, hello retirement."

Whale hello there
PORCUPINE ISLAND ZOO

Chapter Three

Hannah

"You can do it."

"I *can't* do it, Mom!" I hissed into the phone, twirling the cord around my fingers. This beige phone was probably older than me.

"You march into Dawn's office and tell her you quit!" My mother shouted down the line so loudly, I had to cover the earpiece. "You do not want to be a gossip columnist!"

"The *Shoreline Gazette* is the eighth most prominent news-paper in all of New Haven," I said with a cringe. I could practically hear my mother's eye roll along with the gaggle of ladies at her book club in the background.

"How many articles on celebrity baby names and fad diets can you write?"

"Mom!" I whisper-hissed again.

"You're so burnt out, I can smell the smoke from here! Your last headline article was about an heiress buying a house in Watch Hill," she grumbled. "Watch Hill isn't even in Connecticut, Hannah. Why is that local news?"

"No, no, you're right." I moaned. "It's time."

Honestly, if I didn't have rejection sensitivity and had to fight back tears every time I quit a job, I probably would've left already.

"You've got this," Mom said in her relentlessly encouraging voice. "Text me and let me know how it goes. I'll be thinking of you the whole time."

"Thanks, Mom," I said, thinking about how I shouldn't still need my mom to give me a pep talk.

"You'll find another job, sweet pea," she insisted. "One that actually pays the bills. And if you don't, you can always move back home."

I grimaced. I could *not* move back home. Mom's beautiful retirement was hanging in the balance. I needed to show her I could be self-sufficient so she would stop dragging her feet.

"It'll be okay, Mom," I reassured her.

"Okay, I love you," she said. "Good luck."

I set the phone back in its cradle and scowled at the twisted cord. The office chairs still stunk of cigarettes from back in the days when they let people smoke in the newsroom . . . back when the *Shoreline Gazette* was an actual paper and not reporting on the latest viral videos and failed influencer makeup lines.

My computer, a disgusting shade of pale gray, blinked off, the black square of death telling me it had suddenly decided to restart.

Seriously, screw this place.

I shot up from my chair, my tether finally snapped, and marched to the corner office with "Dawn Relenaux" written in peeling gold on the glass. I rapped my knuckles against the window, and a scratchy voice called, "Come in."

I threw my shoulders back and strode into the office, rehearsing my parting words over and over in my head as I walked. I paused when I realized Dawn wasn't alone. A dusty blond-haired man who looked to be in his late twenties sat in front of her desk. He offered me a too-broad smile of perfectly straight white teeth that made him look half shark, half fashion model.

"Oh, Hannah, excellent," Dawn said as she swiveled around in her chair. "I was just about to call you in here."

Dawn was a middle-aged woman with box-dyed black hair, tortoiseshell-rimmed glasses, and orange-hued skin from a generous application of cheap fake tan. She wore the same black dress to work every day and a colorful scarf knotted around her neck to give her a "pop of color." I always wondered if she actually liked dressing like that or if it was what she thought an editor should dress like.

I took a deep breath and said, "Listen, Dawn, I need to talk to you—"

"Hannah, this is Rick," Dawn cut in, gesturing to the man who looked nothing like a Rick. Was there seriously anyone under the age of fifty named Rick?

He stood, straightening his well-tailored suit, and politely shook my hand.

"Hi," I said warily as I sat in the chair beside him. Maybe he was sent from HR? Did we even *have* an HR department?

"G'day," he said, flashing me that shark grin again.

"Australian?" I guessed.

"What gave me away?" he asked with a wink that made my stomach do a little somersault. I was powerless against a hot guy with an accent, even if he was a little . . . odd. Maybe I was just really desperate to get laid. It had been three months since I'd even had a sloppy kiss with anyone and—*oh god, Hannah, you need to get your shit together.*

"What was it you wanted to talk to me about?" I asked in a too-high voice.

Dawn pulled out a manila folder from her drawer and plopped it on the desk. Interest piqued, I grabbed the file and opened it. What would it be this time? A new celebrity sighting? A rumored engagement?

"You've heard of Prickle Island, yes?" Dawn asked.

"It's one of those islands off the coast where all the rich people go for summer," I said. My eyebrows shot up as I opened the folder. "The Prickle Island Zoo?" I asked incredulously, looking over the dossier and then to the Aussie hunk. "You're doing a story about a zoo?"

"*You* are doing a story about the oldest privately owned zoo in the entire country."

"I don't understand." Frowning, I flipped through the pages of the thick document detailing the history of the zoo. "This isn't what we normally write about."

Dawn leaned her elbows on the desk, steepling her fingers. "That is what our handsome friend is here for."

Rick twisted in his chair toward me. "I represent a wealthy investor who has asked for me to hire someone to collect . . . some information about the place."

I narrowed my eyes at him. "You want me to spy for your boss?"

"Investigate," Dawn insisted. "Like any good investigative journalist." She waved her hand up and down at me, her eyes snagging on my nose ring. "I want to give you a story that could really jumpstart your career. You give some information to me, I give it to Rick here and he lets us run any exclusive stories you might stumble across in the process. It's a win-win-win!"

"This seems kind of sketchy." That didn't necessarily dissuade me though. I shut the file and dropped it back on Dawn's desk. "What would I need to do?"

Rick waved my sketchy comment away as if I were being ridiculous. This man was giving off serious mansplaining energy. If he called me "sweetheart," I was going to stab him with my pen, good looks be damned.

"My employer has secured you a job at the Prickle Island Zoo for the summer—working in the gift shop. You don't need to know anything about animals." I furrowed my brow, but he kept going. "Your job is to find out about the zoo's weaknesses. What isn't up to code? What secrets does it have? Rumor has it the zoo has one year to prove its financially viable or the Westworths are going to sell it."

Dawn tossed another bundle of papers onto her desk—a stack of detailed maps and aerial photos of the zoo.

"It was long presumed that the Lachlan family would inherit the zoo when Mrs. Westworth died," Rick continued, "but then Simon Lachlan died before her and now who the zoo passes to is up in the air."

"And your anonymous employer wants to buy the zoo?"

"Maybe," he hedged, flashing that shark smile again.

"That *is* prime real estate," Dawn said. "Multiple mansions, a golf course, luxury shops, who knows? There's gold there and all you need to do is dig for it." She looked back to Rick, prompting him to continue.

"If you unearth secrets that could help my employer obtain the zoo, they will make a generous donation to the *Shoreline Gazette* . . ." He paused before leaning in, holding back the words he seemed to know would seal the deal. "And you will personally get a $75,000 bonus if you get the information my employer is looking for."

I blinked at him, the number unfathomable. I wanted to

say "fuck off" but managed to hold it in. Who was this mystery employer offering this much money to someone who wrote fluff pieces about matching cat pajamas?

"Your accommodation and a weekly stipend will be provided for you as well, along with your normal zoo wages," Dawn added with glee. "I think that'd push you over six figures, Hannah."

My mouth fell open. Six figures. Mom could definitely sell her house!

I could sublet out my apartment for the summer and have some time to figure out my next career move too. This was a life-altering amount of money, and all I needed to do was a bit of snooping. I debated grabbing the good-looking, albeit patronizing, Australian and kissing him. Instead, I asked, "Why me?"

"Most of the summer employees are university-aged," he said, eyeing my pink hair. "We need someone who can blend in."

My mind quickly spun through the list of *Shoreline Gazette* employees. I was probably only one of a handful under fifty.

"Duncan is an idiot," Dawn said as if reading my mind. "Teresa would never take a job that could ruin her manicure. Joyce has kids. And *you* are the only person with the skills to write a killer article about all of this when you get back."

I swallowed. She hadn't given me many opportunities to prove that I was a good writer before, but she'd seen it all the same. I could still quit . . . *or* I could hang in for the summer, get my big fat paycheck, and then quit. Who would pass that up?

"I'm guessing that's a yes?" Dawn asked.

I didn't speak. Six figures? I'd be a fool to say no.

Dawn didn't wait for my response before she nodded.

"Good. I knew you were too smart to say no." She grinned. "Your ferry leaves tomorrow. Go buy some work clothes."

"I have work clothes." I cocked my brow down at my green, striped button-up and gray chinos. "I thought I worked in the gift shop?"

"At a zoo gift shop, not the MET." Throwing her head back, Dawn let out a nasally laugh. "You need work boots, rain gear, you know . . . outdoorsy stuff." She slid an envelope across the table, stuffed with money. "Your first stipend."

I lifted the envelope and opened it, gasping at the crisp hundred-dollar bills.

"I'll be getting this much each week?" I asked, darting looks between her and Rick, who was already texting someone on his phone, smiling like a fox.

Dawn clapped her hands together, her smile widening. I wondered how much money was promised to her personally for brokering this as well. "I'll expect weekly progress reports from you. Be discreet."

"An undercover job," I said with excitement, already imagining myself in a trench coat and trilby hat with a giant magnifying glass.

Dawn rolled her eyes at my enthusiasm and waved her hand, dismissing me.

I hustled back to my desk, my phone already buzzing with texts from my mom asking how my resignation went. I fished my phone out of my pocket and dialed her back.

"Mom, you aren't going to believe what I'm about to tell you . . ."

Whale hello there

Chapter Four

Hannah

We idled through the wharf of million-dollar yachts and out past the smaller private islands that hugged the shoreline before sailing into the bay. The Prickle Island ferry reeked of rotten seaweed and rust. I thanked the weather gods for the wind that brought wafts of fresh ocean air cresting over the bow. I stared longingly at all of the rich people on private boats that zipped past us, cutting through the waves and out toward the island.

Pulling my lavender fleece tighter around me, I braced against the brisk winds, still surprisingly chilly for the end of May. I read over the stack of documents Dawn had hidden inside the standard welcome packet for all the front-of-house staff. In just one week, the island would swell to fifty times the winter population. Along with the old-money families, a slew of workers to clean their houses, cook at the restaurants, and caddy at the golf club flocked to the island each summer . . . as well as a dozen extra staff members to run the visitor side of the Prickle Island Zoo.

Two people broke off from the crowd huddled at the side of the boat and wandered across to me.

"Are you heading to the zoo too?" the first one asked, glancing down at my ripped black jeans and then back at her friend. I wasn't sure what about my outfit marked me as zoo staff.

They both looked college-aged. One was tall and slender with braids embellished in shining golden rings that I gawked at like a magpie. She wore leopard-print leggings and a tight, striped sweater. The other came only to the tall one's waist; she had a white-blonde pixie cut and wore baggy jean shorts and an oversized hoodie with a tie-dyed cow on the front.

"Yes," I said, sweeping a stray lock of hair behind my ear.

"Us too!" the shorter one exclaimed.

"How did you guess?"

"The hair," she said, waving a hand at my messy bun. "Not many jobs on the island allow brightly colored hair, so we figured you must be going to the zoo." She toed my beat-up duffel bag that was mostly constructed out of duct tape at this point. "Also the bag." She extended her hand. "I'm Mae. That's Tessa. We're part of the front-of-house team. That's the café and gift shop," she added conspiratorially when I gave her a questioning look.

"That's where I'll be too," I said, lifting my folder filled with the long history of the zoo that I was meant to have memorized in one week's time. Along with serving at the café and selling overpriced stuffed animals, we'd be required to give tours through the zoo, so I needed to learn a shit ton of fun facts and quickly.

I should've known it was too good to be true when Rick had promised I didn't need to know any animal facts. I wondered what else he was lying about . . .

"Awesome!" Tessa spoke in an equally vibrant tone, her peppy voice perfect for wrangling groups of summer camp kids and shouting coffee orders.

"Is this your first year working on Prickle Island?" Mae asked.

"Of course it is." Tessa chuckled to her pint-sized friend. "We wouldn't have been able to miss you on a small island for three months. Even if you were working on the links or in the bars, we would've caught up to you eventually."

"How many years have you been doing this?" I asked the duo.

"This is my third year, her second," Tessa said, hooking her thumb at Mae. "We're seniors at UConn. How old are you?"

"Oh, um." I glanced around, realizing I was probably the oldest of the group. Maybe it would be suspicious . . . I glanced down at my folder again, the one that included a fake name: Hannah Newton. Job: Master of biology student at Wesleyan. And my age was six years younger than my actual one. "Twenty-two," I said, peeking up from my file.

I hoped they didn't scrutinize the bags under my eyes too carefully. Surely twenty-two was close enough to the truth to not draw suspicion?

"Oh, perfect!" Mae's hazel eyes widened with delight. "You can buy us drinks."

I cringed. "How old are you guys?"

"Twenty," they said in unison.

"I'll be twenty-one in two weeks though," Tessa added, as if buying her drinks was okay because she was *almost* the legal drinking age.

I knew already these two would definitely not help me lie low. They were already peppering me with more questions than I had the answers to, but . . . having a few allies who knew the place would certainly help me on my mission. Was mission the right word? Task? Challenge? Quest? I didn't know, but they all sounded way more awesome than writing articles about designing your bedroom for your body type.

"Did they assign you accommodation with the volunteers or off-property?" Tessa asked, looking at her own folder. Hers probably didn't include a secret identity sheet though. The song "Secret Agent Man" played over in my head on a loop. I really needed to learn to do a side roll—

"Or did you get an apartment with the front staff?" Mae asked, cutting off my secret spy daydream.

I looked back into my folder. "It says I'm in the lighthouse?"

"Yes!" They both cheered. "Us too," Tessa said. "Oh, this is going to be so good. We're staying in this old, converted—"

"Lighthouse?" I offered.

"Yes!" Tessa squealed. "It's so awesome."

How were they so exuberant? I didn't have this much energy when I was offered $75K, let alone when I found out I'd be staying in an old lighthouse. I needed to drink fifty Red Bulls STAT.

Mae sighed out at the horizon. "I can't wait to see all the animals again. I heard Luna had her baby."

"Who's Luna?"

"The gibbon?" Mae said it like a question, as if I should already have heard of her.

"Oh."

"You're going to have to do some serious studying to be ready for opening day next week."

I glanced at a group of students gathered around the far railing. "Who takes care of the animals in the off-season?"

"The Lachlan family, duh," Tessa said, coming to perch on the bench beside me.

"One family runs an entire zoo?"

"There's Mrs. Lachlan and her seven kids."

"Seven kids?" I exclaimed. "That's insane."

"Yeah." Mae chuckled. "And they're all named after birds too. It's totally wild."

"They sound like that Australian family. The ones with that reality TV show."

"Don't mention the Madigans to the Lachlans. They're, like, sworn enemies," Tessa said. "The Lachlans' kids are older. They had the whole animal name, zoo family thing going for them before the Madigans by like five years or something."

"The zoo version of the Montagues and Capulets?" I asked, darting a look between the two of them. "Am I going to be tested on this?"

"No, but like, I swear the Madigans stole the whole idea from them," Tessa carried on, "and now they are making a bunch of money off the idea over in Australia with their show and they're so cringe and I swear they don't even care about conservation. They're, like, the knockoff brand Irwins if you ask me."

"Blasphemy," Mae said. "The Irwins are conservation royalty."

"Sounds like something out of a soap opera," I said, shoving my folder back in my duct-taped duffel bag. "Who knew there was so much drama at a zoo?"

Tessa grinned. "You have no idea."

I smiled, realizing that maybe digging up dirt would be easier than I thought now that I'd been found by two zoo gossips. I was going to text my mom to call the realtor tonight.

I leaned in to my newfound friends. "Tell me everything."

HAWK'S JEEP
ISLAND ZOO

Chapter Five

Hawk

Sitting on the tailgate of my pickup truck, I fiddled with the keys in my hand as I watched the first ferry of the day fade into view.

"You think they'll be any better than last year?" Finch asked, folding her arms in the way she did to make her biceps look bigger.

"If you don't scare them off, maybe." I snickered, scanning my sister from the top of her dyed black hair to her Doc Martens.

"Everyone loves me." Finch placed a hand on her chest in mock offense. "I'm a gentleman and a scholar."

"Gentleman?" I rolled my eyes. "You slept with every non-male staff member over the age of twenty-one last year."

"Giving them memories of a summer they'll never

forget." Finch wiggled her eyebrows. "How many do you think I can get this year?"

"Not this year, Finch," I said tightly. "Not until the Westworths sign over the zoo to us. No more philandering."

"Ooh *philandering*." She shook her hands at me. "Did you get the thesaurus out for that one, or are you so far up Westworth's asshole that the fancy words just tumble out?"

"We need to be on our best behavior this summer," I said pointedly, hoping using the word "we" would soften the blow, but we both knew I meant *her* specifically.

"It's ridiculous," Finch grumbled. "We've been helping run the place since we could walk. This is the future Dad wanted for us."

My eyes dropped to the keys in my hand, which I now held in a white-knuckled grip as the memory flashed back to me. It had happened right here. In this parking lot. On this truck.

Finch and I would have to live with that moment for the rest of our lives. In some small way, I was grateful the rest of my siblings hadn't been there to see it—that Finch drove us straight down to the boat while I did compressions on Dad in the back.

At least the rest of them had still been asleep. But I was certain they'd always remember the sound of my voice over the radio, the way it cracked, calling them all back to the prep kitchens. I'd walked them down to the production gardens, somewhere we didn't go too often. For some strange reason, I didn't want to tell them in a spot that they walked through every day, as if once I shared that news, that piece of pavement would forever be scarred—

"Hawk." Finch's voice pulled me from the haunted memory.

"What?" I snapped and then cleared my throat.

She nodded to the cluster of heads standing at the railing at the front of the ferry, watching as it pulled up to the docks. "Which one do you think is going to be the first incident report of the season? My money's on the tall blonde to the far right."

We made this bet every year. If I won, Finch had to scrub my buckets for a week. If she won, I'd have to clean out the vet hospital cages for a week. Inevitably, someone would do something stupid on their first day. Sometimes it was small, like accidentally stapling their hand when hanging garlands in the shop. Sometimes it was huge, like accidentally grabbing the electric fence . . . the one with giant yellow signs hanging on it *well* above head height. I still wasn't sure how they'd pulled that one off.

I sighed, trying to push the memories away. I glanced at the cluster of heads in the distance, noting the pastel one in the middle.

"My money's on the pink one," I said and shook Finch's hand. "She looks like trouble from a mile away."

Whale hello there
LE ISLAND ZOO
shop

Chapter Six

Hannah

My ass had completely fallen asleep as I sat in the bed of the rickety pickup truck as we arrived at a giant, metal back gate. Barbed wire mounted the chain-link along with a warning about the electric fencing at *both* the top and bottom—which honestly felt a little overkill. Who would be stupid enough to grab an electric fence?

A booming howl ricocheted through the dense trees. I jumped, eyes flaring wide.

Tessa leaned into me, giving my arm a squeeze. "It's just a little howler monkey." She indicated the size with her hands, and I got distracted admiring the delicate gold jewelry around her fingers. I seriously had the attention span of a goldfish. "It's about the size of a loaf of bread."

"That is a very arbitrary measurement to pick," I replied. "Are we talking artisanal loaf or . . . ?"

Another howl sliced through the air. I stared up at the trees looming above us, the way they jostled in the wind, and waited for the water in my bottle to start forming perfectly concentric circles. "Why do I feel like a T-Rex is about to storm through the trees?"

Mae practically leapt up at that, her overexuberant hands flying from her hoodie pocket. "Well, actually, in *Jurassic Pa—*"

"Listen up!" the Lachlan sibling driving the pickup shouted.

"That's Hawk," Tessa whispered. "Isn't he ridiculously hot?"

"Seriously," Mae whispered back. "What do they put in the water here? Have you seen the tatted-up sister? She is an absolute goddess."

Hawk rolled down his window and banged a hand on the truck door, and we all quickly shut up. "Those of you staying in town can leave your belongings in the storage room at the front. You're to meet with your supervisors first and then can take your lunch break to unpack. *Do not* leave the zoo without signing in with your supervisor."

"Wow, someone really has a stick up his ass," I muttered, garnering titters of laughter from my two new friends. I looked up to find Hawk watching me in the rearview mirror and my cheeks turned to fire. I swore he was hiding little devil horns under that perfectly wind-tousled brown hair.

He couldn't have heard me, could he?

Hawk typed something into the gate's padlock and it groaned open, lights flashing and sirens beeping as if he were landing a plane. The truck pulled in through the gap, and the gate immediately closed behind us.

My stomach plummeted as I stared back at the now-shut gate. "This feels straight out of a bad slasher movie. Are we sure this isn't the start of *Hostel?*"

Mae cupped her hands around her mouth to deepen her words into a Hollywood movie trailer voice. "When a group of college students go to Prickle Island for the summer, the adorable zoo is about to become their worst nightmare, dun-dun-dunnnh . . ."

The group chuckled.

"It's a zoo, Hannah. They've got to have fences." Tessa pointed to the mural along the back barn—a jungle scene that my mom would've loved. I wondered if they took artist commissions.

No, nope, I scolded myself. *You can't send your mother back to the scene of the crime. You're meant to be sleuthing, not pulling your mom out of semiretirement to paint giraffes. Although, she does really love giraffes . . .*

Mae pulled out her Chapstick and swathed another layer onto her already shiny lips. "I'd be more concerned if we pulled in and a bunch of lions were just wandering around. Wouldn't you?"

"Good point." The sudden rustling in the trees made me scan through them again, my eyes snagging on a beige-yellow monkey-looking thing in the distance. I elbowed Tessa and pointed at it. "Is that thing meant to be there?"

"*That* is Luna," Tessa said, "and yes, she's meant to be there. That's the gibbon enclosure. You just can't see the rest of it from here."

"Can you see her baby?" Mae practically shrieked, pushing between us.

I arched my brow at her liveliness. "Shouldn't there be a roof over her enclosure?"

Tessa snorted. "There is in parts. They have a whole interior building, but she has her own little island so she and her husband can climb to the top of the tallest trees. She's like a pirate sitting in the crow's nest."

"*Husband?*" I asked, amused by the word.

"No formal matrimony was involved," Tessa amended. "I suppose you could say mate, life partner, male she monogamously copulates with? But that's not as cute. You really haven't read much about this zoo, have you?"

Mae nudged Tessa, her icy blue eyes cutting her friend a look even though her overly Chapstick-ed lips bore a smirk. "She's got a week to learn. Give her a break." Mae turned back to me. "Sunny is the black one with white cheeks, hence the name white-cheeked gibbon."

"Sunny and Luna," I mused. "Very clever."

The two chuckled. "I think one of the younger Lachlan sisters named them. I wonder what the baby's name is."

"I still can't believe there's seven kids running this zoo—"

"They're not kids," Mae said. "Well, not most of them. Wren is a teenager, I think, but Hawk is like, in his thirties or something."

"Ancient," I muttered, thinking about how I was only two years away from that age myself. "Still, it's a lot for a handful of twenty-somethings to be running an entire place like this."

"They're not the only staff members," Tessa amended. "They've got their mom and a couple of townies who work here in the winters too. Our manager, Mateo, lives on the shoreline and does a bit remotely in the winter—ordering new stock, sampling new vendors—but he says it's mostly closed outside of the summer—no café, no visitors."

"Yeah, in the winter, a lot of the locals pick up shifts here when their restaurants and bars are closed down," Mae said. "I had a thing for this one German girl who lived here for two full years doing house renovations in the off-season. She said if she came and raked leaves off the path a couple hours a week, they'd let her go feed the giraffes and play with the meerkats and stuff—"

"Supervised by a staff member obviously," Tessa quickly added.

"Still, I'm so jealous!" Mae whined. "Could you imagine having the whole zoo to yourself? Wouldn't that be awesome?"

"See, these are all good things to know for my imminent career in tour-guiding," I said with a smile. "Wintertime zookeepers and all that."

I made a mental note to write this all down. I wasn't sure trading leaf raking for meerkat feeding was *illegal*, but every little bit helped.

"I think the townies do more of the maintenance, cleaning, and food prep and stuff though," Tessa said, grabbing her folder and diligently flipping through it again. "I don't think there's anything about it in the info pack, but the Lachlans are the only ones who take care of the animals in the off-season. You're going to get a lot of questions about the Lachlans on your tours, but try to steer the conversations back to wildlife conservation wherever you can. They want the animals to be the story, not them."

"Right." I tucked that morsel of information away to add to my notes. What secrets were they hiding that made them not want to be the story? I'd made a special file on my computer labeled "Taxes" because even if someone managed to crack my password and peruse my documents, no one was opening that folder. "That's still a lot of work to put on one family."

"Yeah, but the Lachlans *are* Prickle Island Zoo. Their great-great-grandfather built this place. Their ancestors are buried on this island by special approval from the state."

"That's so creepy." I cringed, imagining an Addams family-style mausoleum somewhere on the property. "They put that in their information packet?"

Tessa shrugged. "I think it's nice they have a family plot."

"Where do they bury the animals?" I wondered aloud.

"I think they cremate and then bury them," Tessa said. "They have an incinerator that's pretty big, but I reckon they're not getting a giraffe in there without a chainsaw."

I gagged. "Are you sure this isn't a horror movie?" I asked as the truck stopped abruptly, jarring us all forward as Hawk stomped on the brakes.

"What a dick," I muttered.

I scowled up at the head zookeeper in the rearview mirror. I was certain he'd slammed the brakes on purpose. My legs had numbed from sitting on the hard steel bed, and I stood on jelly legs, pins and needles prickling down to my toes. I clung to the side of the truck as I stood and swung the strap of my bag over my shoulder . . . a little too vigorously.

My tingling legs did nothing to stop the momentum of my bag sending me flying over the side of the truck. Tessa yelped as I fell, my newfound friends reaching for me as I tumbled. I braced for the impact of the unyielding asphalt when a pair of muscled arms shot out, halting my fall.

I already knew who it was before I even looked up.

Hawk's brooding face was inches from my own. Staring daggers into mine, his dark eyes seemed more cognac brown from this distance . . . which was a really weird thing to be thinking about as he held me like I was a bride he was about to carry over the threshold. Quickly, he dropped my legs with an unceremonious thud, but he kept his arm around my shoulders, steadying me. He smelled like hay and musk and that distinctive outdoorsy people smell, like he was plucked straight out of an old-growth forest.

His sister whistled as she got out of the truck. "Nice catch, Hawkeye. First injury of the summer gallantly avoided."

"There's still time," he shot back, but I had no idea what that meant.

"Th-thank you," I said as I hastily released my death grip on Hawk, stepping out of his warm, strong hands.

Stop thinking about his hands, Hannah!

"I wasn't going to let you fall." His intense eyes pierced into mine. "Even if I'm *such a dick.*"

All the blood drained from my face. "You heard that?" I realized if he hadn't heard me, I'd just confirmed it for him anyway.

The muscle in his jaw popped out, and I had the sudden urge to touch it. It was like a fucking golf ball stuck out the side of his face. He was like a professional jaw muscle body-builder. I swallowed and shook my head, trying to clear the thought.

I wanted to say his growly, pouty behavior was not helping the dick-ish label bestowed on him, but words seemed to fail me as my eyes dropped to his mouth.

"Well, uh . . ." I stared one second too long at those lips surrounded by dark stubble. "Uh, thanks anyway." *Jeez, Hannah.*

No. I wasn't going to be one of those girls who swooned for a grumpy, emotionally unavailable guy . . . even if I had suddenly lost all ability to speak with him standing within kissing distance to me.

Hawk. God, that was such a fuckable name.

Tessa and Mae came rushing over after climbing sensibly out of the back of the truck bed, which broke me from my spiral of trying to think of the least fuckable names. Chad? Bob?

"You okay?" Mae asked, grabbing me by both elbows.

Hawk turned toward the truck and started roughly offloading luggage.

"What a dismount," Tessa said. "Ten out of ten."

"I'm okay," I reassured Mae, who was clearly scanning me for injuries.

I turned back toward Hawk, but he'd already unloaded the luggage and gotten back in his truck.

The rest of the summer staff headed into the back door of what looked like an industrial barn.

But I lingered, my eyes tracking that rusty red truck as it pulled back up the hillside with those dark eyes still fixed on me in the rearview mirror.

Whale hello
there
TURTLE ISLAND ZOO
Shop

Chapter Seven

Hannah

The front of house was actually a puzzle work of buildings that included a main entrance, where guests had to weave through the gift shop and a café complete with an indoor tube slide and a wall-to-wall aquarium that guaranteed visitors lingered and—more importantly—spent money.

We walked around, taking it all in. My mouth dropped open as I admired everything, from the toy monkeys swinging on a makeshift zipline via a train track glued to the ceiling to the giant giraffe sculpture made of miniature giraffe figurines. My inner eight-year-old couldn't help but bounce on my toes as I inspected it all. This place was like a zoo-themed Santa's workshop. I couldn't wait to see a bunch of dazzled little children checking it all out.

A portly man clapped his hands and gathered us around

the magnet wall that displayed everything from little animal portraits to bottle openers to little fun facts scrawled across enamel squares in jaunty letters. The man bore a name tag that said "Mateo" with a smaller "Manager" underneath. He appeared to be in his mid-fifties, with warm brown skin and short gray hair peppered with black.

"Welcome, everyone, to the Prickle Island Zoo," he said in a friendly tone that easily pulled us all closer. He wore a khaki button-down emblazoned with the zoo logo of a porcupine in black. Instead of cargo pants, he wore black business slacks and shined black leather loafers—clearly denoting him as a front-of-house staffer and not a zookeeper. No one was hiking all around the zoo through monkey poo in those pristine shoes.

"It's so nice to see so many old faces," he said, beaming at a few heads in the crowd and smiling broadly at Tessa and Mae. "I'll be relying on you to help our newcomers get ready for the summer." He gestured to a row of empty shelves beside him. "We've got plenty of stock still to unpack. Decorations to hang. Pamphlets to distribute. And uniforms to issue." He rubbed his hands together with a mischievous smirk. "And I've gotten the chef to agree to a tasting of all of our summer menu, so don't eat too much during your lunch break."

A round of whoops and clapping echoed across the room.

"Best boss ever!" Mae whispered beside me.

"Some of you will be working in the café, some in the shop, and some will be heading up the information and tours desk, but we are all part of a big front-of-house family, or should I say troop?" The group chuckled again. "Or pride? Or ambush?"

"Ambush?" I mouthed to Tessa.

"Tigers," she whispered back.

"Okay, well, that's the coolest thing I've ever heard." I tucked that fun fact away to info-dump on my mom that evening.

"No, I think we should be one big prickle of porcupines," Mateo concluded, and the group cheered again as we all looked at the zoo mascot painted across the sliding doors.

Of all the friendly, welcoming animals to pick as a zoo mascot, porcupine didn't really seem like the best choice, but it was apparently part of the zoo's history and the others seemed to love it, so I kept my mouth shut.

"Okay, now, for the most fun part of my welcome speech, health and safety." The group groaned, and he held up placating hands. "I know, I know, but of all places to know about safety, it's a zoo. If a sun bear comes waltzing in here, I want you all to know what to do. Also, those of you first aid certified will be very busy here with all the scraped knees and head bumps and such. Wherever there is a zoo, there's also a hundred toddlers on any given day making sure we have a steady turnover of cartoon animal Band-Aids."

Mateo launched into his long health and safety briefing then sent us over to the café, where a stack of papers and pens was waiting for us to read and sign. It was a very thorough list of all the things he'd just gone over. After the signing of many contracts, we broke for lunch, some of us lingering by the offices to wait for our uniforms, others venturing off to wander the zoo, some going to the dorms to unpack their things.

Mae and Tessa led me straight to the radio bank where a sticker printer and line of radios sat. Apparently, there was a hierarchy of good radios that I was unaware of and they were determined to get first dibs on them.

"Write your radio and key numbers in your information packet," Tessa said, pointing to the long strip of giant black radios charging along the banquet. Across the way was a steel bench top with a mini fridge, microwave, and toaster for us to heat up our lunches, but according to Mae, everyone just bought their lunch from the café or the Peckish Peacock—the restaurant in the middle of the zoo that did burgers, fries, ice creams, et cetera.

"I need a radio?" I asked, inspecting the shiny new radio that had a strip of yellow-and-blue electrical tape on it. I wrote the color combo down in my info packet. On the back was sticky-tacked a laminated sheet of radio calls and names that I already knew I was never going to remember.

I bicep-curled the radio. The thing was way heavier than I thought a radio would be. I had the idea they'd be kind of like the walkie-talkies I had as a kid—although being an only child, I was pretty sure my mom "lost" them after how much I pestered her to play with me. But this radio was a frickin' brick. No wonder they all needed those big belts to keep their pants up.

"You probably won't use it," Mae said. "But just in case there's an emergency, everyone needs one."

"The uniform cupboard is managed by the front staff, so they'll supply you with everything," Tessa said. "We can grab those on our way back to the lighthouse this afternoon. They never run out."

"Okay," I said, feeling suddenly completely overwhelmed. This was way more than I thought I'd take on. I thought I'd be scanning a few stuffed hippos and calling it a day.

"We'll have an orientation tour after lunch," Mae said. "Hopefully, there will be some more news about the changes to the zoo."

I perked up at that. "Like what changes?"

"Well, you know how old Mrs. Westworth is, right?"

"Yes." I leaned in, putting my imaginary Ray-Bans on

and steepling my fingers. Okay, now I was venturing off super spy and more into evil genius territory.

"Well, now that she's looking to give the place to the Lachlans, maybe there will be some upgrades."

"What kind of upgrades are you hoping for?" I prodded.

"More rain cover for one," Tessa said with a huff. "More spots for photo ops. You know, Instagram-able locations, that kind of stuff."

"Right."

"Some new animals would be nice too," Mae said. "And maybe more activities for little kids."

"Are visitors even really needed when the zoo is privately owned?" I asked. "It doesn't matter how many visitors they have through the gates."

"Well, so that's the thing," Tessa whispered. "Mr. Lachlan wanted to buy the zoo. But then he'd need enough money to make this place profitable without their funding so . . . that's why we're here. Give tours. Sell coffees and merch. Delight visitors. Get more people to travel over and spend more money."

"Hundreds, sometimes thousands of tourists visit the island every day over summer," Mae said. "They just need to get the zoo to be a place they have to stop between the beach and barhopping."

"This summer will be a good one," Tessa said, giving my shoulders a shake. "I have no doubts."

"Shall we go check out the gibbons?" Mae asked as she secured her radio into her belt. She checked her watch. "We've got forty-five minutes before we need to be back for food tasting."

Seeing an opportunity to do a little sleuthing, I said, "I might just go for a little wander by myself."

"Overstimulated?" Mae offered with a knowing look.

"That was a lot of information and a *lot* of people in a tiny space."

"Yeah," I said, realizing once again that that was probably part of the cause of my overwhelm. *How* did I never notice it until someone else pointed it out?

"The zoo is a great place for finding a quiet bench amongst the trees and regrouping," Tessa said. "See you in a bit."

She waved to me, and I was grateful my newfound barnacle friends didn't push me any further. I took off at a clip up toward the top of the zoo, hoping I would find something—anything—that I could email to Dawn that night.

HAWK'S JEEP

Chapter Eight

Hawk

I really wanted to get through one summer without filing any police reports. That nose-ring-wearing, cotton-candy-haired tornado was going to get us splashed across newspaper headlines, I was sure of it. There was something about her . . . I wouldn't be surprised if she was a cursed mermaid and this was her first day with legs.

"Just what we need," I muttered to myself, "another hazard."

I made a mental note to email Mateo and ask him to keep an extra close eye on the pink pixie. I drove the truck up around the hill and out of sight of the vet hospital, parking it at Mom's house and taking off on foot from there. Heron had already taken the golf cart up to the top of the zoo and had graciously left my feed buckets up there to save me the trip.

I cut through the middle of the zoo, up past the aviaries, enjoying the quiet and knowing in one week it would be teeming with summertime visitors. I still needed to check the expiration dates on all of our med kits and call Dotty from the ice cream truck place to see if she'd be coming this summer and organize the face painters for opening day . . . The list droned on and on in my head—one I'd written many times over but still felt like I needed to remind myself of. Dove had illustrated all the banners plastered around the Prickle Island shops. Opening day graphics were shared on our socials and website, and I prayed for a sunny, warm day.

It had to be sunny.

This summer *had* to go well.

My phone buzzed.

LARK

Did you call Dotty about the ice creams yet?

ME

Isn't it the middle of the night there?

LARK

I'm getting ready for bed.

ME

Then get ready for bed.

LARK

I saw these people who do glittery hair decorations and kids crafts. I bet we could get them to do some animal print ones. I'll send you the link.

ME

Go to bed, Lark.

LARK

All of the old opening day run sheets are in
the file on your desktop I organized for you. If
you need anything, let me know.

ME

I need you to put this energy into running
your own farm. We've got this.

LARK

Okay, just one more link.

She sent me the link to a group of unicyclists dressed as
zebras because of course she did.

LARK

Good night, I love you.

ME

Love you too.

I rolled my eyes at my phone as I tucked it back into my
pocket. I knew even half a world away, Lark would make sure
I didn't forget anything. She had eased off—well, whatever
Lark's definition of "eased off" was—since last year, but she
and I still texted several times a week and I was pretty sure
she texted every single one of our siblings that often.

The lionesses were grunting at the back of their enclosure
when I reached them. "Okay, okay," I said. "I'm sorry I was a
little late this morning."

I radioed Heron to let them know I was entering the lion's
access area. I needed to check in with them every ten minutes
once I passed the first lock. It was one of our many safety
protocols that Dad instituted, even though we now also had
cameras in all the back enclosures that Mom or Aya would be
currently monitoring from their offices down by the prep

kitchens. We also had digitized locks that meant one door couldn't be opened before another was secured closed, yet another way we made sure that I wouldn't end up in the same place as a lion. Dad had been hypervigilant about safety even before we had the technology. Every time there'd been a zoo incident anywhere in the world, he'd call a team meeting and we'd all sit down and debrief about how to prevent it from happening to us.

I missed that.

We still had family dinners but not so many team meetings. Maybe I should call one? I'd been twenty when Dad died—the same age as Heron and Crane were now, which was wild to think about. Dad and I had always done the carnivore run together. The night he died was the first night I did the carnivores solo. I cried the whole time and have never cried since, my entire emotional well drained out on that day. Instead, I poured my energy into the animals, like the hangry lions in front of me now.

Lucy (Lucifer) and Lilith were our two girls, Sammy our boy—yes, I'd been going through a *Supernatural* phase when I named them. Sammy had a brother named Dean who went off to the Atlanta Zoo when he was a cub. Sammy was the ripe old age of eighteen and still going strong, although he'd been a little off his food recently, which gave me cause for concern. I'd prepped a special leg of goat for him today—hair, hoof, and all.

The sound of the first of three sets of locked doors was like a dinner bell to the lions, and the girls came running to the back of their nighttime enclosure. The lions had three enclosures: two for during the day and an inside one at night. The sisters bolted over to the left of the grated door, Sammy lazily following to the right. I stepped through the second set of doors, and the lionesses started pacing in front of the grating like house cats to the sound of a can opener. Their size never stopped being impressive, their power and stealth undeniable. Meanwhile, Sammy, who was twice their size, lounged against the grating like the sleepy old man he was.

Lucy dramatically banged at the metal slide, making the cavernous space echo. She slid a paw under it and lifted it three inches up until it hit the lock mechanism and then dropped it again. Over and over, she repeated opening the gap and shutting it, making sure I knew how impatient she was for her breakfast. She watched me pointedly as she did it, just in case I wasn't sure why she was causing a riot. It didn't matter that she was hundreds of pounds heavier than a house cat; she had that same stubborn cat stare that demanded she be noticed.

The sisters watched me with bright golden eyes as I came through the last set of doors, now only chain-link separating us. I opened the lid of their bucket, pulled the feed chute lever, and slid their chicken and mince down the slide. They pounced like they hadn't just eaten a whole bucket of venison the day before.

I moved over to Sammy's side. Once the three of them had eaten, Sammy could hang out with his ladies for the rest of the day, but Lucy and Lilith were too eager to be fed with Sammy around. He'd never get a bite in otherwise.

"Here you go, big guy," I said to Sammy as I slid his goat leg down his feed chute. Sammy sniffed the air but didn't rise. "Come on, I brought you hoof and all. You love the hooves!" Sammy let out a deep grumble that honestly sounded like indignation. "Come on, buddy, don't be stubborn."

Sammy yawned, completely unbothered by my prompting. "All right, old man, I'll give you some time." I gave him a look. "But when I come back to clean the night enclosure, if this leg is still here, I'm going to call Finch. Yes, Finch. The one who has the pointy things that draw blood."

I gave him the "I'm watching you" gesture and then went back out my three sets of locks. I radioed Heron to let them know I'd passed through the third door. Within a minute, I was radioing them again to let them know I was entering the tigers' back enclosure. I finished the rest of the morning food run, cleaning where I could and letting most of the animals out for the day. I doubled back to check on Sammy one more time, but he still hadn't eaten that goat leg.

I sighed. "Well, now you've gotta get stuck, old man," I lamented.

I picked up my radio and waited for the beep. "Carnivore to vet team." I waited a couple breaths before I heard the beep of Finch's radio.

"Vet team, go ahead."

I pushed the button in and let out another long sigh—a habit I constantly admonished my other siblings for doing. No one wanted to hear you breathing over the radio. "Uh, yeah . . . I'm thinking I might need you to come do a wellness check on Sammy today. He's not eating his goat."

Finch instantly replied, "Copy. I'll come up on my lunch break."

Even as the words left my sister's mouth, I'd already decided I was going to go scrub out the cages for her so she'd be able to take her lunch off. We really needed to hire a full-time vet nurse . . . and probably another keeper so we could actually take sick days without feeling guilty for our siblings picking up the slack.

"Copy. Thanks."

I wandered down the trail to the servals when I spotted a

flash of ballet-slipper pink amongst the windswept bamboo. What the . . . ?

I went in the other direction, curving around the behind-the-scenes trail to head them off, and ran smack dab into the mermaid-haired hazard who nearly toppled over in front of me for the second time today.

Whale hello there

Chapter Nine

Hannah

This was the second time in a matter of hours that Hawk Scowly McSerious Lachlan had saved me from biting it on the concrete. He steadied me by my elbows as I regained my footing. I felt like Bambi on ice, except I was wearing sensible Converse and the asphalt path was in no way slippery.

Hawk's hands lingered on my elbows for a second as he waited for me to straighten. But when I did, his face was nothing but stone. I'd met the man for all of thirty seconds and he looked at me like I was already a constant thorn in his side.

"What are you doing back here?" he snapped.

I swallowed the lump in my throat and met his storming brown eyes. "We were told we could check out the zoo during our lunch break," I said in a pathetically high squeak. I cleared my throat. I wasn't a school kid getting reprimanded by a principal here, but god, did it feel like it.

"And you thought that by 'check out the zoo,' Mateo meant climb over two ropes that say 'no entry' and some very strategically placed bushes to keep visitors out?"

"I'm not a visitor," I said sheepishly as I wrung my hands together.

Hawk crossed his arms, his muscles straining the sleeves of his shirt—which I probably shouldn't have noticed. He crouched down to meet my eye line. "When you are anywhere outside of the front building, visitor rules apply to you, understand?"

"Yes." *Satan*, I added in my mind, giving myself a mental high five for that comeback. Even if I was definitely the one in the wrong here, his patronizing tone was infuriating.

Hawk looked like he wanted to say more, wanted to go off on a whole health and safety tirade and then beat me to death with the code of conduct. But instead, he said, "Come on, hazard, I'll walk you back to the visitor part of the zoo."

"That's the worst nickname I've ever had," I muttered.

"It suits you," he said tightly, keeping his gaze straight ahead and marching like a surly soldier.

"Unfortunately, I can't entirely disagree," I grumbled, wrapping my arms around myself. Hawk's shoulders lifted and dropped in a nearly imperceptible movement, and I couldn't tell if I'd made him laugh or cringe. "So what are you all hiding back here?" I hedged, filling the silence between us as I followed a step behind him down the narrow path. "What don't you want the visitors to see?"

"Besides the ritual sacrifices?" he asked. I gaped at him for a second before his lips twisted up and one cheek dimpled. Quick as a flash, he was back to his frown again.

"Your sense of humor is dryer than a freaking desert." I

let out a relieved laugh that morphed into a very unsexy giggle/snort combo, and his smile flashed for the barest of seconds again.

"There's nothing back here we don't want visitors to see. In fact, we do tours and encounters back here all the time, under the supervision of a keeper," he said pointedly. "The last thing we need is some David Attenborough-wannabe getting his hand bitten off by a tiger." He glanced at me. "Or a pink-haired mermaid—who already has a penchant for tripping—falling into the crocodile moat."

I wasn't going to lie, I kind of liked that he thought I looked like a mermaid. But the flattery disappeared at the second part of his sentence. "You don't have fences around your crocodile moat?"

"Oh, we have fences," Hawk said, eyeing me. "But I have a feeling if anyone could find a way to fall over them, it would be you, hazard."

I was certain the tips of my ears were turning an unseemly shade of tomato. "Nothing to hide," I said. "Got it."

"We take pride in how well we care for our animals," he said, unclipping one of the thick ropes I climbed over and stepping back to allow me through. It felt like he was marching me to my execution the way he stomped behind me.

"Pride, huh? Is that a lion joke?" I asked. Hawk let out a derisive huff but didn't reply as we continued down the curving path that cut through the towering bamboo. "Why carnivores?"

"What?"

"Why are you in charge of the carnivores?" My tour-guiding packet had a list of keepers to radio with questions about each species. Hawk was the one to talk to about all of the carnivores.

"I'm the eldest," he said simply. "I was the first given the job and my dad trusted me to follow procedures and keep my siblings safe." He looked out toward Kangaroo Point and the turbulent ocean beyond. "I set the standard that they follow."

I hummed, considering his words. "You sound like a good older brother."

"Not really."

So far, this place was all standards and procedures. I didn't think I was going to get any juicy gossip this way. Dawn wanted something salacious, but I doubted I was going to stumble across a pit of dead volunteers or an underground drug ring. I needed to find a computer with the zoo finances on it—that was what Rick really wanted anyway. The answers were probably hiding in the numbers, not in some bad practices.

Still, I pushed, "Why don't the lions have more room?"

"Are you interrogating me?" Hawk's brooding eyes turned back toward me, and I immediately wished I could redact the question. "This is all in your information packet."

"I'm asking you."

"I don't see you concerned about the spider monkeys," he pointed out. "They travel much greater distances every day than lions do. Size of the animal doesn't equate to the size of the enclosure they need to have a good life. There are standards for these things, and our zoo far exceeds them on every count. I'm proud of the way we care for our animals. I'm proud of this zoo," he said tightly, his words filled with frustration, as if he'd had to make this argument many times before.

"Okay, okay, sorry," I conceded. "I didn't mean to strike a nerve."

Hawk was on a rant now though. "Our zoo supports conservation and rehabilitation programs all around the world," he continued. "We release more shorebirds than any other wildlife center in the entire state. We are a go-to rehabilitation site for shoreline wildlife, but not all animals are fit to release and we provide them with forever homes too." He ducked under a low-hanging branch that I easily fit under, and I was reminded again that he was at least a foot taller than my five-two self. "This isn't fucking *Tiger King*. We are an accredited organization that has consistent exemplary standards. There are zoos and then there are *zoos*, and we here at Prickle Island Zoo are the latter."

I blinked as his rant fell off into silence. I now understood why they paid perky people like Mae and Tessa to give tours and not surly giants like Hawk Lachlan.

"Jeez. Sorry," I said. "I didn't mean to ruffle your feathers."

He huffed. "Another zoo pun?"

"Come on, I quack you up."

His frown deepened, and I couldn't help but smile at how easily I got under his skin.

We arrived back at the main thoroughfare between the insect house and the Peckish Peacock. He lifted the chain up for me to duck under. "Stick to the paths from now on, okay, hazard?"

"Right." I turned back to look at him one last time. "Nice to meet you, Hawk."

"I don't know if *nice* is the word. But it's certainly interesting meeting you . . ." He stopped me with a featherlight touch on my elbow, and I looked down to where his calloused fingers brushed across my arm. "What's your name?"

I looked up into his intense eyes, breath stealing from my lungs. "Hannah."

From this distance, I could see the rings of gold and hazel in his eyes, smell the coffee on his breath, feel the heat emanating from his broad hand hovering over my forearm. His eyes searched my face for a moment, and my cheeks tingled under his gaze before he finally said, "Welcome to Prickle Island Zoo, Hannah." I swallowed, nodding my head and stepping out of his touch. "Don't come behind the scenes again, got it?"

My tentative smile morphed quickly into a grimace. I needed to stop letting that gorgeous face distract me from the fact that he was a total dick.

"Got it," I gritted out, whirling around as he watched me with that hardened, no-nonsense gaze.

I clamored back through the rest of the narrow bamboo path and spilled out onto the main trail, my heart thundering in my chest all the way.

HAWK'S JEEP

Chapter Ten

Hawk

I finished my top sweep of the zoo, checking for any other wayward staff members who needed a telling-off on their first day, before heading down to my mid-camp office behind the invertebrate house. I sat at my dusty beige desktop and started going through my work emails.

I handled most of the day-to-day husbandry things, but that ended up bleeding into all areas of the zoo, not just the carnivores. I was the head keeper and my siblings' supervisor, which meant I usually took most of my breaks at my computer. Aya managed most of the enrichment acquisitions and food orders. Mateo covered all of the front-of-house business. Mom was the head honcho of everything though payroll, building contracts, construction planning, grants, et cetera. Half of my inbox was emails that I didn't need to actually read and was only copied in on in case of future issues. Lark had diligently made subfolders for all of the different categories of work emails, and my morning coffee break was spent moving them into their allotted folders.

One such email I'd been CC'd in on was from Mateo with the final staff numbers for the summer—usually a few college kids dropped off between the hiring and first day. Normally, I wouldn't have given it as much as a cursory look, but a pink head of hair flashed in my mind and I decided to open the attached file. The title of clumsiest creature in the zoo was officially being stripped from our three-legged goat, Prudence, and being re-awarded to Hazard Report Hannah instead. I scrolled through the names, searching for Hannah's. I was debating whether I could justify this as a health and safety concern and not a serial killer-level of stalker crazy when I came across her name.

Hannah Newton.

She was a master's biology student at Wesleyan. Impressive.

First summer at the zoo. Yeah, I definitely would've remembered her otherwise.

Age: 22.

Oof. My gut clenched at that.

I was nine years older than her. Finch likely wouldn't bat an eye at that age difference, but that was probably the outer limit of age gaps in my opinion. Finch had a rule that anyone over twenty-one was fair game, but now that I'd tipped into my thirties, I wasn't sure if that rule could still apply. Not to mention I was a senior staff member, and while I wasn't *technically* in Hannah's chain of command from Mateo to Mom, it still felt like a power dynamic I shouldn't be playing with. How many times had I told my siblings no sleeping with volunteers? Hannah technically wasn't a volunteer but . . .

Any time I thought of the word "technically" this much, it was always bad news.

Whoa, why was I even thinking about this?

The girl was maddening. She was going to be the death of me by the end of the summer; I knew it already. The difference in our ages meant nothing, only reconfirmed how much I needed to keep an eye on her. No part of me wanted another agent of chaos in my life—wild animals were plenty, thank you.

But God help me, I couldn't stop thinking about the way she looked up at me. Those bright blue eyes. That freckled nose. The generous curves that—

I groaned and dropped my head in my hands.

What the fuck was wrong with me? I probably just needed more coffee. Yep, that was it.

The door rattled open, and I closed the staff file like I was getting caught watching porn on a work computer.

"You look like you've either had too much coffee or too little," Mom said with a concerned frown as she walked into the office. She strode over and put her hand on my forehead. "You feeling okay?"

"Fine," I said, leaning out of her touch. "What's up?"

"I had some ideas for opening day I wanted to run past you," she said. "What are your opinions on unicyclists?"

I glanced down to the stack of run sheets in her hands. "Lark's gotten to you too, huh?"

Mom laughed. "I tried to dissuade her, but she said it made her less homesick and—"

"Ah, she got you with the emotional manipulation," I said, pointing my pen at my mother. "Classic."

"We might have it in the budget to hire a bouncy castle," Mom suggested. "Or maybe a live band up by the Jeep?"

I shook my head. "The music freaks out the tigers," I said,

knowing it wasn't just the tigers but that I didn't want large crowds messing up my favorite spot in the zoo. "It'd have to be closer to the Peacock. And where exactly are these funds coming from?"

Mom shrugged. "I set some aside for conservation trips," she said and then leaned in. "But between you and me, I don't think the rest of the conservation world is ready for us to unleash Heron and Crane Lachlan on them yet."

"Agreed." I chuckled and rubbed my eyes. "Why don't you just save that money? Opening day will be fun enough, and it'll look better to the Westworths if we're being frugal."

Mom sighed. "Honey," she said in a way that made me tense up. I knew that sigh. I knew that "honey." It was the sound she made before she was about to give one of us some tough love. I clenched my jaw as she continued, "Why don't I call in some favors from some of our conservation friends—"

"No," I said, holding up my hand.

"They would help us out. I'm sure of it."

"We need to prove we can do this ourselves," I insisted.

"No man's an island, Hawk," Mom said, concern in her eyes. "Even if he lives on one." She smiled as if she hadn't made that joke a thousand times before. "It's okay to ask others for help."

"We need to do this on our own," I insisted, turning back to my computer. "It's what Dad would've wanted."

"Oh, honey." This time, the "honey" meant I'd crossed a line and she was about to let me have it. "I will remind you that *I* am the chief executive of this zoo and I have no plans on resigning anytime soon. So while I think it's noble that you want to continue on in your father's footsteps, I will be making the final decision when it comes to this."

I didn't know how she did it, but I swore I shrunk three inches down into my chair from her glare alone. Even in my thirties, she could make me feel like a little kid. Mom was a warm and gentle optimist, but she turned full mama bear in a flash when she needed to.

Mom turned toward the door, hand poised on the handle. "And what your father would've really wanted is for his children to not be so stubborn that they aren't willing to do whatever it takes to keep this family together."

And with that proverbial nail in the coffin, Mom pranced out the door with her chin held high.

Whale hello there

Chapter Eleven

Hannah

My brain had been blendered—was that a word? Tornadoed? Minced?—by so much information that when I finally dragged my duct-taped duffel bag to the lighthouse down the road from the zoo, I was less than enthused by what I found. I just wanted a long, hot shower and to go to sleep on a comfy bed.

But when I arrived, those hopes were quickly dashed. This place felt more like an empty grain silo than a lighthouse, or at least what I thought a lighthouse would look like. Standing in the very center, I could see up five floors to the lookout platform high above us. Each cylindrical level had a balcony that looked down to the common room on the bottom floor.

The kitchen was on level one, a curving disarray that had been haphazardly converted into a makeshift cooking space. It had a single-burner cooktop but two microwaves, which told me everything about what kind of *meals* people ate here.

The "dining" area was a mini fridge and yet another microwave gathered around a giant wood table that had beer pong circles painted on it. Every single plug in the place was in use charging people's cellphones and laptops. In the whole lighthouse, I didn't spot a single window except for the skylight far, *far* above.

At least the metal slider doors were open. The sea breeze wafted in, cutting down on the smell of rust. Summer staff crammed on couches made out of pallets by the door to get a peek of natural light.

I was beginning to understand now why Dawn had seduced me with all the bonuses—this wasn't going to be an easy job.

The front doorway was converted into a coat room with a drain on the floor for washing muddy boots, and a closet with five computers straight out of the nineties lined the wall of the common room.

The bathrooms were on the third level—three toilet/shower units bisected into a peace sign by flimsy half-walls.

Great. Nothing said group bonding like people being able to hear—and *smell*—each other poop.

The bunk room was up four sets of tight spiraling stairs and consisted of little more than a hallway with bunks built three high all the way around. I guessed I would be sleeping in a C-shape for the near future.

I tried to find the silver lining. I liked cohabitating with others after all. In classic **ADHD** fashion, I was great at making friends and terrible at keeping them. My childhood felt very lonely despite my mother being the most kick-ass mom in the world—a point I felt I always needed to make even to my own subconscious, like even my inner monologue wanted to make sure I didn't offend her or not give her enough credit.

"We saved you a bunk," Tessa called, pointing to the top bed inches above her head. Mae sprawled across her coffin-sized bunk below her.

I huffed and puffed my way up the stairs. "How many people live here?" I panted.

They shrugged. "It can sleep eighteen, but there's usually less."

I leaned over the railing and stared up at the skylight that used to house some sort of beacon. "What's on the fifth floor?"

"It's the games room," Mae said as she toyed with a zebra-striped fidget spinner. "Ping pong table, pool table, bookshelf, lots of board games with missing pieces. I'd steer you away from attempting any puzzles."

"There's some chairs and hammocks up on the top deck that are great places to sit and read," Tessa said. "You can watch the sun rise over the ocean if you don't mind the height."

"My mom would love this place," I murmured.

"Your mom?"

"She's an artist," I replied with a shrug. "This place would be like her dream home." I tried to say it lightly, but it was clearly implied that this was not, in fact, *my* dream home.

Neither Mom nor I had ever liked the white-picket-fence life, even when we moved out to the suburbs. Everything we did had to have a quirky twist, and I loved my mom for it, but I'd also craved normalcy as a child in a way I knew she could never provide. Now, I realized I was my mother's daughter. There was nothing normal or consistent about me. Eventually, I stopped fighting it and embraced my chaos.

I chucked my duffel bag up onto the bed, barely able to wedge it between the mattress and the ceiling. I groaned, debating sleeping in the bean bag chair on the first floor or the hammock on the deck instead. Otherwise, I was doomed to sleep three inches below a giant fluorescent lightbulb that I had a feeling I would have no control over when it turned on and off. I chucked my bag onto the bunk and stared out across the open spaces that were meant to be kitchen, lounge, dining room . . .

"I feel like we're in an army barracks," I grumbled.

"Oh, come on, it's fun." Mae rolled off her bunk and landed on all fours, as if that were a normal way to dismount out of bed. "It reminds me of the hostels we used to stay in when we were backpacking around Europe."

I bit my lip to keep my mouth from curving downward. *This* was the difference between twenty and twenty-eight. Not so long ago, I loved stuff like this for the adventures and the stories. Sleeping in hammocks and festival tents and old converted railway cars were once fun things I'd be able to take photos of and brag about later. But now . . . Now, I'd already lived a lot of those crazy stories and I was blissfully old enough that I didn't care what was cool or not. Now, I could proudly state that I preferred sleeping in a comfortable bed and staying up way too late scrolling funny cat videos instead of partying. But I was meant to be twenty-two-year-old college student Hannah Newton, not twenty-eight-year-old homebody Hannah Murphy, so I just smiled and nodded.

My phone buzzed in my freshly starched, new cargo shorts.

DAWN

Anything?

I glared up at Mae and Tessa. "It's my mom," I said a little too enthusiastically. "I'll go up to the deck to chat with her."

Why did I need to make that so awkward? Like they'd be able to infer from my "Dawn: Anything?" text that I was a secret spy trying to find issues with the zoo that could discourage the wealthy zoo patrons from bequeathing it to the Lachlans? That's a lot to read into one word . . .

"Are you coming to the Salty Dog tonight?" Tessa asked as I started back toward the spiraling stairs, my legs barking in protest. I'd been on my feet all day and was desperate to be horizontal. "You could buy us drinks?"

I tried to hide my sour expression. Buying drinks for them all night sounded like the worst babysitting job ever. I'd thought I was fun. I'd thought I was a high-energy golden retriever girlie, but my battery was officially *tapped*.

"I have zero spoons left," I called back. "Rain check?"

This day had been a whirlwind, and the idea of having the place to myself to snoop around was also a bonus. Tessa and Mae left it at the spoons comment, praise be all the neuro-sparkly gods.

I wandered up to the top deck and perched on a surprisingly comfy, crocheted hammock. The view from here was incredible. I could see all of the town and a good chunk of the zoo too, including a bunch of houses and buildings behind the vet hospital that weren't on the visitor map. The lights of a golf cart drove up the hill, and I wondered what a Sunday night in the Lachlan family looked like. I imagined them all eating dinner while zebras and monkeys and parrots raced around their house like something out of an Ace

Ventura movie. Then again, Grumpy McStuckUpFace was one of them, so I doubted it would be anything so fun.

I pulled out my phone and replied to Dawn.

ME

It's my first day, let me settle in a little please?

DAWN

A lot of money's on the line, Hannah.

ME

That money is not contingent upon me finding a whole Pandora's box of zoo secrets on my first day, is it?

DAWN

You certainly have a way with words

ME

That's why you hired me ;)

DAWN

Just keep an eye out.

ME

For what exactly? This place seems like a well-run zoo. What am I supposed to be looking for? Is there a zoo drama bat signal I'm missing?

DAWN

Save your quips for your work. An animal escape would be pretty amazing. Or signs of bad animal husbandry? Something true crime-esque would be fantastic. Any mysterious disappearances? Every family has skeletons in their closet.

ME

I don't see that happening here.

DAWN

You could make something happen there . . .

ME

You want me to free a lion or something????

DAWN

Maybe not a lion, maybe a snake or
something exciting but less . . . deadly.

ME

That is NOT what we agreed to.

DAWN

Well, what do you have so far?

ME

The eldest sister, the vet, is a party animal.
She's apparently slept with half the island
and brings alcohol to the staffers.

DAWN

Hm . . . That's a start at least. We need more
of that. Get me some profit margin details
too. Paperwork isn't as sexy but it's probably
what Rick wants.

My jaw clenched at the mention of Rick. What was I doing here? Trying to find a way to sabotage the zoo to get six figures? It felt more slimy than it had the day I'd agreed. I thought I was going to report on anything amiss, but now I felt like I was being tasked with ensuring it *did* go amiss . . .

ME

They don't exactly leave a stack of
paperwork around with all of their financial
details.

DAWN

They might. Otherwise, it's time to get
access to your boss's computer.

ME

Awesome

DAWN

You didn't think this summer would just be
petting fucking monkeys, did you? Get your
shit together. We need answers and a
newsworthy story and some insider details
for Rick. Unless you'd like me to send Oscar
to replace you?

I let out a frustrated growl and gripped my phone so tightly, I thought it might crack. No. I needed this money. Mom needed me to have this money. She wouldn't move on with the retirement she deserved until I could prove to her I was a responsible adult . . . God, I was twenty-eight, not eighteen anymore. I'd spent a whole decade job-hopping instead of picking a ladder and climbing it. Where had the last ten years gone? It was time for me to get serious about a career—*any career*—and this money was the catalyst I needed to be responsible future Hannah. An image of me in a suit flashed through my mind and I wanted to gag. Okay, maybe not a corporate career, but something other than writing articles about celebrity star signs.

I could do this.

I could get onto Mateo's computer and find some financial reports for Rick and get that money. *Sharing* information was less sketchy than releasing a snake into the zoo, right? I hated the acrobatics I had to do to make this fit my morals. My eyes tracked the lights of the golf cart again. There were real people on the other side of this now—a real family—no, I couldn't think about it. Me passing along information didn't mean Rick's employer would be able to actually do anything with it. Everything might just tick along as normal with me $75K-plus the richer.

ME

Don't send Oscar. I can handle it.

Dawn didn't respond.

HAWK'S JEEP

Chapter Twelve

Hawk

The eight of us crammed around Mom's dinner table. I'd bribed Wren two years ago with pygmy goats to secure me one of the only dining chairs that didn't wobble in perpetuity. She better never move out of Mom's house or I'd be relegated to a teetering barstool again.

A giant pot of cheese fondue sat in the center of the table with little skewers stuck into chunks of stale baguette and apple wedges. We had a family dinner every Sunday — or *Sunday Funday Fondue Day*, as it had come to be known — a Lachlan family tradition for as long as I could remember.

"Wren," Crane said, showing my sister a photo of animal poop on his phone.

"Red pandas, easy," she said through a mouthful of fondue-covered bread.

I took a swig of my soda from Johnny's Rockin' Candy Emporium. It was a new summertime shop that had just opened for the season. Mom had immediately swooped in and befriended the owner, whose real name was actually Norbert. I didn't blame him for choosing a different name for his old-timey confectionary store. Norbert's Rockin' Candy Emporium just didn't have the same ring to it. Mom had traded zoo passes to Norbert for a steady supply of summertime sodas.

Wren's soda was apparently cotton-candy flavored, Crane and Heron had birch beer, Dove—grape of course (anything purple), and Mom had orange, while Finch sipped on a sarsaparilla drink that made my teeth feel fuzzy when I stole a sip.

"No freaking way!" Dove exclaimed, lifting her phone and showing it to Finch.

"Shut the fuck up," Finch said, holding a hand over her Caesar salad-filled mouth.

Mom tapped a hand on the table. "Goldfinch Goodall Lachlan, language, please," she admonished.

"Why the expletives?" Heron asked, leaning over to look at the news headline on Dove's phone. "No way! The Madigans are getting a divorce? That's epic!"

I nearly snorted cream soda out of my nose. "They what?"

"After twenty-eight years of marriage," Dove read aloud. "Gaz and Beverly Madigan are calling it quits. The reality TV patriarch has been caught cavorting with a bevy of other women on more than one occasion over the years—"

"Wow, this is really juicy," Crane said, scrolling through his own phone. "It literally names all his mistresses. It just keeps going and going and going."

I couldn't help the spark of enjoyment from hearing the

demise of our arch nemeses. The Madigans deserved every shitty thing that happened to them. I hoped the divorce bankrupted them too and their show got taken off the air . . . which seemed a little bit petty, *but* Dad hated Gaz and Dad didn't hate anyone, so I knew I was vindicated in my ill will.

"This is insane," Crane said. "What's going to happen to the Wildlife Park?"

"It's on every Aussie news station," Lark said, eyes scanning frantically as she sent link after link to the family group chat. She held up a remote control and gaped at her TV screen. "It's all over our news too."

Lark video-called in to our Sunday Funday Fondue Day, and we placed the laptop at the head of the table like she was our evil boss and we were all her henchmen. Occasionally, the twins would even pretend to feed her fondue while she sipped her morning coffee, just waking up for the day in New Zealand.

Crane kept elbowing Heron and showing them his phone screen. "Who knew Gaz was such a whore?"

The room was in hysterics, everyone's phones out now as we all relished in the demise of the Madigans . . . all of us apart from one.

I glanced over to my mother, who was swirling her bread in the fondue pot with that tight-lipped smirk she did when she was trying to bite her tongue. "Mom," I said, making my siblings all turn to her. "What do you know that we don't?"

"Oh, what?" She pretended to look surprised by the question. "Nothing."

"*Mom*," Finch and I said at the same time. "We can tell that you're lying."

"What do you know?" Lark asked.

"Spill it," Heron said, pointing an accusatory finger at her.

Mom weighed her head side to side as if debating with herself before setting her fondue fork down. "Okay, fine," she said with a shrug. She waved her hands through the air like a floundering penguin. "Gaz and Bev have always had an . . . understanding."

I gritted my teeth at the way she said Bev like they were friends. They *were* friends way back in the day before I was born. But Dad and Gaz had a massive falling out and our families had been unspoken rivals ever since. Our parents had seven kids named after birds, so Gaz and Beverly had eight kids, all named after animals. Dad wanted a state-of-the-art zoo, so Gaz built a state-of-the-art wildlife park. The one thing Dad never wanted? The fame.

The show *Madigan Mountain* had been a staple of Australian reality TV for over a decade, but instead of being a conservation-driven show like the *Crocodile Hunter*, this was the Aussie zookeeper version of *Below Deck*. The melodrama alone was enough to put me off my dinner.

"What does 'understanding' mean?" I asked.

"They have an . . . open relationship," Mom said, taking a long sip of her soda as we all gasped. "Although Bev was always much more discreet about it than Gaz was."

"What?" The table erupted into a clamor of questions and people shouting over each other.

Mom held up her quiet coyote hand like she did when we were children and, despite us all laughing at the gesture, we did all, in fact, shut up.

"One at a time," she said.

"Do their kids know about their open marriage?" Wren asked.

Mom shrugged. "I'd assume so."

"How do they even know if all of those Madigan kids are

Gaz's?" Crane asked, elbowing Heron. "That Cricket one doesn't even look like the others."

"They're all his," Mom said definitively. "They had a schedule."

"A schedule?" Finch spluttered, bits of lettuce flying from her mouth. "Like a procreation date?"

"Basically," Mom said.

"Oh my fucking god," Finch said. "That is *insanely* creepy."

Dove leaned into the table to catch Mom's attention. "So how do you know about their 'copulation schedule' if you guys weren't talking before Fox was even born?"

Fox Madigan was the slimiest piece of shit I'd ever met. He and I had run into each other at a few conservation events and conferences in our youth, and he had the most punchable face I'd ever seen. Arrogant, rich, and acted like everyone should know he was famous.

Seriously. Fuck the Madigans.

"We've run into each other a few times," Mom said defensively. She started fiddling with her food again.

"And you two talked about your sex lives during these run-ins?" Finch asked incredulously.

"What is with the inquisition?" Mom barked, giving us the patented mama bear stare that made us all instinctively look down. "Bev and I were good friends for a long time. That didn't immediately fall apart when your father and Gaz had the implosion of *their* friendship. Still, I never thought Bev would finally kick Gaz to the curb. Good for her."

We all exchanged glances around the table. I had a million more questions but could tell Mom was flustered and upset.

So, being the eldest and the diplomat of the family, I instead took out my phone.

"Oh, I've got a good one," I said, scrolling to find one of many photos of animal poop. I showed it to Crane, carrying on our game of "It's feces but what species?"

"Hmm . . ." Crane squinted at the screen and grabbed my phone from my hand. Heron leaned in from one side and Wren from the other.

I stole a glance at my mom, who mouthed the words, "Thank you."

A family our size always had a penchant for drama, especially when it came to our rivals. But Mom had been through a lot since then. Losing Dad with seven kids and a massive business to run should've broken her, but she'd found a way to push through, to give us all the best life, to honor Dad's memory and show up with this boundless positivity even when it was sometimes tinged with sadness.

I felt very protective of my mom after all she'd been through, often positioning myself between her and my siblings, taking the brunt of their anger for unpopular decisions.

"Okay, well, Quillith and Waddles had the runs. That's not fair," Crane bemoaned when it was finally revealed that it was porcupine poo. "New rule: only healthy specimens."

"Nope," Dove said.

"Uh-uh," Herron said. "We debate that rule every year and every year it's rejected."

Finch chuckled. "Not up for the challenge, Craniac?"

Crane frowned around the table. "We need more bread," he said, pushing back from his chair and going to grab more provisions from the kitchen. "Don't start highlights of the week without me!"

At the end of every Sunday Funday Fondue Day, we'd go around and share our highlight of the week—something Mom picked up in some team-building book. But, like with many things around here, the tradition stuck. I already knew what I was saying as my weekly highlight: finally getting the cheetahs to recall on the first command. I'd been working on it with them for over a year and today was the day they did it on the first try. Big win for me.

The conversation carried on, a wild and varied mishmash of topics and chaotic segues, but instead of my successes, my mind kept wandering back to the most stressful part of my week: a pink-haired hazard falling into my arms . . . twice.

Whale hello there
PRICKLE ISLAND ZOO
t Shop
FF

Chapter Thirteen

Hannah

"What is the only big cat that can't roar?" Mae asked from where she teetered on a ladder, stocking the top shelf of squirrel monkey stuffed toys.

"Cheetah," I said diligently, sticking my tongue out at the corner as I focused on my drawing on the entry chalkboard that currently had a picture of a whale with a penguin surfing the spray coming out of its blowhole with the words "Whale-come!" across the bottom. I shook out my sore hands. I'd been clenching the chalk too tight. "Cheetahs can purr like smaller cats, which big cats like lions and tigers cannot." I pointed a finger victoriously to the sky.

"Nice," Mae said with an approving nod.

I was starting to get the hang of all this information. Everything from emergency evacuation drills to the lifespan of giraffes. Stretching my neck to the side, I groaned. I was going to need a spinal surgeon if I slept on that thin, little mattress in the lighthouse too much longer.

Over the last few days, I'd averaged maybe four hours of sleep per night. With some people stumbling back at all hours, staying up late playing beer pong and pool, and others like the German barista, Hans, waking up at four-fucking-a.m. to blend a green smoothie in a house without doors and walls . . .

I glared through the glass partition covered in zoo animal decals to the café side of the front building. Hans, who was cheerfully cleaning the espresso machine, looked up at me and waved. I smiled back as I snapped my chalk stick in two. If he wasn't careful, I would put *him* in the blender tomorrow morning.

Needless to say, the lighthouse wasn't exactly the cohabitating setup I'd been dreaming of.

"Name the miniature donkeys at the farm," Mae said as she moved the ladder over a shelf and hoisted another box of stuffed animals up it.

"Colin—"

"That's the cow," Mae said in a knowing singsong.

"Gregory?"

"Yes, and?"

"I don't know, some other old-man name!" I crumpled forward dramatically, rubbing my sleepy eyes. "I'll just look at the placards around the petting zoo area if I'm ever giving a tour. Please, dear lord, just let me sell keychains and not give tours."

"You're doing great," Mae said. "And the donkey's name is Benedict."

"Benedict!" I exclaimed, exasperated. "They should've named one of the chickens Benedict. That would've made more sense." Mae arched her brow at me. "Chicken. Eggs. Benedict? No? Anyone?"

She snorted and shook her head. "The Lachlan siblings name them. Usually after favorite TV and movie characters. Sometimes inside jokes. Sometimes just because they're cute names. I don't know why they do what they do."

Mateo left his office and waved to us. "How's the newbie going, Mae?"

"She's doing great!" Mae said in her extra-peppy voice that made me want to pretend to gag, but I refrained, offering an embarrassed smile at Mateo instead.

"Great," Mateo said. "Why don't you two take a break from that? You can show Hannah how to print and cut the bumper stickers."

I waited until Mateo turned and walked away to say, "Delightful." Okay, I needed like eight more cups of coffee because my normal golden retriever optimism was really failing me today. *That's what sleep deprivation will do to you.* My mind went back to my run-in with His Lordship Crabby von Grumblesburg and I decided that maybe the attitude was contagious.

"It's not that hard," Mae said, tugging on my elbow and pulling me to stand.

I dusted my chalky hands down my gray zoo T-shirt with a bright orange porcupine printed across the pocket and followed Mae into the office. We sat at the computer beside Mateo's, and I noticed his was still unlocked, his desktop full of neat lines of folders, including one that said "annual reports."

Bingo.

Now we were finally getting somewhere. Hello, six figures. Goodbye, neck pain and cows named Colin.

"Um, Mae," I hedged, trying to find a reason for her to leave. "Do you . . . have any tampons in your backpack?"

It was the first thing I could think of. What happened when I got my period two weeks from now? Either I'd have to keep it a secret or tell them I had *really* short cycles. Hopefully, once the zoo opened, it would be so chaotic that Mae wouldn't be counting.

"Of course!" she said in her Girl Scout voice. "I'll go grab you one. Do you need painkillers or anything?"

Gosh, she was like a freaking apple pie-level of sweetness. I kind of was beginning to adore it about her. She seriously put me to shame. I was more hot mess than sweet.

"No, just a tampon is fine, thank you so much. Lifesaver," I said with a wink.

She grinned back and bounced off like the frickin' fairy-tale princess that she was.

I returned to the folders on Mateo's desk, my heart thundering as I clicked on the first file and immediately grabbed out my phone and started snapping photos as I scrolled through the massive report document. I would read what it said later. Right now, I just needed to get as much info as possible.

Scroll. Snap. Scroll. Snap. Scroll. Snap.

My eyes darted back to the door, my ears straining for the sound of the handle clicking. When I heard the scuffle of footsteps outside and the jangle of the door handle, I practically vaulted out of my seat. With shaking hands, I clicked out of the document and rolled away from Mateo's desk . . . a little overenthusiastically and banged my hip into the corner of the far desk.

Mae walked back in, mistaking my pinched expression and hand on my hip for cramps. "The worst!" she said, passing me a tampon.

"Thank you," I croaked, taking it and fleeing out of the office to the bathroom.

I prayed to all my lucky stars that my phone now held the key to my escape from this fever dream of a place.

Hello, normal bed and Mom's dream retirement, I thought to myself as I hustled toward the bathroom.

I spotted a mop of dark hair and a tall, muscled figure standing between me and my bathroom escape. Hawk was grilling Mateo about putting down anti-slip mats during rainstorms before one of our flip-flopped visitors got a concussion.

I tried to move around him without notice, but my foot hit a patch of spilled water beneath the water fountain and one foot went skidding off like I was trying to do the splits.

Hawk snapped his hand out without even breaking from his conversation and steadied my elbow as I clung to the water fountain like a crazed koala.

"See?" Hawk said to Mateo. "It's unsafe."

I backpedaled out of Hawk's grip, grimacing. "I'm just gonna . . . go to the . . . toilet," I said, turning and fleeing the situation.

I could feel Hawk's eyes tracking my every step. "You might need to build a safety wall of stuffed animals around that one," he muttered to Mateo.

That one. Great. I was "that one" to Hawk now. Hazard Report Hannah. That name had really stuck. The asshole zookeeper felt more like a middle-school bully than a boss by now. I walked into the bathroom and locked the door behind me, pulling out my phone and the dozen new photos on it.

I smiled as I scrolled. *I'll show him just what a hazard I can be.*

Whale hello there
PORCUPINE ISLAND ZOO
Shop

Chapter Fourteen

Hannah

Despite now having the computer photos at my disposal, I decided I needed to do a bit more detective work before sending them off to Dawn . . . That was the *only* reason why I hadn't sent them yet. Annual reports weren't going to paint a full picture, and if the zoo had a slight increase in visitor numbers from the previous year, they'd make it into the green, which wouldn't be a front headline story. I needed more dirt on Captain Grumpypants and the rest of his porcupine clan.

I tried to go about my day with my investigative journalist hat on, but the only excitement in the front building was caused by *me*. I'd spent my shift being trained at the café and had managed to fuck up at least a dozen mock coffee orders, burnt multiple pieces of banana bread in the toaster, and started a small fire when I put a muffin in the microwave and accidentally pressed ten minutes instead of ten seconds. After putting the fire out with water from the aquarium instead of the readily accessible fire extinguisher, Mateo decided I was "better suited" for the gift shop and took me off the café rotation completely.

It was awful. By the end of the day, I was sore and sweaty and smelled like burnt muffin and aquarium water.

I needed a win.

After the front closed up for the day, I told Tessa and Mae I was going to sit out at the café's picnic tables and write in my journal for a bit before heading back to the lighthouse. It wasn't *technically* a lie. I'd been cataloging interesting things around the zoo, details about the animals and the people. Writing was like a release valve after a stressful day for me, probably why I was pulled into writing for the *Gazette*. None of it was really useful for the salacious gossip that Dawn expected of me, but I'd rather write about zoo animals than journal about myself, so that was what I did.

There was a beautiful serenity to the place after hours. The whoops of gibbons and calls of the lemurs, the chirps of the otters and squawks of the parrots, the wind rustling through the trees. I took a deep breath of the briny sea air, enjoying the afternoon sun that was still not so midsummer scorching that I couldn't bask in it.

I waited until the last stragglers had wandered off and looked at the front emergency exit: a metal wheel thing that looked like a medieval torture device. It was like a sideways turnstile that meant visitors could get out but couldn't get back in. That was where I was meant to exit through after finishing writing in my journal . . . *or* I could turn back toward the zoo and go snooping.

I tucked my notebook in my backpack and left it stashed

behind a flower bush by the after-hours exit before turning and wandering off through the front of the zoo. I wandered down the leafy alley of trees toward the farm, ducking through one of the "staff only" trails. There were dozens of secret little buildings hidden throughout the zoo, ones that weren't marked on the visitor maps. Maybe one of those would have something noteworthy. I found a couple of containers painted in camouflage to blend in with the trees, but there was nothing interesting inside, just a bunch of folding tables and chairs for events and stacks of old animal crates.

I moved farther down the path and froze when I heard voices. The Lachlan twins, Crane and Heron, were walking through the farmyard area, holding buckets in each hand and chatting loudly over each other—one about the Roman Empire, the other about the *Barbie* movie. I tiptoed behind the container, holding my breath as I waited for them to pass.

When they faded out of earshot, I picked up my pace and focused on the Rainforest Walkthrough to my left. Unfortunately, that meant I ignored the fact that there was a building to my right and I almost walked out in front of three dudes chatting in French while chain-smoking. I leapt back behind a sparse tree that really did little to hide me as I stared at the three of them standing out on the back deck of the house. I narrowed my eyes at their bright orange T-shirts.

Volunteers.

I'd forgotten that the volunteers lived on the property. They weren't allowed to leave the volunteer house after hours at least, so if I just crept backward out of sight, I'd be fine. I waited until they snubbed out their cigarette butts and walked back inside. Keeping my eyes glued to the door, I tiptoed in reverse, edging away from them . . .

. . . which felt like a smart tactic until I tumbled backward over a waist-high fence and plunged into a pool of icy water.

My head breached the surface as I gasped at the biting sting of cold water, a thousand needles stabbing into my skin. I flailed frantically like I was in a scene from *Jaws* as I remembered Hawk's threat that I might tumble into the crocodile moat. I swirled around in the water, unable to touch the ground, searching for a giant reptile coming to eat me when I came face-to-face with . . . a one-winged, little blue penguin.

The penguin stared at me, and I stared back—both of us equally unsure what to do about this situation. His name was Chicken Wing, as I had learned from Tessa and Mae's constant quizzing, and he was the easiest penguin to identify considering he was missing an arm.

"I'm sorry," I whisper-hissed to the bird. "I'm just leaving, okay?"

Chicken Wing flapped his one little wing at me expectantly, like I might have some food. "I know I'm wearing a zoo uniform, but I don't have any fish." He shook out his little body like a wet dog, puffing up and hopping onto a higher rock. The penguin let out a little vibrato cooing sound, and three other penguins waddled out of their nesting boxes to watch me. "I said I don't have any fish! Dammit, Chicken Wing! Be quiet!"

I then realized I was in a one-sided battle with a group of penguins and decided continuing to argue with them was a sure sign of madness.

I swam over to the side of the pond, the walls incredibly steep and slick with algae. I tried to scramble up the side but slid back down again. The walls were shaped in a deep V up to a high edge and I couldn't scramble up the slick sides . . . *probably by design to keep the penguins inside, Hannah!* Little did they know the enclosure was also human-proof. I started to swim over to where the penguins all stood, and they erupted into a chorus of pitchy honks again.

"Shut it," I hissed.

If I went any closer, they'd make a riot of sounds and a keeper eventually would come running. Or maybe I'd freak out the penguins enough that they'd attack me.

Death by penguin.

Great. I'd be front-page news for being drowned by their tiny, adorable webbed feet.

I was both grateful and disappointed I left my phone in my backpack. I could probably shout for help and the next volunteer to pop out for a smoke would come rescue me, but then I'd also probably be fired.

No. No one could find me like this.

I spotted a hook halfway up the slick wall and tried to scramble up to reach it. I tried three times, but it was just beyond my grasp. My brain took this opportunity to remind me of all the times I'd judgmentally watched rock climbing competitions thinking it didn't look that hard . . . I decided if I ever made it out of this pool that I was going to start practicing pull-ups.

It didn't help that my boots were waterlogged and the weight of my wet clothes was dragging me down. But I couldn't leave my boots floating in the penguin pond! No evidence could be left behind. I just needed to get to that hook. If I could hoist myself up that far, then I could reach the lip of the enclosure. If only I had a rope . . . or maybe I could make one?

Deciding it was better not to think too much about it, I whipped my zoo T-shirt off and twisted it round and round into a makeshift rope. I tossed the wet shirt up toward the rock and it snagged on my first attempt.

"Hell yes! Catwoman has nothing on me!"

I pulled myself up to the hook, hearing my shirt rip as I went. Thank God they'd issued us three. No one would have to know. I rested at the hook, huffing and puffing like I'd just run a marathon, before summoning the energy for the last push up to the retaining wall. I grabbed onto it and yanked myself up with arms that I didn't know if they were trembling from adrenaline, the cold, or exhaustion. I rolled unceremoniously over the side, collapsing into the leaves with a wet *thunk*.

I decided then and there that I was done with this sleuthing business. Boring spreadsheet evidence only from now on. Next time, it might actually be the crocodile moat, and now that I knew I was terminally clumsy, I wasn't going to risk it. I turned back to the penguins and flourished a bow.

"Good day to you gentlemen," I said, striding back the way I came, a bounce in my step that I'd managed to survive that misguided escapade. My arms and legs buzzed with adrenaline.

A little fuzzy head popped up from the farmyard gate as I stalked past. The miniature cow let out a groaning moo that was loud enough to wake half the zoo. "Not cool, Colin."

Slicking my wet hair off my face, I picked up the pace back through the main path to the front exit. I couldn't have any more animals making noises and giving me away.

I was almost to the gate when I heard a gruff human voice behind me.

"Do I even *want* to know?"

HAWK'S JEEP

Chapter Fifteen

Hawk

Hazard was definitely an appropriate nickname for her. Hannah stood there by the exit completely soaked in her boots, shorts, and a navy polka-dot bra that made me choke on my own breath. She held her rumpled gray T-shirt in her grip and looked at me with a scrunched face like a cat stepping on wet grass.

I held her gaze like my life depended on it, but in my periphery, I could see the swell of her breasts rising above her bra with each deep breath, saw the soft curve of her sides pebbled in goose bumps above her soaked, baggy shorts . . . which snapped me back into business mode.

"*Why* are you walking through the zoo shirtless, looking like a drowned rat?" I barked. I rubbed my forehead, muttering under my breath, "Looks like Finch will be cleaning my buckets for a week."

Hannah frantically rung out her shirt and pulled it back on, revealing a tear that ringed around the collar, and I wondered if she'd intentionally taken scissors to it to give it a zany boatneck. I wouldn't put it past her.

She squeezed more water from the hem of her shirt and pockets of her shorts, patting herself down in odd, random movements like she was playing a game of Simon says that only she could hear. "Sorry, I didn't realize anyone was still here," she said.

"I live here."

"Right, yes, of course." She aggressively nodded like a bobblehead in an earthquake. "I knew that. I just thought you wouldn't be coming down the front of the zoo this late in the day. Don't you live up behind the vet hospital or something?"

"The zoo is closed, hazard," I snapped. "You shouldn't be here." My eyes dropped to her belt. "Especially without your radio. What if there was an emergency?"

"I was just leaving," she said, hooking her thumb behind her and walking backward to the door. I held up an exasperated hand, and she paused before nearly toppling backward into the flower bushes.

This was the last thing I needed right now—another wildling to keep tabs on.

"I'll ask you again," I said, speaking louder and slower. "*Why* are you wet?"

"I, uh, just decided to, uh, have a quick mist in the splash pad because it was so hot," she said, fanning herself as if acting it out for my benefit.

I looked from her goose bumps to her chattering teeth to my polar fleece.

"A mist in the splash pad?" I asked skeptically. Beside The Farm, we had a little splash pad we turned on during the hottest days of summer. It had little jets that shot out of spitting animal sculptures and misters circling an inch-deep splash pad for toddlers to play in.

"Yeah." She said it like *I* was the obtuse one.

"The jets and misters weren't turned on today," I pointed out. The air still had the springtime chill to it, especially with the winds sweeping off the ocean. As we got further into June and the temperature shot up, we'd turn them on. But not now, which meant . . .

"Oh, of course, yeah, I know." Hannah's words were like scattershot, flying out of her mouth like one single word. When she finally took a breath, I narrowed my eyes at her. "I just lay in the water for a sec to cool down after a hot day."

Today had been chilly, mild at best. I scrutinized her up and down, imagining her lying in the inch-deep water and having to roll herself across it to get as thoroughly soaked as she was now.

I rubbed my forehead again. This woman was giving me a permanent headache. "I don't understand you."

She flailed her arms around like some sort of Jim Henson creation while trying to explain herself. "Today was a really intense day at the gift shop. Super busy. I personally tagged and hung up fifteen boxes of keychains and designed some really gorgeous new zoo-branded bumper stickers—you can thank me later—I just got a little overheated with all the unboxing and ladder climbing and lanyard hanging, and then there was the fire—"

"What fire?"

"Oh, what? Nothing," she said as her words sputtered out of her like shrapnel. "Tessa said I should put ice packs under my armpits because that's how they taught her to deal with heat stroke when she was in the Girl Scouts, but I was like ew, gross, then the ice packs will smell like my BO, and I—"

I held up a hand to silence her rapid waffling, and she took a deep breath, holding her side as if she'd been sprinting and got a stitch. "Please, just . . . go home. Now."

She gave me a mock salute. "Will do, sorry."

"I'm emailing Mateo," I continued, trying to push down on my frustration. "I need to make sure he watches you leave before he clocks out for the day."

"Please, don't!" She clasped her hands together, her saucer-wide eyes pleading with me. She looked like she might cry, which made my gut twist into a knot. I couldn't deal with tears. If she started crying, I'd need to call Mom in for backup. "I don't want to lose this job, and I think I might not be Mateo's favorite person after today."

Wow, if she managed to rile up Mateo, who happened to be one of the most even-keeled people I knew, then maybe she was as hazardous as I suspected.

"Fine," I gritted out, watching her shoulders visibly sag. "But this is your last chance. No more trouble."

Her blush grew even more furious, creeping across her cheeks and down her neck, dipping below the ripped neckline of her T-shirt.

"Right, okay," she said, quickly grabbing her backpack and fleeing out the exit.

I turned and headed back to my office, planning on sending a zoo-wide memo about closing hours and staff conduct. I wouldn't be specific or call Hannah out by name, but it needed to be said. This summer was too important.

I stormed up the hill, trying to focus on everything I still had left to do for the day but instead thinking about

Hannah's wet, bare skin. Maybe she really was a fucking mermaid who got caught walking out of the ocean. It would honestly make more sense than half of the things that came out of her mouth.

Not that I had any desire to think about her mouth.

HAWK'S JEEP

Chapter Sixteen

Hawk

"I think we should have it done by next summer," I said, opening the door for Mom.

She and I wandered through the vet hospital and up the back stairs to the half-finished second floor. Mom had caught me raking leaves long, long before the sun came up and decided to rescue me from my pedantic ways by having me take her on a tour of the new apartment.

"I know Finch is so grateful you're helping her," Mom said approvingly. "I think she's ready for a little more privacy. Maybe it'll help her grow up from her bachelor lifestyle."

"I wouldn't hold my breath," I muttered. "You're probably ready for a little more peace and quiet too. Can't imagine living with Heron, Crane, and Wren is exactly tranquil."

"I'll be honest," Mom said as we navigated up the spiraling steps. "I kind of hope at least one of you will always be in the house. I don't think I could handle the quiet."

"We'll buy you ten more dogs," I assured her.

"Phoebe would never allow it." Mom huffed, glancing down at Phoebe, who walked up the steps behind us. Phoebe was Mom's elderly mutt, some strange combo of pit bull and border collie. She had become the unofficial mascot of The Prickle Island Zoo. Dove even had a porcupine costume made for her for special events.

"We'll all be on the same property together still," I pointed out. "Once I finish off this apartment, I'll get started on the cabin."

"Cottage," Mom countered.

"It's a cabin," I gritted out.

Mom rolled her eyes. "The toxic masculinity of it all," she bemoaned. "I raised you better than that. A man can't have a dream cottage? Is the word too whimsical for you?"

I mirrored my mother in her exaggerated eye roll. A cabin was a sensible log dwelling. A cottage evoked the idea of flower gardens and pastel fairies with glittery wings frolicking around a wisteria trellis. I couldn't help but picture Hannah, freckle-nosed and pink-haired with fairy wings and a flowing white dress . . . probably toppling over a bird bath and collapsing on a toadstool. That was what I thought of when I thought of the word *cottage*.

I'd been planning and plotting building myself a cabin up behind the lion enclosure for several years . . . pretty much as soon as my sisters followed me to the renovated monkey enclosure. Now, I was helping Finch make her dream apartment and then I'd set to work on my forever home at the zoo.

"Besides," Mom continued. "You won't all stay here. It would be naive to think any differently. I can only hope that some of you will want to stay and continue your father's legacy. But I'm not going to hold you back if your dreams are elsewhere." Mom paused as we wandered through the freshly drywalled space that would become Finch's living room.

"I miss her too, Mom," I said, knowing she was thinking of Lark. "But she's coming back for Christmas. It won't be that long now."

Mom paused and turned to me with a knowing smile. Evelyn Lachlan always knew when to call bullshit. "You don't have to always protect me, you know? It's okay for me to be sad. I'm not going to crumble just because I have feelings." She gave me a pointed look as if to say, "You should try it sometime."

"Okay," I said tightly.

"Maybe if you were a little more open to feeling your emotions," she continued, unnecessarily driving her point home. "You wouldn't push everyone away who didn't have Lachlan as a last name, hm?"

"Okay," I repeated through clenched teeth. I'd never liked the phrase "beating a dead horse," but that was exactly what she was doing.

There was no point fighting her on this. I had a fine relationship with my feelings. Yeah, I was a little terse and maybe sometimes intense, but I was plenty friendly enough to all the locals, and honestly, I didn't have the capacity to make any more friends with summertime visitors. Trying to keep up with them all was exhausting. People needed to just suck it up and deal . . . *Okay, maybe she might have a point.*

But what did she want me to do? Get out a guitar and sing "Kumbaya" and just hug and cry all the time?

I didn't cry. The capacity just didn't exist in me anymore. I was too busy, too productive, too hardwired to care for my family. I didn't have time for Mom's wishy-washy sentiments.

"I think Lark made the right decision." Mom put a hand on my shoulder and squeezed. "She's so happy in New Zealand, and I'm happy for her, even if I miss her a lot too. I can feel more than one thing at once. We're all so close. It's hard to see one of you go, but I knew eventually some of you would grow up and move on."

To have seven kids and still miss the one. I knew that feeling. Knew there wasn't a limit to the love we had as a family unit. It was why I was hellbent on getting these houses built and maybe even re-renovating the monkey house to make it more appealing too. Finch and I had a bet about who would be the next sibling to fly the coop. Her money was on Dove. Mine was on Heron. Heron seemed destined for a cool, quirky job in an international city. But at least they'd all have a place to stay when they came back to visit.

"This is coming along so fast," Mom said as she swung open the door to the kitchen. "I can't believe you did this all yourself—cheese and fucking crackers!"

Leave it to Mom to swear when attempting not to swear.

I peeked over her head to see what she was looking at, as Finch and a hot chick were flying apart from each other. The voluptuous raven-haired beauty's shirt was askew, revealing a lacy black bralette. Her yoga pants were pulled down to mid-thigh showing off a matching black thong. Apple red lipstick was smudged across her cheeks. Meanwhile, Finch's lips were swollen, bearing an echo of the same lipstick shade.

"Hi, Mom," she said, shifting to cover the girl behind her as she yanked up her pants and straightened her shirt. "Hawk."

"Finch," I said with a shake of my head.

The woman grabbed her discarded sandals and fled barefoot past us. She paused at the threshold to the stairwell and shouted, "Call me!"

"Yep!" Finch called back, folding her arms and tucking her hands under her armpits.

The sound of rapid footsteps disappeared down the stairwell.

"And *who* exactly was that?" Mom whirled on Finch.

"Sunflower is a Portuguese yoga instructor working at the Rosenburg estate this summer," Finch said with a waggle of her eyebrows.

I rubbed a hand across my jaw, shaking my head at my sister. "Of course her name is Sunflower."

"Not often do I meet someone with a name as strange as my own." Finch chuckled and then quickly added, "Sorry," to Mom, as if it were a personal offense.

"You couldn't even let your brother finish your new apartment before you had sex all over it?" Mom reprimanded.

Finch leaned her hip on the drop cloth covering the kitchenette. "We weren't having sex *all over* it. Just the kitchen." She flashed a mischievous grin.

"When are you going to get serious about someone?" Mom folded her arms in the same position as Finch, and when Finch noticed, she immediately changed her posture, fiddling with the waistband of her gray sweatpants.

"How do you know Sunflower and I aren't destined to be?" Finch asked.

Mom let out a haughty laugh and popped her hip. "Are you?"

"God no." Finch snorted, her shoulders bunching around her ears at the thought. "She and I couldn't have a thirty-second conversation about anything but yoga and breathing techniques, which is all good fun when she's demonstrating those yoga poses without her clothes on, but . . ."

Mom groaned. "Finch, why is your brother making all of

this space, two guest rooms—one that could easily be a nursery," she added, "if you don't plan on settling down?"

"Well, one of them is going to be a sex room—"

"Is my only hope for having grandbabies going to be halfway around the world in New Zealand?"

"Jeez, Mom, Wren isn't even eighteen yet. Can you fucking chill on the grandbaby talk?" Finch shot back.

I pushed into the room in front of Mom, mouthing, "Let her have this!" and Finch immediately shut up. One more word and Mom would probably pivot all her grandbaby rage on me and ask me why I hadn't settled down yet either.

It was no use explaining. Mom and Dad had met and instantly fallen in love. It was a "heart eyes across a crowded room" situation. Mom had cursed us all when she said, "When Lachlans fall in love, they fall hard and they fall fast." Maybe that had been true for Mom and Dad . . . and Lark too, but it definitely wasn't going to happen for Finch and me.

Dad said he knew Mom was "the one" from the first time he saw her. That set us all up for an unrealistic expectation of what our own future romances would be—Finch, of course, having *many* more failed romances than me. But not a lot of people wanted to fall in love with a zookeeper and spend their life on a little island taking care of wild animals. There wasn't a zoo version of Tinder . . . Well, there kind of was for organizing animal breeding programs . . . but there wasn't one for the humans who looked after them.

"The guest room will be for Lark and Logan when they come visit over Christmas," Finch offered instead. "And the second room can be for all of *their* children."

Mom, momentarily acquiesced, turned back to me. "Okay, let's continue the tour." She glanced at Finch. "Go pee and put some fresh underwear on. You don't want to get a UTI."

Finch dramatically slung her forearm over her eyes. "I'm almost thirty, Mom! And I'm a doctor! I don't need your medical advice, thank you."

"Maybe we'll do the tour later," I said, steering Mom by the shoulders out the door and away from Finch, who looked like she was about to put her head through the freshly painted drywall. "I told Petey I'd come pick up the repaired chainsaw before he heads off the island this morning."

"What are we going to do with her?" Mom groused as I led her back down the stairs. "I am not one to slut shame. She could have a million partners if it actually made her happy, but . . ."

"I know, Mom," I said. "I know."

Whale hello
there

Chapter Seventeen

Hannah

I'd given up on the bed designed in the seventh circle of hell. Seriously, one more night and I'd need a permanent neck brace. I took my lumpy pillow and blanket, climbed to the lookout, and found one of the comfy hammocks to lie in. They were lined up three in a row, and I took the far one by the wall to get the greatest amount of awning cover just in case it rained.

The ocean breeze swirled around me, the sounds of the waves soft and lulling. I sighed. This was so much better.

Four hours later, I was awoken to the sound of wet lip-smacking and low moaning. My hammock jostled as the one beside mine kept swinging rhythmically into me. The haze of sleep cleared enough for me to realize what was happening: people were having sex in the hammock next to mine.

Gross.

I grabbed my pillow and pinned it against my ear but could still hear the drunken, "Shh!"s coming from beside me.

Really? They couldn't have found any other place to shack up that wasn't right beside me? When did I end up on Fuck Boy Island?

The hammock started rocking more wildly and my hammock rocked along with it, making me feel like I was unwittingly participating in this late-night hookup.

"Ew, no, nope, I'm not a part of this," I muttered, trying to gracefully exit.

As I grabbed the edge of my hammock in the darkness, a sweaty slab of flesh smacked into the back of my hand. I leapt the rest of the way out, mumbling, "Please be a shoulder or arm or something, fuck!"

I abandoned my blanket and pillow, stumbling through the darkness back to the stairwell. I caught the faintest sliver of light on the horizon, the sky slightly more gray than pitch black. It must be close to dawn. We'd probably need to be up in another hour.

As I plodded down the spiral steps and over to my bunk, I decided going for a walk was better than an hour of lying on a bed of nails. I grabbed my baggy gym shorts, crop top, and hoodie, changing in the darkness before wandering the rest of the way down to the front door.

I had no idea which way I was going to turn; I figured I'd just roam for a while and let the morning take me. Maybe even see the sun come up.

I wandered down past the rows of closed-up shops, finding little remnants of a seafaring town of yore, from the barnacle-covered buoys to old fishing nets to oceanscape paintings hanging in the windows. It was an odd mismatch of old New England boathouses and fancy new boutiques catering to the rich elite for the summer. Quaint confectionary shops sat beside luxury sunglasses stores, as if Prickle Island couldn't decide what aesthetic it was going for. I wondered what it would be like in the winter, when the town was quiet and all the luxury stores were closed up. Would it just be the general store at the end of the street then?

I took a side road, cutting through a lavender garden beside an old fountain. As I wandered off the main thoroughfare, the buildings grew sparser. Tall hedgerows and roped-off dirt roads with signs saying "Private Entrance" or "No Entry" were emblazoned across giant iron gates that made me feel like if I were to slip past them, I'd be transported back in time and enter a scene from *Downton Abbey*.

Instead, I veered left, shaking my hands out as I thought about that meaty slap of skin in the hammocks. It made me want to gag. Who even was it? I bet it was Hans. Fucking Hans.

The paved road turned to gravel, and then the gravel turned to sand, hugging the shoreline to my left. Soft early morning waves gently lapped upon the rocks, filling the tide pools as gulls lazily bobbed on the gentle surf, too early for their morning caws.

I found an old, abandoned wharf, its boards splintering from decades of ocean waves. Jumping over the broken and missing beams, I wandered down until I was at the very tip. Surrounded by the dawn fog rolling off the ocean, I held up my arms to the sky and took a deep breath.

The sky grew paler, color returning to the bleached white horizon, starting pale blue and fading to pink.

I strained my ears, wondering if I could hear the animals at the zoo and their early morning calls. I glanced up at the zoo poking up above the fog on the far hillside of the southern peninsula. It sat like a monument, a proud beacon of quirky buildings and a mixture of exotic and native trees. Something about that zoo was like nothing I'd ever seen before. It felt like some sort of alternate universe, like a weird Willy Wonka-esque version of what a zoo should be. It was equally alluring and eccentric, and I kind of loved that about it.

A twang of guilt strummed through me. I was going to ruin this place. Those photos I took weren't anything incredibly damning, but it did show that the zoo needed to earn quite a staggering amount of money to become solvent by the end of the summer. It was exactly what any developer needed to buy the zoo out from under the Lachlans. I'd saved the photos in a locked folder on my phone . . . but several days later, I still hadn't sent them.

The Lachlans had the rest of the summer to make that money and . . . Crap, I didn't know what I was going to do. I had a photo that could hurt them in my pocket. And even though Hawk was like a health and safety demon, the rest of his siblings seemed like kind of cool people. His mom seemed sweet albeit a bit quirky, like my mom. She didn't deserve what I was doing to her.

The animals could find new homes, surely. Maybe the Lachlan kids would then feel free to move away and do other things, I tried to justify to myself, but it all felt hollow now.

Fuck. Fuck. Fuck.

I was supposed to spy, not be charmed by this place and the people who run it. My loyalty should be to *my* mom, not Evelyn Lachlan. Mom needed to get out of that old house in the suburbs and start living her life, and I needed to stop being such a fuckwit. This money was life-changing, morals be damned.

The sound of an old car rattled past, the hum of the engine slowing and then stopping. I glanced over my shoulder and spotted a rusty red pickup truck parked at the end of the wharf. As if summoned by my thoughts alone, Hawk cut the engine and stepped out like an even grumpier and more attractive Mr. Darcy as the dawn haze lifted.

ISLAND ZOO
HAWK'S JEEP

Chapter Eighteen

Hawk

She moved down the wharf and out of the fog like a siren, like a dream, one I didn't want to wake up from. Had all that talk of cottages magically conjured her out of my imagination? I leaned against my truck, fighting the urge to walk out to her. With her track record for clumsiness, she might very well trip on one of those wobbly, old boards. But she moved with a surprising amount of steadiness, as if the early morning made her go slower. Maybe her 3X-speed brain didn't start until sunrise.

Hannah reached the end of the wharf and paused. "What are you doing here?" I liked the way her lips curved up as she asked it before she could remember herself and force her expression back to neutral. Her voice was husky with sleep, a pleasant sort of scratch to it. I was probably the first person she'd spoken to today and I didn't know why, but I kind of liked that thought.

"I could ask you the same, haze," I said.

"Haze?"

"Short for hazard."

"You gave my nickname a nickname?" she asked incredulously, even as an amused smile split her face.

"It suits you," I said, trying to sound nonchalant. "So why are you here?"

"Hammock sex," she said as if that were a complete sentence.

"Excuse me?" I choked out. "There's no way I could've heard you right."

Hannah lifted her palms to the sky, her hair swirling around her heart-shaped face as the stillness of the fog began to lift. "I couldn't sleep another night on that god-awful bunk bed, so I decided to sleep in one of the hammocks at the top of the lighthouse, but *then* I was woken up by two drunken college students banging like frickin' bunnies in the hammock beside me." I let out a soft chuckle. Her full-speed brain was clearly back online now. "So I decided instead of just lying there, rocking with them"—she pretended to gag and my smile uncontrollably widened—"I decided to go for a walk and get away from the love shack. I don't know how I ended up here. I guess I thought I could watch the sun rise."

"Ah," I said. "That might be a problem."

"Why?"

I pointed behind me. "The sun rises from that side of the island."

"Oh," she said, bashfully tucking a strand of hair behind her ear. "Right, I . . . knew that."

"Of course you did," I said, turning back to my truck. "Come on. I'll take you to a better spot."

She paused, her eyes narrowing at me suspiciously and then to the bed of my truck as if she'd just caught me burying a body. "Why are you down here before dawn?"

I reached into the truck bed and lifted our freshly repaired chainsaw. When Hannah's eyes flared, I set it back down and laughed. "I needed to get it fixed because I'll be trimming back the trees around Kangaroo Point today. Petey, the local handyman, is heading off-island today so I needed to pick it up early. It's not to murder you with, in case you were wondering," I added. If she didn't think I was burying bodies before, she definitely did now. Maybe this whole over-sharing, ranting thing was contagious?

But Hannah let out this easy, light laugh that made my muscles ease involuntarily. She wore her emotions on her sleeve—an open book—and I could read all of the feelings flashing in rapid succession behind those big blue eyes.

"Well, now that you've said that . . . ," she said jokingly, looking in every direction, like she didn't know which way to go. "I guess I could use a ride."

I tipped my head to the passenger-side door of my truck and got in on my side, starting the engine as I waited for her to climb in. We rode in silence, bumping over the uneven gravel road that hugged this side of the island. I cut through town and out toward the east, where the horizon was still a sliver of pale pink and yellow.

Good. We hadn't missed it yet.

I didn't know why I cared if Hannah got a good view of the sunrise, just another thing I was going to tuck away in the "better to not think too much about it" folder in my mind.

I glanced over at Hannah as I turned down the road toward the zoo and found her watching me, a questioning look making her chin dimple and brows knit. When our eyes connected, she quickly darted her gaze away.

"Something you want to ask me, haze?"

She chewed on her bottom lip, debating with herself. "We are going to circle back to this whole nickname thing," she muttered and then took a stealing breath, as if she were psyching herself up to say what was really on her mind. "Why are you being nice to me right now?"

"What?" I didn't look at her as I pulled up the hill toward the southern peninsula. At the Y, I took the steep road up to the lookout that sat just beyond the zoo's parking lot.

"You don't like me," she said—a statement, not a question. "You call me hazard. You think I'm a nuisance. Why are you taking me to get a good view of the sunrise?"

That hit me like a ton of bricks. She thought I hated her. Awesome. She wasn't exactly on my list of favorite people— she had "troublemaker" and "pain in my ass" written all over her. Hell, she had a shiny beacon over her head that said "Warning!" in flashing lights. But that didn't mean I didn't like her. All of the very pointed things Mom said to me this morning echoed through my mind. *Why* did she always have to be right?

Instead of saying any of those things, I just shrugged. "The best view is right next to the zoo. It's on my way. No big deal."

"Oh," Hannah said, deflating slightly, and I knew that I had somehow picked the wrong answer. "Okay."

I pulled to a stop at a little area of picnic benches by the flagpole, the Prickle Island Zoo flag flapping gently in the predawn breeze.

"You don't need to stay," she said, glancing at me as I cut the engine and moved to open my car door.

I grabbed my thermos of coffee that I'd intended to nurse on my way back from Petey's but still hadn't touched, distracted by my mermaid rescue. I shrugged. "I need somewhere to drink my coffee."

"Coffee?" She perked up like a meerkat popping out of a burrow.

I chuckled, climbing out of the driver's side and opening her door for her. I unscrewed the cap of my thermos and filled it, passing it over into Hannah's eager hands. "I hope you don't mind that it's black."

"Anything with caffeine is good right now," she said, even though she grimaced at the first sip. She peeked up at me from the lip of her makeshift cup, steam swirling up past her freckled cheeks. "Thank you."

And fuck if that wasn't the most arresting thing I'd ever seen. I thought my heart stopped for a second with the way she looked at me before I took a long, bracing swig of coffee. Maybe that would knock some sense back into me. I ambled over to the picnic tables, trying not to think about those big doe eyes or the curve of her ass in those running shorts.

Damn you, early morning Hawk.

I took another sip of coffee, trying to clear the cobwebs from my mind and focus on something other than my traitorous libido. It didn't mean anything. I was just tired . . . and, fine, a little horny.

Hannah wandered over and perched beside me, close enough that her hoodie brushed my jacket . . . something I had no business noting.

She nursed her coffee as the gibbons began to sing. Her eyes widened to saucer-level huge, and she looked up at me. "That is incredible. She is quite the songstress."

"It's two of them. Sunny," I said to one trill of song, then when another longer whoop replied, "Luna." As if I were the one conducting their little duet, I added, "Sunny. Luna."

"They sing a little love song to each other," Hannah said,

setting the thermos lid aside to smoosh her cheeks together. "That is so painfully adorable it makes me want to hug something to death."

I let out a surprised laugh. The only thing that was painfully adorable right now was her: the way her hoodie-covered hands cupped her cheeks, the delight with which she listened to the gibbons. It was like discovering these animals all over again with new eyes.

Hannah cleared her throat as if realizing herself and picked her coffee back up.

"Luna's a lucky girl," she said. "We don't all have boyfriends who serenade us with love songs every morning." I hummed in agreement, and she glanced at me. "So there's no Mrs. Grumpyface then, I presume?"

"No." A one-syllable answer that I was hoping would clearly indicate I wasn't interested in the direction of this conversation.

Hannah either didn't see the indication or—more likely—chose to ignore it. "Is your sister in New Zealand the only one of you with a partner?"

"It depends on your definition of partner because one could argue Finch has quite a few."

"A long-term partner," Hannah corrected.

"Right."

"Is Lark the only one?"

"Mm-hmm," I hummed.

"Do you want me to stop talking about this?"

"Yep," I said.

She nervously toyed with the drawstrings of her hoodie. "Okay, got it, sorry."

We stared back at the sunrise, the pale pinks brightening to burnt oranges as the sun peeked above the horizon and cast the morning ocean in its golden glow. We watched in silence as it slowly rose, the clamor of animals behind us rising as everyone woke up for the day and started demanding their breakfasts.

At every squeak and roar, Hannah's face morphed into one of glee, and after a few minutes, I realized I wasn't watching the ocean but was watching *her*, studying the little ways her face morphed and shifted in response to each sound. Her delight was infectious. She glanced back at me, and everything in me tensed at the look in her eyes.

Fuuuuuuuuuck.

I reared backward. This was bad. So bad. For so many reasons. She was a summer employee. She was a tornado of chaos. She was *twenty-two*. And she was someone that in three months, I would never see again.

I stumbled up to a stand, snatching the now-empty thermos lid. "I need to go feed the animals," I said with a half-hearted wave. "I'll see you around."

I departed—more like *fled*—to my truck and hauled ass up to the zoo service entry. When I looked in my rearview mirror, Hannah was backlit by the morning sun and I couldn't tell if she was turned out toward the ocean or looking back toward me, but I had a terrible, excited, pit of my gut instinct that she was watching me.

Whale hello there

Chapter Nineteen

Hannah

Our first open week was an absolute clusterfuck of over-sugared children and rich, preppy people who looked like they were getting ready to hit the courts at Wimbledon. Surprisingly though, my week went by without a hitch. We had a couple lost children who were quickly reunited with their parents while Tessa and I distracted them with elaborate reenactments of *The Lion King* with our stuffed toys—obviously glossing over the Mufasa part because we didn't need to give the next generation that kind of trauma.

One old man was disgruntled that the penguins weren't visible, and Mae calmly explained to him that they were probably sleeping and bandied about the word "crepuscular" several times before telling him to come back at their feeding time in an hour and offering him a coffee voucher to the café.

It was all going smoothly, and Mateo seemed pleasantly excited by the visitor numbers.

The face painters and ice cream truck really seemed to draw a crowd. There were even unicyclists dressed like zebras —it was well and truly *wild*. Dove and Heron wandered around the front entrance with snakes and parrots for the kids to touch while waiting in line. We'd turned the process into a well-oiled machine, moving people through and getting them into the zoo.

Friday went by in such a blur, filled with adrenaline, that it felt like only an hour had passed by when the keepers started sweeping the last of the stragglers from the top of the zoo and we were selling our last season passes to the elderly couple in golfing attire.

The weariness of the day was just starting to seep in when Tessa hefted in the chalkboard and leaned it against rolling doors. "Um, guys," she said, getting Mae's and my attention. "I think there's a lost dog out front. It won't let me get close enough to read its tag though."

Instantly revived, Mae and I rushed out the front door.

An old black cocker spaniel sat under one of the outdoor café tables. He had gray around his face and dappled into his coat. His tail thudded against the ground, but he didn't move as Mae approached.

"Aren't you just the cutest," Mae crooned, and the spaniel's ears went back as it growled at her. "That's okay." She took a step back and glanced over her shoulder at us. "Who knew a dog would be the most dangerous animal at the zoo today?" she quipped. "Hannah Banana, you want to try?"

I clenched my jaw, thinking about how, if I got bitten, Mateo would probably have to write up an incident report and Hawk would probably read it and then he'd be back to calling me "Hazard Report Hannah" instead of the much nicer—and cuter—"haze."

That moment at sunrise still echoed through me days later. Something beautiful, almost sacred, had passed in the silence between Hawk and me. I didn't know what it was about those moments: something about the awe I felt hearing the zoo come alive as the sun rose over the ocean, the fact he was there in that memory, the way he looked at me before that guard snapped back down. I was probably projecting. I told the guy he didn't like me and he hadn't denied it. That was pretty damning. Still, I couldn't shake that light and jittery feeling low in my belly whenever I remembered his face lit up with the golden glow of the morning sun. When he left, I'd immediately had to stop and write it down in my journal—a memory I wouldn't be letting go of anytime soon.

The dog in front of me barked, pulling me out of my daydream as Mae nudged me forward. I slowly crept toward the dog like I was trying to pat a tiger.

"Hey there, buddy," I said, crouching down and giving the spaniel a scratch behind his ear. He melted like butter into my scratches, his tail picking up in tempo. My whole body relaxed as his anxious posture turned into one of calm and he flopped down on his side and lifted his leg for belly pats. "Is that the spot?" I asked in my dopey baby voice as his foot started scratching the air. "Is that the widdle spot?"

Tessa clapped me on the shoulder. "Hannah, you're a freaking dog whisperer!"

The dog's whole body waggled in delight as I reached for his collar and grabbed the tag. "Walter," I read. "Are you lost, buddy?"

"Is there a number on the tag?"

I flipped it over and found a cellphone number. "Yeah." I read it out while Mae dialed.

Mae tapped her foot, waiting for someone to answer. "Hi, this is Mae from the Prickle Island Zoo gift shop." Her voice rose an octave as she put on her customer service voice. "I think we've found your dog? Walter?" Her eyes went wide. "Oh. Oh. Okay. Awesome. We'll send someone over with him now." She shut the phone and gaped at us. "That is Ethel Holloway's housekeeper's dog."

My mouth dropped open. "Holloway? As in Holloway Art Museum? As in *Holloway Times*, Holloway?"

"Money to rival the Westworths," Tessa said. "Let's go return this dog to the housekeeper. Maybe they'll pay us in gold doubloons for finding him or something."

"The guy on the phone said the housekeeper isn't there," Mae said. "He told me to go to the back gate and meet him there for further instructions."

"Further instructions?" I wondered.

"I don't know." Mae shrugged. "He's just the messenger of a messenger of a messenger. Telephone game down the hierarchy of staff, I'm guessing."

"How many people work on these estates?"

"In the summer? Dozens. In the winter, only one, if that. Usually, a local gets hired out to keep all the pipes from freezing over, mow lawns, and protect against any storm damages and stuff," Mae said. "But in the summer, they bring whole households with them: chefs, gardeners, stylists, masseuses, you name it."

"That's . . . intense." I picked up Walter by the belly and tucked him under my arm. "I suppose if you have enough money to name museums after you, helicoptering in a hairdresser probably seems like an everyday thing."

"Let's go scope out the mansion," Tessa said, bouncing on her toes. "We've already finished up anyway and apparently 'all staff members have to promptly leave after work.'" She put on the deep, surly voice of Hawk, repeating the words from his staff-wide memo.

My stomach instantly curdled at the memory.

The radio on Tessa's hip crackled. "Lima Three to Tango Five."

"Ugh," Tessa grumbled at the sound of Mateo's voice. She picked up her radio and pushed in the side button, waiting for the beep. "Tango Five, go ahead."

"Hey, we have a family at the visitor kiosk wanting a private tour." We all exchanged looks. Private tours meant big money and usually big tips. Not a casual visitor, but some rich family. I guessed our closing hours didn't apply to them. "We need two cart drivers. Can two of you come show them around?"

It wasn't a question, even though it was worded like one.

Tessa lifted her radio. "Roger. Be there in five."

Mae groaned. "Guess you'll be going to Holloways' all by yourself. Jealous."

"I can take a tour if you want to go," I offered, even though we all knew I was the worst tour guide on staff.

Walter snarled and snapped at Mae's hand, and she yanked it away. "Jeez. Yeah, no, you're on your own with the hellhound."

"Easy, Cujo," I told him.

Mae looked at me, confused. "What?"

They were definitely too young for the reference. I mean, I *also* was way too young, but my ADHD liked collecting pop culture references like a dragon hoarding treasure. So here I was, name-dropping a Stephen King novel from the eighties about a rabid dog—a book which I had never read.

I realized it would take too long to bring Tessa and Mae on that particular mental adventure, so I just waved my hand. "Never mind."

Tessa ducked inside and returned with a cartoony visitor map of the Prickle Island shops. She drew on it in pen instructions of how to get to the Holloways'. The "staff entrance," as she put it, was only a ten-minute walk from town.

It wasn't that far; surely I could handle it.

"I'll see you guys at the lighthouse," I said with false confidence then headed off toward the Holloway estate with the fair-weathered Walter tucked snugly under my arm.

ISLAND ZOO
HAWK'S JEEP

Chapter Twenty

Hawk

I sat at the kitchen island, reading the day's report from Mateo as Finch and Dove heated up Peckish Peacock leftovers for dinner. It had been a crazy day and we were exhausted, but it had also been record-breaking, and we were all proud of that.

"Today went surprisingly smoothly considering three *thousand* people passed through the gates," Dove said, knocking on the wooden cutting board. She opened the fridge and grabbed out a hard cider, holding it up in silent question to Finch and me. Finch nodded, and I shook my head. She took out another cider and then tossed me an IPA.

Thank God for sibling telepathy because I didn't have the energy for any more conversation. Even the twins had decided to call it a night and not come down to our house to

bother us all evening. The sun was still setting as we all show-
ered and began to unwind. I loved these long summer days.
Soon, I'd be falling asleep at a sensible eight-thirty, or maybe
nine p.m. if I were feeling dangerous.

"I've got a date with one of the face painters tonight,"
Finch said while doing a little shimmy dance.

"Of course you do," I muttered as I typed out a reply to
Mateo, who was only just now leaving for the day.

"I've got a date with my sweatpants and YouTube," Dove
replied, spearing her fork at a chopped salad in a to-go
container.

My phone began buzzing, and I pulled it out of my
pocket to see an unknown number across the screen. I sighed,
preparing myself for a spam call but knowing I needed to
answer it. There were too many vendors and staff members
and locals who had my number and it could be something
important. One time, I'd ignored a call and it was Kirby from
the Salty Dog letting me know that one of the peacocks was
roosting on her patio.

"Hawk speaking."

"Oh, hi, Mr. Lachlan, this is Katie Henshaw, Mrs. Westworth's PA," said a woman in a slick PR voice.

I straightened in my chair. "Katie, hi, how are you?"

My sisters looked at me with questioning expressions.
"Who is it?" Finch mouthed, and I waved her away.

"I am well, and you?" Katie asked, doing the formalities
charade that I'd come to expect from these people.

"Well," I said tightly.

"Wonderful! I know you've all had a busy day so I won't
keep you. I just wanted to pencil in a time for you to meet
with Mrs. Westworth to discuss your annual reporting
numbers."

"Those are usually finalized in August after the last day of the season," I said, a question in my voice.

"Yes, but unfortunately, that's not going to work for us this summer," she said. "Mrs. Westworth is planning on heading back to New York after the annual zoo gala, so we'd like to schedule you in for July twelfth. How does two p.m. work for you?"

"But we won't have all of our numbers by then," I blustered. "That's only half of the way through the summer."

My sisters were now both leaning across the kitchen island, staring at me with concerned expressions. Finch grabbed the phone from my grip and put it on speaker.

"I understand," Katie said, clearly not understanding. "But we're going to go ahead and take whatever numbers you have then to make our final decision." I ground my teeth at the way she said "we" even though we all knew she was speaking for Mrs. Westworth alone. "We'll factor in the projected sales figures into your final report."

"Couldn't we hold this meeting virtually at the end of the summer?"

"That's, unfortunately, not going to work for us," she said. "Mrs. Westworth would really like to settle her affairs here before she departs. We'll see you on the twelfth at two. Have a good evening, Mr. Lachlan."

She hung up before I had time to respond. I pounded my fist on the table, making all the dishes clatter.

Finch frowned at the phone. "Fucking bitch."

"That's too soon." I groaned. "It's not enough time to cobble together the money."

"Why don't we start looking at my social media plan?" Dove asked. "We could also start doing more private events, weddings—"

"We can't set up a wedding planning service in four weeks," I cut her off.

"But we could factor it into our reporting for future revenue," Dove countered. "We could do special holiday events outside of the summer. And online ones! And we could open the zoo to other people who need a location for photo shoots and film sets and stuff."

"It's not going to happen, Dove," I said, shoving back from my chair.

"You're such a dick," Dove snarled. "You could at least take my ideas seriously. You're so stuck in your ways, we're about to lose the fucking zoo, asshole."

I just gave her the finger and stormed out the back door. "I'm going for a walk."

"No point working on your house, Hawk!" Dove shouted, already knowing where I was going. "Not when they're going to take the zoo from us because of your pride!"

I marched away at double the pace and headed up the hill toward the building site for my cabin, suddenly having some energy again. Might as well keep working on the foundation even if the Westworths bought the place and leveled it again. Maybe they'd just sell the zoo to another rich family who would use the place like their own personal trophy and let us all still stay here.

Jumping over the rope barricade, I rushed up the back pathway. I couldn't keep living with my sisters. They'd drive me fucking crazy.

I set to work, moving piles and raking leaves from the site. A few minutes later, Heron and Crane showed up, probably having been called by Finch to check on me. I braced myself to tell them to fuck off too, but when I saw Crane was carrying a toolbox and Heron a bag of greasy food, I let them stay.

The twins got busy, silently helping me to blow off the steam of that phone call as we started on the groundwork for the cabin. The sibling telepathy was a double-edged sword. Dove knew how to cut me in just the right way—*was I really too proud?*—but the twins also knew how to help me regroup after. They somehow knew I needed silence and to think, my brain buffering as I tried to come up with a plan to save our family's zoo in only a few weeks.

I didn't even know if this cabin would ever be built. Maybe my siblings and I would all be living in different states with different jobs in a year's time. Maybe Dove was right and I'd waited too long and now I'd killed my dad's dream. Maybe this was the end of the Prickle Island Zoo's legacy.

Whale hello there
ICKLE ISLAND ZOO

Chapter Twenty-One

Hannah

The exhaustion of the day was really starting to wear on me as I walked the twenty-five minutes it took to get to the "Staff Entrance" sign of Holloway estate. I only managed to get lost twice on the way, which felt like a win to me. Walter seemed perfectly content to be carried in my arms even though I'd made a makeshift leash for him out of gift shop ribbons. His stubby little tail thumped against my waist as I turned down the perfectly trimmed hedgerows to the back gate.

A high-tech buzzer sat discreetly to one side. It looked like something out of a Batman film, and I wondered if Alfred was about to ask me to scan my eyeballs or something.

I pushed the buzzer and the video screen flickered to life, a red dot indicating it was recording as my black-and-white picture appeared.

"Uh, hi," I said, awkwardly shifting my weight. Pink hair and a nose ring weren't exactly synonymous with the Holloways, were they? "I'm from the Prickle Island Zoo. I have Walter here." I held Walter's schmoopy face up to the screen and wondered if there was such a thing as a dog retina scan.

"Take a left through the gate and follow the signs to Sycamore Cottage, please," a deep voice said. Then the gates buzzed and started opening.

I did as he instructed, the sandy road turning into pristine white gravel. I took in the sweeping estate. This place looked straight out of a Regency romance novel. The main house was so far in the distance, past a labyrinth of gardens, ponds, sitting areas, and gazebos, that I had to squint to make out the front door. A beautiful cursive sign that looked like a wedding invitation said "Sycamore Cottage" with an arrow.

I set Walter down again, and this time, he seemed happy to toddle alongside me. "You are one spoiled dog," I murmured as he lifted his leg to pee on a topiary unicorn.

I didn't know which way to turn or what to look at. The whole place was like a movie set. As we wound our way through the garden, Sycamore Cottage finally appeared. The house was beautiful, painted all white with gray and black trim. It had box hedges and white flower bushes growing out the front, the whole place devoid of color.

A man in a perfectly pressed navy suit stood at the front door, his hands clasped behind him.

"I am Mrs. Holloway's butler, Alfred," he said in a mild British accent, and I couldn't help but snort. So this really was a Batman movie?

Alfred didn't seem to get the joke; instead, he assessed me with judgmental disdain. "This is usually the part where you state your name," he said impatiently.

"Oh, sorry, I'm Hannah." I placed a hand on my chest. "Newton," I offered, not sure if I should curtsy or bow or something, so I just settled on a floppy-handed wave instead. "I bet the housekeeper was really worried about their dog," I hedged, trying to fill the silence.

"The housekeeper no longer lives in the cottage," Alfred said cryptically. "The woman who owned the dog now works in Martha's Vineyard."

"Oh, that's weird." I probably shouldn't have said that out loud. "So who's looking after the dog?"

"The staff do," Alfred said. "Mrs. Holloway likes to take a walk through the gardens each morning and picks up Walter to spend the day with her in the main house. She returns him in the evening as part of her afternoon exercises."

"So the dog is Mrs. Holloway's now?"

"The dog is the former housekeeper's," Alfred corrected. "He just travels with us everywhere, including the island for the summers where he resides in this cottage."

"That kind of sounds like he's her dog," I pointed out. Alfred just stared at me and I blinked back, trying to make sense of what he was saying. "So this cottage is actually just a big beautiful dog house for an elderly cocker spaniel?"

Alfred pursed his lips at the way I described it but nodded.

"Wow, well, the more you know, I guess," I said, feeling like I had just entered the land of the *Real Housewives*. Rich people really did live in an alternate reality. "Glad Walter's made it back safely. I guess I'll, uh, go now."

"One moment," Alfred said before I could take even a step backward.

"What's up, Freddy? Alfie?" I swung my arms back and

forth, feeling jittery under the butler's scrutiny. "May I call you Alfie?"

"You may not." He looked at me like I was an annoying little gnat buzzing around his ear. With a frustrated sigh, he finally added, "We have a proposition for you."

"Well, that doesn't sound ominous." I flashed him an awkward grin. "You're not going to ask to harvest my organs or something, are you?"

Alfred didn't seem amused. He waved a hand up and down at me. "You work at the zoo, yes?"

I dropped my gaze to the Prickle Island Zoo logo emblazoned across my T-shirt. "What gave me away?"

"Which means you're probably staying in either the lighthouse or the dormitories," he continued, ignoring me. "I am proposing that you stay here," he said, gesturing to the cottage. "Free of charge, naturally. You will have a fully stocked kitchen and access to the golf buggy for driving around the island and to your job at the zoo."

My mouth fell open as I tried to hold in a slew of expletives. "And in exchange?"

"In exchange, you will feed Walter twice a day, let him out to relieve himself in the evenings, and give him his morning heart medication before you go to work."

"You'll let me stay here if I pet sit?" I asked, gaping at him. "Why me?"

Alfred released his hands that were, up to this point, held behind his back and showed me fingers covered from nail to knuckle in Band-Aids. "It seems you are the only person apart from Mrs. Holloway that the dog won't assault."

I gaped at his bloody, bandaged hands and then stared down at the sweet, little, old gentleman sniffing through the grass. This couldn't be the same dog.

"You and I have some work to do on etiquette, buddy," I

murmured out of the corner of my mouth. I looked back at Alfred. "I . . . I don't know if it's appropriate that I—"

"We'll pay you a weekly stipend of five hundred dollars and you can use the Holloways' credit at the spa in town," he said so quickly, he didn't take a single breath.

Holy shit. Did I accidentally plant a money tree or something? It felt like people were just throwing it at me lately.

I considered Alfred, my eyes snagging on his hands. He was really desperate to pass this dog-sitting gig off to someone else.

I looked back up at the cottage that looked more opulent and beautiful than any house I'd ever dreamed of. I tilted my head to the side and my neck throbbed at the motion. A permanent knot had formed in my back from sleeping on that bunk bed . . . a knot that could be worked out by a masseuse at the spa on the Holloways' credit. I bet the bed in there was glorious, with feather pillows and a million thread-count sheets.

"Okay, fine," I said, and I swore I saw Alfred's shoulders sag in relief for a split second before he straightened again into his perfect posture.

"Excellent," he said with a tight smile. "I'll have Sebastian go collect your things from the lighthouse." He pulled out a giant metal key that looked like something a pirate would use to unlock a trunk of gold and held it out to me. "Why don't you get settled in, Ms. Newton? The feeding instructions for Walter are in the manual on the kitchen island."

Of course this dog had a manual. Weren't all rich people's dogs super high-maintenance?

"Great, thanks, Jeeves," I said as I plucked the key from Alfred's grip.

Alfred—as always—was not amused.

Walter and I entered the kitchen, something straight out of Martha Stewart's wet dream, and I had to hold in a shriek of glee. This was my *Princess Diaries* moment. I had this whole gorgeous place to myself for the entire summer!

Walter toddled in and found the nearest plush dog bed—of which there were many—while I immediately pulled out my phone and took a short video to show Tessa and Mae.

TESSA

That is Scrooge McDuck-level fancy.

MAE

Guess we're coming to hang at your house tonight.

ME

IDK, I'm so tired after today.

TESSA

But we need to celebrate our first open week. Also, that house is probably haunted and creepy AF at night so you'll want some buddies around, riiiiiiiiight?!

MAE

We'll bring pizza if you share with us some of that wine on the rack behind you???

ME

Okay, fine. But I will not be held responsible for any Walter attacks.

I glanced over at Walter, who was snoring loudly, already collapsed on his bed, the ribbon leash still trailing over the side.

"Thank you for picking me, buddy," I whispered to him, hoping that this streak of good luck would continue for once. No more falling into penguin ponds and being reprimanded by hot zookeepers. I was fancy wine and white linen couches Hannah now.

I snorted. "Yeah, right."

HAWK'S JEEP

Chapter Twenty-Two

Hawk

"Lachlans!" Kirby called from over the bar. "Surprised to see you here tonight."

Kirby tossed a bar towel over her shoulder and wandered through the crowd toward us. Kirby was a former Londoner who'd owned and operated the Salty Dog for longer than I'd been alive. Normally, we came to staff drinks on Tuesdays, but Finch and I decided we wanted something better than the general store beer we had left in our fridge. I'd invited Dove along as an olive branch.

It was one of the things about being older. My siblings and I didn't fight any less, but we got over it faster.

Kirby gave each of us a peck on the cheek, one of the few Britishisms she'd never seemed to grow out of even after decades of living on Prickle Island.

"Aya and Petey are upstairs," she said, tipping her head to the back stairwell.

"No private parties tonight?" Finch shouted to be heard over the throng of voices.

"It was a hen do," Kirby said, glancing between us and rolling her eyes. "A bachelorette party. They left on a party boat to the mainland about an hour ago."

I checked my watch. It was only six p.m. Getting started early, I guessed.

As the crowd awaiting drinks at the bar grew several people deep, one of the overwhelmed bartenders called for Kirby.

"Go on," she said, nodding to the stairs. "I'll bring up some drinks."

We waved to her in thanks and moved through the crowd, who all seemed to part and give us a wide berth . . . probably because we all still smelled like fermented hay and animal feces. Finch had some sort of suspicious bile on her scrubs that I was guessing came from one of the wallabies with a stomach bug.

"If it isn't the zookeeper Cullens," Petey said when we crested the stairs.

I arched my brow at him.

"Like *Twilight?*" he said. "A bunch of good-looking siblings . . . Never mind. My daughter was obsessed with it back in the day. Must've missed the Lachlan household."

"Oh, it certainly did not," Finch said, grabbing Dove by the shoulder. I was certain Finch was about to mention the Taylor Lautner posters Dove used to have in her room, but Dove gave her an "I'll kill you" death stare and Finch dropped it.

"What's the occasion?" Petey asked.

Petey was a burly, bald man in his early sixties who wore

enough flannel to put a lumberjack to shame. He was a Prickle Island local who did a bunch of odd jobs around the estates and ran the local hardware store/mechanic shop.

"Just felt like some whiskey," Finch said, dropping into one of the plush armchairs. "Whoa." Her eyes snagged on the decor. "That is more penises than I ever wanted to see in my entire life."

I looked up to see a phallic garland hung across one wall with penis-shaped balloons gathered in the corner.

"Bachelorette party," Aya muttered as she held her beer bottle in the air to us in greeting. "And a thousand percent agreed." Aya leaned over to me. "Is it Tuesday already?"

"I needed whiskey," Finch repeated.

"Ah," Aya said like it all made sense now.

Aya was the head of nutrition and animal diets at the zoo. She did all of the food prep and sourced all of the many and varied diets for the animals. She was also Kirby's wife, a fellow Brit of Japanese descent, and fluent in five languages, which had come in very helpful over the years. Aya had made her way over to the island three decades ago to work at the zoo and fell in love with the Salty Dog owner and never left. They were the closest thing we had to aunts.

Kirby came up with a handful of drinks, already knowing what each of us wanted. She dropped a kiss on her wife's head as she rounded the mismatched tables, setting each of our drinks in front of us. The upper floor of the Salty Dog was an odd amalgamation of furniture that Kirby had scooped up whenever the rich estates were reno-vating or redecorating. It was a popular event space in the summer but reserved for us to have staff drinks on Tuesdays.

"I can't believe next summer the twins will be tearing this place up," Aya said.

"There's no way," Petey countered. "They're still, what, sixteen?"

Aya shook her head with a laugh. "I know! Wren is nearly eighteen."

"When did we get so old?" Petey asked, chuckling as he swigged back his beer.

One of the things with growing up in a place as small as Prickle Island was everyone knew everyone. We were all like some weird extended family. Petey, Aya, and Kirby had practically raised us along with the dozen other permanent residents of the island.

I glanced at Finch, who was now unceremoniously popping penis balloons. Growing up here also meant we had the entire island keeping an eye on us as kids. My mom got more than her fair share of phone calls about us getting up to mischief in our youth, especially in the off-season when there were no island visitors and nothing to do but get bored and cause trouble.

Drunken whoops of laughter echoed up and over the balcony. All of the summer staffers were clearly hitting it hard this year—either that or I was getting older and less tolerant . . . probably the latter.

I stood from the leather cigar chair I was sitting in and wandered to the balcony to peek over. When I saw the flash of pink hair, I froze. I'd be lying if I said I hadn't thought about that sunrise every morning since. It had haunted me throughout each day—the look on her face when she turned to me, her smile lit up by the first rays of sun.

I groaned and scrubbed a hand down my face. Hannah was with a gaggle of other front-of-house staffers, one with a headband with a glittery silver "21" atop it. They swayed and cackled, clearly already three sheets to the wind.

I had the sudden urge to go down there and tell them to

behave. Great, I really was a grumpy old man. I decided I should hang around until they left just to make sure they got back to the lighthouse safe and sound. This definitely wasn't about Hannah though . . . This weird, strange protectiveness I was feeling was just me caring about my coworkers' safety. It was about zoo staff conduct, that was all. But when Hannah's big blue eyes seemed to instinctively look up and immediately hook into mine, I knew I was a fucking liar.

Whale hello
there

Chapter Twenty-Three

Hannah

We gasped in unison as the flashlight swept over the rocky tide pools and landed on us. A drunken giggle escaped Tessa's lips.

"Who goes there?" Mae boomed in a deep ogre-like voice, and Tessa and I erupted into laughter.

It was Tessa's twenty-first birthday and I had them over to the cottage for some pre-drinks before we headed to the Salty Dog . . . which in turn ended with us doing some inexplicable late night tide pool exploration. I felt a little more like a big sister/chaperone than a fellow partier though. I watched as Tessa and Mae—who had brought a fake ID with her—took tequila shot after tequila shot while I sipped on a white wine spritzer. I knew they'd be green and sick and painfully hungover tomorrow, and while I was interested in sharing in the celebrations, I wasn't interested in sharing in the day-after regrets.

Still, my body was buzzing pleasantly with the fancy wine we'd pilfered from the cottage, my stomach rumbling as it attempted to digest the quince and cheese crackers we'd scarfed down. What the hell even was quince anyways? Sycamore Cottage was certainly stocked to the hilt with fancy gourmet food, as if they expected someone posh would be residing there. But there was not a Cheeto or Peanut M&M in sight, which needed to be remedied at my earliest convenience.

Goose bumps rippled over my arms as a wine-burp burned up my throat. Did fancy-people wine get you drunk faster? Or was I just extra loopy from another long workday?

"What are you three doing down there?"

I cringed at the voice, knowing exactly who spoke behind the blinding flashlight. Had this man put a tracking device on me or something? Was there some sort of flare that went up whenever I was about to do something embarrassing? I searched beyond the light to try to see his shadowed figure.

"Nothing, *Dad*," I said, dramatically rolling my eyes and making the others shake with barely held-in laughter.

"We're commandeering a boat!" Mae shouted a little too vigorously, and her sneaker slipped on the algae-covered rock.

Tessa cackled as she tumbled into the tide pool, soaking her sparkling, glitter-covered body from head to toe.

"If you're looking for a yacht to break into," Hawk called dryly, "you're on the wrong part of the island. It's too rocky out here to dock."

"Aw," Tessa whined, adjusting her askew "21" headband. Streaks of mascara lined her cheeks from when we'd been crying-laughing as we roamed the tide pools.

The beam of the flashlight landed straight into my eyes. "It's also stealing," Hawk added.

"We weren't going to take it," Mae grumbled, nearly toppling over again as she clambered back toward the stairs. "Just sit on it."

"Then that's trespassing." Hawk's cool voice cut over the sound of waves crashing over rocks.

"We just wanted to celebrate Tessa's birthday." Mae moaned.

"Celebrate indoors." Hawk put the flashlight under his armpit to free up his hands as he moved to the rusty stairwell. He offered Mae his hand to help her out of the tide pool and up the slippery steps.

"The lighthouse was already throwing a party to celebrate something else," she said.

"Celebrate what?"

"Uh . . . the full moon, I think?"

"That seems like a random excuse for the entire front staff to get drunk," Hawk grumbled as he helped Tessa up the stairs.

"Probably," Tessa said, clutching his forearms. "Hans just texted and said Finch was bringing over moonshine. Very on-theme."

"For fuck's sake," Hawk growled. "You couldn't have celebrated before a rainy day?"

"What?"

"The weather forecast is for sun," he said. "Getting shit-faced before a rainy day would've at least given you enough time to nurse your hangovers *before* you had to be sharp for huge crowds of people."

Tessa slung her arm around Mae when she got to the top of the steps. "Well, when you put it like that . . ."

"Come on, Hannah Banana!" Mae sang to me, dancing

down the path. "You've got to get all the way to Camp Holloway before the sun comes up or your soccer Daniel will miss you!"

"Cocker spaniel," I called back.

"You're staying at the Holloways'?" Hawk asked, turning the flashlight my way like a cop interrogating me.

"Will you put that thing down?" I hissed.

"She got a pet-sitting job there. She's staying in the house-keeper's residence," Tessa informed him as I shrunk further under the weight of his surprised stare.

"It won't keep me from my job at the zoo, if that's what you're worried about," I muttered, already bracing for some sort of speech about staff conduct.

I dawdled behind, focusing all of my attention on my soaked sneakers. Hawk kept his hand offered out to me, but I didn't move. I didn't want to look up into his angry, shaming eyes.

"Haze," he said under his breath, extending out his hand farther. The sound of my nickname on his lips in that quiet, little grumble did ungodly things to my insides. All I could imagine was him making that exact same sound with his lips pressed to my ear, his hands in my hair, his—

Jeez. I'd had *way* too much fancy wine. Sober Hannah knew the guy was nothing more than a hot buttwad.

I laughed to myself. Buttwad.

Tessa pointed a floppy, drunken finger at Hawk. "Why does hot, broody zookeeper call you haze?"

Hawk turned toward them. "Why don't you two head back to the lighthouse?" he said. "I can get Hannah home."

"Oh, I bet you can," Tessa said, gyrating her hips and twerking on Mae.

I drew my hand across my neck and glowered at her, but she didn't get the signal.

"Nuh-uh," Mae slurred, pointing an accusatory finger at Hawk. "We don't leave friends behind. You could be a predator for all we know."

"The only predators here are the lions," Hawk said, tipping his head to the electric fence that ran the outer perimeter of the zoo behind him.

Ohhhhhhhh, so that was where we were. It made sense now why he heard us floundering around the rocks. How had we made it all the way down here?

"It's fine," I said, kicking at a seashell. "I'll see you guys in the morning."

"Oh . . ." Tessa sounded suddenly amused. "Right. Right. Right."

I grimaced at my friend's taunting tone. "Happy birthday, Tessa. Drink some water before bed."

Tessa blew me a kiss, and I had a feeling she wasn't listening to me. "I'm freezing my tits off anyway," she said, hugging her arms tighter around her wet top. "We'll see you later. Have fun," she sang.

My pulse rose as their drunken, stumbling steps faded away. Hawk just stood there at the top of the stairwell, arms crossed, unspeaking. The tension mounted until I forced myself to say something.

"So your sister makes moonshine? She really knows how to get a party started," I said lamely, trying to fill the awkward silence.

Hawk guffawed. "Yeah."

"She's not exactly what I thought a veterinarian would be like."

"You must not know a lot of veterinarians."

"I knew the boats weren't down here," I added sheepishly. "I just didn't want those two drowning on their hunt for them, so I figured I'd supervise their rock-pooling expedition.

I didn't realize how close to the zoo we'd got though. How fortuitous."

"You certainly have a way with words."

"That's why I'm . . ." I swallowed, cheeks burning. *A journalist.* I almost said I was a journalist. Out loud. To the man I was meant to be investigating. I took a deep breath. "I knew I could keep them safe."

Hawk scoffed. "And what about the tides?"

"It's low tide right now," I said. "It'd be another handful of hours before I'd need to start reeling them in."

"You're really doing nothing to rebuke my theory that you're secretly a mermaid, you know?"

"What?"

"You learned the tides?"

"You say that like it's a ridiculous thing to do." I folded my arms against a sudden gust of wind. "I'd assumed everyone who lives on a tiny island knows the tides."

"Not the summer folks who live in the lighthouse."

My shoulders rose and fell in a Muppet-y shrug. "Consider me extra diligent."

"Well, haze, you're one less staff member I have to worry about then, I guess," he said with a sigh. "I should be relieved."

"But you're not?"

"No."

"Why?"

"Because all of you are my responsibility and if anything goes wrong this year . . ." He leaned against the rusted railing. "Well, there's just a lot at stake this year."

This was it. He was opening up to me. Maybe I could finally dig up some of that dirt Dawn seemed to think existed. But with every passing day, that began to feel more and more wrong. Before this was a faceless, nameless job. Now, I felt like

I was trying to take something from a real human—a real *family*—and it didn't feel so great, six figures be damned.

"I'm sorry if our little adventure threatened whatever's at stake," I murmured.

"It's not your fault." His voice dropped so quiet, I could barely hear him. "It's mine. I could've secured this place a long time ago for my family if I'd tried harder." He stared out at the water. "I wasn't sure I wanted that pressure. I didn't know if I could ever live up to my father."

I blinked at him. I hadn't considered he wouldn't want to be the owner of the zoo. Who wouldn't want to own a zoo? It seemed like the coolest job ever. "And now?"

"Now I have six younger siblings and five of them I still need to take care of."

"Aren't they all adults?"

"Technically, yes, apart from Wren. Although I don't know if I can ever wrap my brain around Heron and Crane being adults either." He scrubbed his hand down his face, and I suddenly felt the weight of everything upon his shoulders. "I know they're all counting on me to keep our family together. To keep our *home* together. My dad always wanted that—all of us living here, running this place together, carrying on his legacy to the next generation. I know for certain I want that now, but I wasn't always so sure."

"That sounds like an impossible amount to take on."

"Yeah, well." He folded his arms tighter. "Sometimes life happens and you don't have a choice."

"Now *that* I understand."

The moonlight beamed through a break in the clouds. The gentle lapping of waves seemed so soft now compared to the roaring winds and white-capped surf of midday.

"I'm sorry for your loss," I said, finally reaching out my hand for him to help me up the stairs.

He pushed off the railing and took my hand in his own. It was warm and calloused in my cold, clammy grip. He held onto me so tightly, I knew if I fell, he'd hold up my entire body weight from just my hand alone.

My foot slid along the algae-covered steps and skidded out from under me. I gripped Hawk's hand tighter.

"I've got you," he murmured, and I felt those words dance along my skin, wondering what it would be like to have those soft lips on my own.

I blamed it on the wine and moonlight.

I regained my footing and got to the top step, but Hawk didn't let go of my hand. We both stared down at my small hand in his for a moment before he cleared his throat and let go.

"Thanks," I said awkwardly, sweeping a lock of hair behind my ear.

"No problem, haze," he replied, shoving his hands in the pockets of his zoo-branded fleece as if in punishment for his lingering touch. "Come on, I'll walk you home."

HAWK'S JEEP
ISLAND ZOO

Chapter Twenty-Four

Hawk

Why did she have to smell like cinnamon and fresh laundry? How was I supposed to keep focused when all I could think about was burying my nose in her hair and smelling that delicious scent?

Fuck me sideways. This was so bad.

We walked in stilted silence, our shoes chewing up the gravel and the waves breaking on the pebbled shore the only sounds. Inside of me, everything felt like it was building and building and I kept tamping down on it.

My stomach rumbled and Hannah laughed. "Sorry." I grimaced. "It was fondue day."

"Fondue day?" She looked at me with gleeful surprise. "Explain."

"Every Sunday, we have a family dinner that usually

consists of pasta and salad but also always includes cheese fondue," I said, and her mouth fell open like I'd just told her I was a secret billionaire. "We call it Sunday Funday Fondue Day."

"That very well might be the greatest thing I've ever heard in my entire life," she said, bouncing on her toes with excitement. "Well, that and a mini cow named Colin."

"It's silly."

"It's *awesome*," she said. "Really." When my shoulders remained bunched around my ears, she added, "My mom and I have a similar tradition: Pancake Fridays. It's not as cool as fondue, but it was one of the first things I learned how to cook so it stuck."

"I love pancakes," I said.

I love pancakes? I LOVE PANCAKES?

What the fuck was wrong with me? I needed to immediately go back to my vow of monosyllabism. I needed to be slapped with a leather glove duel-style and have someone shout at me to get a grip.

"I love pancakes too, especially blueberry," Hannah replied, seeming to completely ignore my awkward statement. "It must be nice having such a big family." She breezily kept the conversation going.

"If by 'nice' you mean absolute pandemonium, then yes," I replied, and she laughed. I peeked over at her, enraptured by that sound. Her hair danced in the breeze, and I had the terrible urge to reach over and tuck it behind her ear. "Do you have any siblings?"

"None," she said in a sad, little voice that made me quietly ache.

I couldn't imagine. "That seems blissfully noiseless," I tried to joke, but it felt off.

"It was lonely," she said. "I always wanted a big family.

All of that pandemonium, as you put it." She smiled softly. "My mom had me via sperm donor in her mid-forties. And she's the absolute best. Seriously, I couldn't ask for a better mom," she amended quickly. "But she's an only child too, so no cousins, no grandparents, no aunts and uncles. Just the two of us."

I really wanted to reach over and grab her hand then. I wanted to pull her into my chest and wrap her up in my arms and bury my face in her pink hair.

"You are more than welcome to borrow some of my siblings," I offered. "Please, for the love of God, pick the twins to take off my hands."

"A sibling lending library?" She chuckled. "That sounds kind of nice."

We walked down the main strip of shops, lights still on in about half the row, though every store had their "Closed" signs up.

"I don't hate you," I said before I could think better of it.

"What?"

"I know you think I don't like you, but, um, it's not true," I remedied. "I just . . . don't think it's a good idea for us to be . . . friends." I hated that word. It didn't feel anything like the word I wanted to use. I didn't think it was the word Hannah was looking for either, judging by how her lips curved downward.

"Oh," she said.

"I mean, you're only here for the summer," I quickly added, trying to fix that disappointed look on her face. Was she disappointed? Did she want this to be something more? "You probably just want to hang out with your friends and go drunken rock-pooling, which I'm sure seems fun when you're twenty-two and—"

"I'm twenty-eight," she said.

My feet stopped moving, and I lightly held onto Hannah's elbow to make her stop and turn her back toward me. "What?"

"I'm twenty-eight," she repeated, her eyes cagily darting everywhere except my face. "My application had a typo on it. I actually was working for a while before I decided to get my masters in, uh, biology."

"Right, okay." I didn't know why that made a difference. It shouldn't. "All my reasons still stand though," I said more for my own benefit than hers.

"You don't want to be my friend but you don't hate me, got it. Glad we cleared that up," she muttered and kept walking.

I hustled forward and side-stepped in front of her, forcing her to stop walking away. "I'm not doing a good job explaining this," I said, my face scrunching up in frustration. "I would be happy to be your friend. I just feel like . . . ugh." I didn't know what the fuck I was saying now. Seriously, I needed a translator or something because this was ridiculous.

"You just feel like if we hang out, we might venture into more-than-friends territory?" Hannah supplied, finally saying the thing that I'd been thinking since I watched the sunrise with her. "And that would be bad because I'm only here for the summer and it would be destined to not end well?"

"Something like that," I said, rubbing the back of my neck.

"Okay, well, thank you for being honest with me," she said a little more lightly now. "I'd much rather that than you hating me, so . . ."

"I definitely don't hate you," I said again.

"Good," she replied as we continued past the shops and down the road to the Holloways'.

My phone buzzed in my pocket and I took it out.

Of course she'd already talked to Mateo. She really couldn't let this go. I would reply to her when I got home.

I locked my phone and moved to put it back in my pocket when Hannah said, "Oh weird!" She pulled out her phone and showed me the exact same light blue case. "Twinning."

"A sensible brand," I said approvingly. "I'm surprised it's not some sort of tie-dye pink."

Hannah rolled her eyes. "I'm not always eccentric. What made you pick blue?"

"Finch bought it for me for Christmas," I said with a shrug. "You?"

She held the phone up to her face. "It matches my eyes." I chuckled and shook my head. "No, seriously though." She held up the phone to her ear. "Doesn't it make my eyes really pop when I'm taking a call?"

My eyes crinkled. "How often are you *taking calls*?"

Her full lips turned into an adorable pout. "Just let me have this, okay?"

I held up placating hands. "Okay. Okay. Yes, they make your eyes even bluer, like giant ocean-blue saucers."

She bobbed her chin with triumph. God, she was fucking adorable and equally sexy, and I hated the way it made my hands clench in my pockets.

We turned the corner to the staff entrance to the Holloway estate.

"This is me," she said, tipping her head at the towering iron gates. "I'll, um, see you tomorrow."

I shifted awkwardly on my feet, not knowing what to say. I didn't want her to go. I didn't want this to be it. There were a million reasons why she and I shouldn't spend any more time together, but I wanted all of these special, secret moments to continue. This couldn't be the last one.

She turned and was four steps down the pathway before I called out, "Do you want to come with me to feed the lions tomorrow?"

She spun, her eyebrows lifting at my offer. Did she think I was asking her on a date? Was I? Shit. Fix it. Quickly.

"We try to give all the front-house staff a chance during their summer here," I hastily added, and I swore her smile faltered. Fuck fuck fuckity fuck. This was so painfully bad. "It's good for the photo ops and usually keeps morale up."

"You're trying to boost my morale?" Hannah asked skeptically.

Okay, enough of this. It was time to just be honest. I took a tentative step forward and then rocked back on my heels as if being pulled in two directions. "I'm trying to spend time with you."

"Oh. Uh, okay." That earned me a smile. "I'd like that."

"Cool," I said while little cartoon me was leaping around my mind screaming, *"Three-pointer! Nothing but net."* "After work? Five p.m. tomorrow? Meet by the Jeep?" I cleared my throat, really hoping I didn't sound as nervous as I felt.

"See you then," she said with a shy nod, turning to head back to the gate. She looked into the camera and waved. "Hey, Daryl," she said to the security guy on the other end. "How's your night going?"

I chuckled, lingering as she had a quick conversation with the man on the other end. Of course she knew everyone who worked here already. I bet she delighted all of them. Something about Hannah was just pure magic.

I waited until they buzzed her in and the gate swung open

before calling after her, "Make sure you drink lots of water before bed. Tomorrow's going to be a busy one."

She gave me a mock salute. "You got it, boss."

My smile widened, a mirror to the one she was flashing me through the closing gate. "Good night, Hannah."

"Goodnight to you too, Hawk."

I savored the way she said my name as I turned and walked back to the zoo, a little extra bounce in my step.

Whale hello there
KLE ISLAND ZOO
Shop

Chapter Twenty-Five

Hannah

I had never in a million years thought I'd be standing face-to-face with a real-life lion. I'd hoped I'd be as chill as I was on the visitor side behind a sturdy glass partition, but alas, my whole body was trembling, completely out of my control. To be fair, this reaction was probably etched into the very DNA of human existence. Wasn't this literally what our fight/flight/freeze response was designed to protect us against—a mother trucking lion?

All of the intrusive thoughts started pouring in. It felt like I was standing on top of a very large building and I might fling myself off. Except in this instance, I was standing in front of grown-up Simba with nothing but a flimsy chain-link fence between us.

What did my anxious brain think I'd do? Lay my whole

body against the chain-link so it could eat me one nibble at a time? Okay, well, now I was . . .

Hawk's arm landed on my shoulder. "You okay?" I nodded, unable to find any words. This was an incredible, once-in-a-lifetime, permanently time-stamped on my brain kind of moment. "Hannah, meet Sammy. Sammy, meet Hannah." My mouth gaped open and shut like a fish on a hook. "What do you think?"

I finally found my words. "Holy. Shit."

This was *definitely* not on my Hannah bingo card for the year.

I shuffled closer into Hawk's side and then stopped. As if he could protect me if the gates somehow magically evaporated and the lions attacked. It felt like we were in a shark tank—this narrow little chain-link box while the lions had a sprawling faux savanna and heated caves out beyond us. But Sammy, the giant male lion with a beautiful golden mane, was standing right up next to the chain-link, making these happy, little grunting sounds and rubbing his face against the wall like a house cat wanting scratches.

I finally found another statement I could verbalize. "He's so huge!"

"He's average size," Hawk said with a laugh. "But I'm sure he'll take it as a compliment. You want to help me give him his dinner?"

I arched my eyebrow at the meat bucket in Hawk's hand. "You want me to feed that thing with my *bare* hands?"

Hawk reached for the box of rubber gloves mounted on the wall beside a bottle of hand sanitizer, a fire extinguisher, and a first-aid kit. "Actually, you'll be wearing gloves," he said, pulling two out and passing them to me.

"Are these magical lion-proof gloves?" I asked, holding the rubber gloves up to the light.

"You just need to keep your hand flat and you'll be fine." He chuckled, picking up a chunk of raw meat and holding it to the grating.

My stomach turned as the giant lion stood up on his hind legs to reach the food.

"I suppose you're going to tell me he's actually really gentle and wouldn't hurt a fly . . ."

Hawk snorted. "Oh no, he'd kill you without even trying."

"What?!" I screeched, taking a giant step backward.

"One playful swat or love bite and—" He slid his hand across his throat.

"Well, I'm so glad you brought me here, then," I snarked. "Raw meat and the potential loss of life on a first date. How romantic." I quickly realized I'd said all of that out loud. "I mean, not that I think this is a date. This is just me helping you with your job. You said you do this with all the summer staff members. It's no big deal. Date wasn't the word I meant. I was just kidding, and it obviously wasn't funny because you're not currently laughing and—" A sudden waft of a foul scent made me gag. "What is that smell?"

Hawk grinned, ignoring my anxiety spiral. "One of the lionesses is in heat and Sammy has been spraying everywhere."

I wrinkled my nose. "Ew."

"Just beware of any lifted tails and you'll be fine," he said. "If he turns, run."

"Who knew lions were like skunks?" I grumbled even as I put on the gloves.

Hawk lifted the bucket higher for me, and I grabbed out a wad of some sort of meat. I didn't want to ask what it was. "There you go," he said like he was coaching me through some sort of complicated maneuver. "Just put the edge of your palm on the mesh and tip it up."

"Simple as that," I whined. "Just don't mess up or a lion will bite off your fingers."

"You'll be fine," Hawk said, placing a hand on the small of my back that sent fireworks sparkling all the way down to my toes.

"Okay. I can do this," I whispered to myself, taking another step forward.

Sammy's giant eyes tracked my every movement. My stomach plummeted to my feet, my hands shaking, but I kept going. I put my hand on the edge of the mesh and tipped the meat ball up. Sammy gingerly took it in his teeth and stepped back to eat it.

"Oh my god." I gaped at the giant lion inches from my face. "I did it!"

I spun around, relief and glee flooding through me. I flung my arms around Hawk's neck, and he dropped the meat bucket to catch me.

Suddenly, I remembered my whole "this is not a date" fiasco and slowly dropped back onto flat feet.

Hawk's face lingered inches from my own for a split second as his eyes dropped to my lips. I loved the half-smile on his face, so rare, like he couldn't help himself. I loved even more that he was flashing that little smile directly at me. My arms remained wrapped around his neck so I could steal another second. He smelled like sweat and musk and hay, and I had no idea why that smelled so fucking good, but I was beginning to wonder if the lionesses weren't the only ones going into heat.

I cleared my throat and pulled away, crouching to grab another meat ball. "I think I'm getting the hang of this now—"

I turned and was met with a lion butt and a lifted tail.

Shit.

I only had a single heartbeat to close my mouth before a spray of lion piss coated me from the top of my head all the way down to my boots.

Hawk erupted into laughter even as he darted over to grab some paper towels and started blotting my face. I was paralyzed by the stench of it. I held my arms out at my side, my face clenched into a grimace. "I smell like the inside of Satan's asshole!" I groaned. "This is so fucking gross. Why does my throat burn? My eyes are watering. Oh my god, am I going to lose my eyesight?"

Hawk was doubled over now, hands on knees, laughing so hard that his face turned bright red. I would think about how sexy and infectious his laughter was another time, but right now, I had more important things to deal with. I stood there, anxious and frozen, like a cat in a Halloween costume.

"Stop laughing!" I shouted. *Well, at least now I know I can keep my composure,* I thought sarcastically. "What do I do?" I bounced up and down, whining like a toddler who didn't get the gift shop toy they wanted. "I've got to go all the way back to the Holloways' to change STAT!" I groused. "Tell me there's a back way out of here. If I enter the gift shop smelling like this, they'll fire me. I'm burning these clothes."

Hawk seemed to have no qualms putting his bare skin on my piss-coated shirt. His warm hands gripped my sides as he steered me to face him. He still had to take another several breaths before he wasn't laughing when he tried to speak.

"Don't panic. I promise you, it washes out. We've got a closet full of old uniforms back at my house," he assured me. "Come on, it's just behind the vet hospital."

I remained in my frozen—just been sprayed by a lion—position. "You're inviting me back to your house?"

Hawk paused, seemingly missing my implication. "Yes?" His cheeks dimpled in a way that made me forget for a second that I smelled like a rotten sewer. I was more than a little intrigued to see the inside of his home. "The house I share with my sisters," he added.

"Oh yeah, right," I remembered. This wasn't a sexy "come back to my place;" this was an emergency "come back to my place." It wasn't like he was asking me back to his apartment to have really hot, really great sex while I smelled like pepper-spray urine. Jesus, I needed to get my head straight. The ammonia fumes were probably causing brain damage.

"Okay, lead the way," I said.

"Let me just give the girls the rest real quick since they've been so good," Hawk said, turning and opening a feed chute to give the rest of the meat to the lionesses. "Goodnight, you three," he said, looking at each of the lions in turn.

I softened a little at that. "It's nice to see how much their keeper cares about them."

Hawk checked all the locks one more time and then looked at me. He sighed, rubbing the back of his neck. "Sammy was my dad's favorite animal in the zoo," he offered, and I instinctively knew sharing this was something incredibly special. "So naturally, he became my favorite too." He smiled and looked up through the enclosure, and I knew he was staring back in time, remembering his dad. "I guess Sammy is my little part of him that is still with us. He's like this special tie that only Dad and I shared."

We both watched the lions for a beat. "Hawk?"

"Yes, haze?"

"I really want to give you a hug right now, but then you'll smell like toxic sludge right along with me."

His eyes lit up at that and he laughed, turning and wrapping me up in his arms without hesitation. "I'm used to smelling bad," he said with a chuckle as he tucked his chin onto the top of my head. "I'll shower when we get back too."

I squeezed him tighter. The feeling of being completely enveloped in his arms was incredible, even with the nauseating stench. I loved the way his hands gripped me, the way I perfectly fit into his embrace, but when Sammy threatened us with a lifted tail for a second time, I finally relinquished our stinky hug.

"I can't keep smelling like this." I groaned. "But if I let go, then this moment will be over, and I'm scared this is like a 'one-time freak-out thing' and I don't want this to be it either."

"More hugs will be available later," Hawk murmured into my hair, and a tingle zipped straight down my spine at that promise.

"Thank God, because I'm going to throw up."

Whale hello there
TINGLE ISLAND ZOO
Shop

Chapter Twenty-Six

Hannah

I tugged on the khaki fabric, trying to close the gap in the snug button-down. Why had I put on a pink bra? I liked that the color matched my hair, not thinking that anyone would ever see it. Should I have picked more sensible colors or outdoorsy patterns? Did zookeepers wear camouflage and khaki-colored bras too?

I ground my teeth, looking at my bedraggled reflection. At least I didn't smell like piss anymore. I combed my fingers through my hair. The industrial shower had an odd collection of soaps and shampoos, and I selected the only one that had flowers on the front to wash my hair. I might have sniffed a few of the other shampoos and found the one that was definitely Hawk's. When I realized I was huffing his shampoo in the shower, though, I quickly put it back and finished washing. I didn't want to be thought of as a long shower-er or "high maintenance." And while my logical brain told me there was no way Hawk was timing my shower or would even care, the ADHD said: he'll judge you and think you're too needy and this whole thing will all fall apart before it's even begun if you don't get out of the shower right fucking now.

I turned off the water and stepped back out onto the heated concrete floor. The whole place was very rudimentary—concrete and steel fixtures with drain holes in the center of every room. It was an odd juxtaposition to the soft and quirky decor, like the pride flag towels and a flamingo loofa.

The parking lot streetlamps blinked on through the bathroom window as the sun began to set. The final squawks and calls were ringing out through the trees as the animals settled in for the night.

I gave myself one last glance and sighed at the little gap in my shirt. I kept my hands pinned to my sides. If I didn't lift my arms, I'd be fine.

I ambled back down the stairs to the first floor, the smell of stir-fry and spices wafting up the hall. The clamor of banging pots and banter grew until I turned the corner and the conversation instantly died.

My pulse thundered in my ears. Oh god.

Five sets of eyes stared back at me.

"Oh, um, hi," I said, feigning confidence as I waved to the group with little pterodactyl arms to not make my shirt peek open.

Hawk turned from where he was cooking onions and bell peppers in a pan, a white dishtowel thrown over his shoulder and the khaki sleeves of his fresh shirt rolled up like a zookeeper-chef hybrid.

"Looks good," he said, giving an approving nod to my new uniform. "Khaki suits you."

That felt like a serious compliment coming from the head zookeeper. I liked that instant belonging in the acknowledgment too, like I was part of the pack somehow.

I tugged the shirt out and rolled my shoulders. "It's a little snug."

"'Cuz your boobs are bigger than Dove's," said one of the twins—Crane, judging by the chameleon pin on his lapel. Crane was the one who did the reptiles and invertebrates, right? All of that training and quizzing immediately tumbled out of my head.

My cheeks burned as Finch smacked Crane over the head with the roll of tinfoil in her hand.

"Ouch," he grumbled. "It's true!"

Hawk cringed and mouthed, "I'm sorry," to me.

I gave him a small nod, letting him know it was fine.

"Let me introduce you," Hawk said, turning to the gaggle of siblings who crowded around the countertop, some prepping food, others just scrolling on their phones. "Everyone, this is Hannah. She's one of the front-of-house staff."

"Hi," I added with another awkward wave.

"Hannah," Hawk said with a grin, "just got sprayed by Sammy."

His siblings erupted into cheers and guffaws of laughter.

"You've been officially initiated," Finch said in an old-timey bow, swirling her hands like she was bestowing a blessing. "Anointed by the feline gods with the smelliest of golden showers. Welcome to the club. The proud. The few."

"Only Finch, Mom, and I have ever claimed the honors," Hawk added with a chuckle.

"This feels like the 'bird poop is good luck' thing," I said.

"Well, then we're the luckiest bastards to ever roam the earth," Crane said.

I looked around the room, counting heads and wondering

where the rest of the Lachlan clan was. "I thought there were more of you?"

Finch chuckled. "Lars, the one between the two of us." She tipped her head at the one with purple streaks in her hair. "She lives on a farm in New Zealand now, long story but a good one. Our youngest sibling, Wren, lives up the hill at Mom's house. Wren and Mom are having a movie night, and apparently, it's not cool enough for these two." She pointed an accusatory finger at Crane and Heron. "Technically, the twins live up the hill too, but you'd never know it for all the time they spend here."

"Crane is the one with the short hair and the freckle on his left ear," Hawk said.

"Hey!" Crane scowled. "Don't give it away."

Hawk grinned at his brother's angry expression. "Save your tricks for the visitors, wrecking ball."

"I'm the one who's less of an asshole," Heron offered with a cheeky smile. "Also, I'm a they/he kind of chap," they said, tipping an imaginary hat to me.

Crane adjusted the snake wrapped around his neck. "I'm not an asshole . . . all the time. How are the apartment renovations going, Finchy? We can help with the build if you'd let us," he taunted. "Then we can move in here."

"Please, no," Dove whined. "I just got away from you two." Her words carried no heat though, and Heron leaned a shoulder into her and she leaned back.

Finch returned to slicing zucchini beside Hawk. Dove leaned on the countertop beside her, rapidly typing on her phone. She adjusted her round wire-rimmed glasses and gave me a quick smirk, as if sensing my anxiety standing in the middle of their chaos.

I pointed to the macaw perched on the high back of the third barstool. "And who is that?"

"His name is Viago," Heron said with a smile. The macaw squawked in response, his head tilting as he tip-tapped down the chair to grab another pumpkin seed from Heron.

Finch finished chopping and moved over to the wooden dining table that looked incredibly out of place in the all-concrete room. It had a reddish-brown stain, was long and narrow with ornately carved legs that looked like something from a vintage shop, maybe a family heirloom even. I watched in horror as Finch diligently started covering the dining table in tinfoil.

"Are you performing surgery on the table?" I joked.

Finch chuckled and flipped the roll over in her hand like she was a bartender mixing a fancy cocktail. "It's nacho night."

I quirked an eyebrow. "And you're . . . decorating for it?"

"I knew I liked you," Finch said with a laugh.

Hawk shifted over toward me, hooking a finger in the belt loop of my shorts and tugging me closer into his side. My hand casually brushed down the side of his leg as I tried really hard not to flash a pleased smile. I wanted to linger, to stay tucked into his warm side like this, but then I realized I might be way overstepping. Before I could spiral out about it, I shifted away from Hawk.

"Well, I'll leave you to it," I said, giving a half-wave to the room. "It was nice meeting you all. I'll return the shirt tomorrow, thanks."

Hawk's hand reached out as I turned. His fingertips grazed the inside of my palm, barely a touch but enough to stop me in my tracks. I bit the inside of my lip. The action was so small, but it made my insides somersault.

"Why don't you stay for dinner?" Hawk offered, garnering a few surprised looks from his siblings. "We always make way too much and it's better than whatever crudités and caviar they have probably stocked at the Holloways'."

He wasn't wrong there. When I'd gone hunting for something edible in the stocked kitchen, there was not a Cup Noodles in sight but four tins of anchovies and six jars of capers. Six!

"Stay," Hawk insisted again, and a little thrill zipped through me at the way he said it like a command.

Ooh, I liked that *way* too much.

Finch leaned over and nudged her sister with her elbow. Dove didn't look up from her phone, but her cheeks dimpled and eyebrows raised in silent acknowledgment—classic "girl code" move.

I held up an apologetic hand even though I stayed firmly planted by Hawk's side. "I don't want to impose."

"Aw, come on, newbie," Finch said, beckoning me with a tattooed hand. "We like collecting summer friends. There's always a random assortment of guests over for dinner, and you're the first of the summer. We're all really sick of each other by now. Stay."

"Yeah, stay," the twins echoed.

"Okay, I will, thanks." I walked over to the table where Finch stood opening bags of corn chips. "Let me help."

I picked up a bag and opened it, pouring the chips out in a matching circle around the table.

Hawk sautéed the chopped vegetables and greens, covering them in red and orange spices. The room filled with a delicious aroma that made my stomach growl. A man who liked to cook was the golden unicorn of the dating pool, especially if that skill extended beyond grilling meats—bonus points for baking too. I wondered if Hawk baked . . . Yeah, there was no way I could casually work that into a conversation.

I loved the rhythm of this house. It was like some sort of wild dance the way they all moved around each other. Something about me craved this joyful chaos. I was always jealous of my friends who had aunties and cousins and dozens of people who would always show up for them.

"Dove," Finch called to her sister as she manhandled open a jar of salsa. "Help us set out the toppings, please." Despite her ex-rockstar appearance, she had a motherly tone, and I wondered how much of her life had been spent raising her younger siblings. Finch leaned across the bench to the twins. "Go put Matilda and Viago back and then wash your hands. Twice."

"Fine." Crane looked at his twin with a mischievous grin. "I'm bringing Stella to dinner."

"Nope." Hawk instantly spun toward his brother and waved his forearms into an X. "Stella stays put."

"Do I even want to know who Stella is?" I murmured out of the corner of my mouth to Finch.

"A Mexican red-knee," Finch said.

"A what?"

"A tarantula."

My shoulders scrunched to my ears. I suddenly felt like my skin was crawling.

Dove chuckled, walking over to the table with a bowl of guacamole and setting it in the island created by the ring of corn chips. "Don't worry, I can't handle arachnids either," she offered, giving me a free pass to be freaked out.

"Oh good," I said, bouncing on my toes and shaking out my hands. "I thought you'd kick me out if I said I think they're creepy AF."

"I don't mind being covered in muck and inspecting feces for parasites," Dove said. "But the thought of that thing crawling over my hand makes me want to vomit."

I laughed so hard I snorted. I covered my mouth, morti-fied as the twins laughed at me.

Finch stepped in front of me and raised her eyebrows at the twins. "Animals. Back. Now." She flicked her hands at the back stairwell and they scattered.

Dove returned from the kitchen island, placing a bowl of salsa on the table while continuing to scroll through the phone in her right hand.

I caught a peek of what she was looking at. The hot-pink and neon-blue frames of the photos told me enough. "Is that Morph?"

Dove looked up from her phone in surprise. "You're on Morph?"

"I have a profile, but I'm not very good at it yet."

"I have six thousand followers," Dove said, suddenly animating before my very eyes.

"No way! That's incredible."

"Do I even want to know what Morph is?" Finch inter-rupted, setting down the sour cream bowl between us.

"It's a new social app," I said. "It started as a gaming thing, but now everyone is using it. It's just beginning to really explode, mostly teens, but a lot of people think it's going to be the next big thing."

"I keep telling these guys we need a zoo account," Dove said.

"That would be amazing!" I exclaimed then looked to Hawk, who was paused, holding the pan midair as he watched the two of us. "You should definitely do it."

"See?" Dove glared at her brother. "There are ways to increase our income that we're not exploiting right now."

"A bunch of gamer nerds aren't coming to a zoo on an island off the coast of Connecticut," Hawk countered.

"No, but they might buy merch, sponsor animals, lots of things," Dove protested.

"She knows what she's talking about," I cut in, pointing at Dove. "They had over one million new subscribers last month."

He turned his questioning gaze on me. "How do you know about this?"

"I need to keep up with the latest social news for—" I caught myself just before I said *work*. "School."

"I thought you're studying biology?" Finch asked.

I blanched. Had she remembered the profiles of every person they'd hired for the summer? Or had Hawk already mentioned me to his sister?

"I am. I . . ." I looked between Finch and Hawk. "I had a few other odd jobs in social media marketing before I went back for my masters." Okay, first I said it was for school, now I said it was for a past job. Shit. They were definitely going to catch me in this lie. My stomach roiled. They were all going to find out who I really was and were going to hate me for the rest of my life. Wonderful.

"That explains your age," Dove said with a nod. "Wondered what a twenty-eight-year-old was doing here."

Shit. She knew my actual age? Did that mean Hawk had been talking to her too?

"I had Dove update your file," Hawk said quickly.

"Anyway, I'm studying biology but I'm interested in psychology too, particularly how to convey messaging on apps like Morph." I tried to cobble together a decent explanation, but the Lachlan siblings seemed to not pick up on my panic —one of the silver linings of always seeming like I was on the verge of a panic attack, I guessed . . .

"I have so many ideas!" Dove grabbed a plate and passed

one to me. "Come eat out on the deck with me. I want to tell you about this 'meet an animal' VR idea I had."

"Oh, awesome!" I grabbed the plate from her and started dishing up.

Hawk's mouth fell open. He darted looks between the two of us, seemingly dumbfounded, like I'd cracked some sort of sister code.

"I'll join you," he said with a smile, his gaze hooking on mine and catching.

HAWK'S JEEP

Chapter Twenty-Seven

Hawk

"I've never seen anyone talk to Dove that way," I said as I strode beside Hannah through the nighttime zoo. Most of the animals were asleep in their indoor enclosures for the night, but some were just getting their day started. The porcupines were happily snuffling around their foraging boxes, the penguins were swimming around their pond, and the owls, of course, were flying around their aviary, their soft hoots intermingling with the buzz of insects and chitters of summertime crickets.

Hannah's shirt kept peeking open, giving flashes of the bra I now knew for certain was pastel pink. God, that pink was so branded into my mind that I could probably go to the hardware store and find the perfect matching swatch from memory alone.

I wondered if Hannah picked the bra to match her hair. That seemed like a very *her* thing to do. *Bra to match the hair, phone to match the eyes . . . the dark khaki shirt to match mine,* I thought absentmindedly. With only the light of the moon, the colors faded to shadow, but I still knew her shirt was peeking open every time she swung her arms and it was killing me. It would take nothing, the slightest tug, and those buttons would come flying off.

I clenched my jaw, trying to think of anything else besides her gorgeous, full breasts and . . . fuck. I took an awkward step, adjusting myself when Hannah turned to look at the sky.

"She's got some great ideas," Hannah said, eyeing me in a way that made my skin burn. "You should listen to her."

"Maybe I can hire you to be the sibling liaison and translate for me," I replied. "You're good with them."

"A sibling keeper?" Hannah chuckled, rubbing her hands up and down her arms.

"Cold?" I asked, unzipping my jacket.

"Oh no, I'm fine," Hannah said, but I was already wrapping it around her shoulders. She hummed, pulling the fabric around her and sighing in the most delicious way. "You're like a furnace. Are you always this hot?" Her eyes crinkled in that little way they did, and I knew she was blushing. "I mean . . . don't answer that."

"Even in the summer, the ocean winds can bring unexpected cold fronts." I shoved my hands roughly into my pockets because I had no idea what to do with them. Hannah made me lose all ability to move like a normal person and not like a secret alien failing to blend into human society.

We carried on up the hill, the bamboo rustling on the gentle breeze. A curious red panda peeked out of her den, but when she realized we weren't carrying any buckets, she went back to sleep. I knew the cheetahs wouldn't even give me cursory glances as we passed in front of their enclosure. They were like the greyhounds of the cat world: incredibly fast but acted more like couch potatoes.

"Thank you for inviting me to dinner," Hannah said, filling the silence.

"I'm sorry if it was too much. I know my family can be a lot—"

"No." She shook her head. "It was awesome. I . . ." She pulled the jacket tighter around her. "I used to watch these TV shows as a kid, all these big families, *Cheaper by the Dozen* style." She laughed to herself. "And all my school friends who had a bunch of siblings. I always wondered what it would be like. It seemed like chaos, but a really happy kind, you know?"

"Well, you certainly got the chaos part right."

"I was envious," Hannah murmured. "To always have a friend or even an enemy. To always have *someone* to talk to. To never be lonely."

We walked another few steps before I couldn't contain myself anymore. My hand reached out and took hers, threading my fingers through her own. I never wanted her to be lonely. She looked down at our joined hands, and I gave her fingers a little squeeze.

"Can I show you something?" I asked.

She let out a little, contented hum in reply.

I led her off the main path, heading in the direction of the giraffe enclosure. We made it to the top of the hill and stopped at the Jeep. It was built to look like an old safari truck but was actually a playground for kids; above it were two tree-houses connected by a rope bridge. Honestly, it was one of the most popular attractions in the zoo, probably even more so than the animals for children of a certain age. I released

Hannah's hand and hopped into the driver's seat, and she went around to the passenger side.

"Are we going for a ride?" she teased.

I pointed up through the open windscreen. "This is the best spot for stargazing on the entire island."

Hannah looked up at the night sky, and it took great force of will to break my gaze from her to stare up at the stars too. It felt brighter than it had a moment ago, the lights of the main path leaching some of the detail from the constellations, but up here . . . the constellations actually looked milky, not just singular twinkling lights but whole shrouds of color: white and blue and silver.

"It's beautiful," she whispered, reaching out and finding my hand again.

"It is. I come up here when I want some peace and quiet," I whispered back. "With six siblings, we all needed to find places to be alone. I claimed this one."

"I bet you bring all the girls here." She laughed lightly, but I knew it was a question.

I turned to look at her with a grin. "I think you're confusing me with Finch."

She bit the corner of her lip. "I can see how easy it would be," she whispered, keeping her gaze on the stars. "A new girl each summer."

My fingers subconsciously gripped hers tighter, as if she might evaporate into thin air. "That's not me."

"How exactly do you date when you live on an island?"

"The dating pool is pretty small, I'll give you that." I let out a half-hearted laugh. "I've had a few relationships over the years. One pretty serious after college, but she didn't want to live on an island forever and that was that. I dated a private chef from one of the mansions on the eastern peninsula . . . but she got a better job on the mainland and . . ."

"That was that," Hannah echoed.

"Yep."

"One day, you'll find someone who wants to stay," she whispered.

I turned my eyes to her, my lips parting. "One day."

She leaned in, the tiniest movement, and my eyes hooded. "But for now . . ."

I leaned in, her hot breath brushing against my cheek as my lips hovered just above hers, waiting for her to close the distance between them. She didn't hesitate. Her lips met mine in a soft, torturous kiss that flooded my veins with molten heat. So gentle, so sweet, it made me ball my hands with restraint.

She kissed me again, this time her hand snaking up to cup the back of my neck as my tongue brushed the seam of her lips. Restraint be damned. A deep sound rumbled through my chest as I slid my hand to the small of her back. I pulled her off the seat and onto my lap as I deepened our kiss, my tongue diving into her mouth. The feeling of her body pressed against mine set every nerve ending on fire.

The shrill ring of a siren wailed, jolting us apart.

"Shit," I cursed. "Jackie got out again."

"Who's Jackie?"

"The spider monkey." Hannah snorted. "It's not funny!" I said even as I laughed along with her. "She keeps getting out and trying to steal Chicken Wing."

"The penguin?"

"Yep."

"No way!" Hannah cupped her hands to her cheeks as she threw her head back and cackled. "You can't be serious! Star-crossed lovers!"

"I think Jackie thinks he's more of her involuntary pet," I countered. "We've set up cameras but can never catch her.

How does she do it? Spider monkeys don't even have thumbs!"

Hannah laughed harder, her shoulders shaking as she wiped tears from her eyes.

"I've got to go." The last thing I wanted to do was leave, not after that kiss, not with all of the ideas I had swirling around in my mind, ones with Hannah and me and much less clothing. But as the siren whooped again, I said, "I'm sorry."

"Go, go, it's fine. Before another penguin heist." Hannah wheezed. "The Holloways' is just downhill from here. I'll use the emergency exit. I'll call you if I spot any spider monkeys . . . or penguins."

I grinned and grabbed her face, pulling her back into one last quick, burning kiss—one that I hoped would tell her everything, that promised this was only the beginning. And I knew then for certain this was the start of something that was going to shatter me.

Whale hello there

Chapter Twenty-Eight

Hannah

I kept Hawk's jacket in my backpack, trying to find a quiet time to return it to him all morning. I still couldn't believe we'd kissed. The memory of it flooded through me over and over throughout the day. I didn't know a kiss could be that electric—my lips still tingled even thinking about it. And the way he grabbed me and pulled me onto his lap like he was just as desperate for me as I was for him . . . I was never looking at that Jeep the same way again.

Speaking of the Jeep, I had a little idea that I'd been toying with all morning. I spent my lunch break fiddling with the sticker machine to finally get it right. Then I debated throwing it out several times, but finally I decided to stuff it into my pocket to worry about later.

The afternoon moved by in a frenzy. The sun was shining

and the crowds were pouring in. Even Mateo seemed stunned by how many families were coming across the bay. He said the ferries were packed.

The gift shop was doing a roaring trade too. We sold out of zoo-branded sun hats, and I spent most of the day restocking the limited-edition animal pins to keep up with demand. It felt like a team effort, a communal victory of the day. Everyone was bright and chirpy by the end of it.

Maybe the zoo would survive this year and everything would be okay. Maybe all of the dirt I'd dug up on them would still amount to nothing. I kind of hoped it would. I needed the money, but I was starting to become team zoo, and I wanted this David to defeat the Goliath of whatever land developer wanted to buy this place from them.

It wasn't until we were pulling down the roller doors and locking up the place for the night that I heard Hawk's voice on the radio and remembered that I needed to return his jacket.

"I'm just taking the freezer enrichment up to Ptolemy and then I can come down and help with the final sweep," Hawk said. "There's still some stragglers by the crocs."

"I'm going to go out the back gate," I said to Tessa and Mae, seizing the opportunity to find Hawk alone. "I'll see you guys tomorrow?"

"No dinner tonight?"

"I think I'm just going to crash and eat fancy crackers," I said. "I'm exhausted. But today was amazing. Fingers crossed tomorrow is the same!"

They waved me off as I grabbed my backpack and headed into the zoo. The back exit by the Jeep was the closest way to the Holloway estate and would make it easy to take a little detour at the tigers to find Hawk.

I hustled up the hill, wanting to catch him before his

siblings or any volunteers spotted me. I made it up to the tiger lookout without anyone spotting me. The weighted door shut with a bang as I pushed through a curtain of thin chain-link strands that kept the free-flying birds inside their aviary. I spotted two of the blue-and-green parrots already huddled on a branch together, seemingly unbothered by my late-afternoon interruption. I pushed out the other side of the metal curtains and into the hut that looked down on the tiger enclosure.

Judging from the radio still echoing out of the tiger service area, Hawk still hadn't left.

I anxiously held the bundled jacket to my chest, waiting for Hawk to come back through the roped-off trail hidden amongst the bamboo. The zoo was eerily quiet at this time of day, all of the animals seeming to settle in for the afternoon after a wild day of visitors, talks, and feedings. I remembered the sticker in my pocket and pulled it out just as Hawk turned the corner and paused.

The way his surprise morphed when he saw me into a smile he couldn't quite hide made my insides melt.

"Hi," he said, setting down his empty buckets beside the fence and wandering over to me.

"Hi," I replied, rocking back and forth, the memory of that kiss at the Jeep echoing through me again. A kiss had no right to be that good. It lit up every corner of my body like twinkling Christmas lights. "Oh, uh." I realized I was just staring at his lips as he wandered over to me. "Your jacket and the shirt I borrowed," I said, proffering out the clothes. "Thank you for letting me use them. I would've probably vom-ed in the bushes if I had to walk all the way home."

Hawk chuckled as I silently shouted at myself for saying the un-sexiest thing ever. I really didn't want to be conjuring images of me vomiting in this guy's head.

Hawk took the khaki shirt from the top of the pile but left his jacket in my grip. "Do you have a zoo jacket?"

"No," I lamented. "It costs extra to buy one and it's usually warm enough in my uniform without it so—"

"Keep it," he cut in. "It looks cute on you anyway."

My lips curved. He thought I was cute! I fought the urge to skip around at that. I tucked the jacket back under my armpit, delighted that I could still sniff that Hawk scent wafting off it.

"What's that?" Hawk tipped his head to the bumper sticker in my hand.

I instantly regretted making it. There was no way he would like this.

"Oh, what? Nothing," I said a little too quickly, trying to shove the sticker back into my shorts pocket, but Hawk was faster and snatched it out of my hand.

He looked down, perplexed at the bumper sticker I had made with the writing "Hawk's Jeep" on it with little cartoon hawks on either side.

"I, um, just made this for you," I said, tucking my hair behind my burning ears. "It's stupid. I thought you might want to officially claim your special spot."

Hawk's eyes lit up as they lifted from the bumper sticker to meet my gaze. "You made this for me?"

"Yeah," I said sheepishly. "I'm not a graphic designer or anything . . . I could've probably done a better job—" I tried to grab it out of his grip, but he held it higher. No fair. He was already so much taller than me.

"Oh no, I'm keeping this," he said with a laugh. God, I loved that laugh. It felt like it was hard won. Hawk Lachlan didn't give out his laughs for free. "It's perfect," he said, grinning down at me. "It's definitely going on the Jeep."

I realized then that in my attempt to retrieve the sticker, I was standing a hair's breadth from him. His towering body curled over mine as his mischievous smile shifted into something warmer. His gaze dropped to my mouth—an invitation —one I was more than eager to accept. Like a moth to the flame, I lifted up on my toes and kissed him.

HAWK'S JEEP

Chapter Twenty-Nine

Hawk

Her mouth was utterly intoxicating. I quickly put the bumper sticker in my pocket and wrapped my arms around Hannah, pulling her flush against me as I bent to kiss her deeper. We fused together, her fitting so perfectly against me. She had this spicy cinnamon taste to her mouth, and I couldn't help but breathe her in, reveling in the smell of her.

We moved so easily, like we'd done this a thousand times before, like this frenzy was from months of dating and not one single kiss. A satisfied, little breath escaped her lips as I licked into her mouth, and my cock twitched at the sound. I needed this little siren so badly it hurt, needed every single little sound and breath, needed to feel her soft skin pressed into mine.

I lifted Hannah by her ass and she let out a squeak of

surprise as I set her on the railing . . . and then I quickly pivoted her away as I thought about us getting carried away and falling into the electric fence that lined the tiger enclosure below. That would *definitely* be one dramatic way to ruin this moment.

I carried her over to the aviary door and slid the lock across so I could lean her against it—and prevent any of my siblings from opening the door and interrupting us. Hannah clung onto me, her mouth crashing into mine as if she were just as overcome with need as I was. I'd hoped that kiss in the Jeep had been buzzing through her mind as much as it had for me.

There was something completely magnetic about her, something so different than anyone I'd been with before. I'd always gravitated toward the sensible, stoic types who looked good on paper but were far too tame for the kind of life I led. Hannah was so antithetical to everything that I thought I wanted in another person, and yet here she was, a hurricane, one that I had no choice but to get swept up in.

Hannah's fingers dove into my hair and roved down my neck, back, arms, as if she needed to map out every inch of me. Each touch pulled me closer into her as my hips settled against her core. When she rocked against my hardening length, I groaned, my mouth feasting on her, my hands more urgent. What was this frenzy? I'd never been so completely overridden by lust in my life, and Hannah seemed just as desperate.

One hand held her up by her gorgeous ass, and the other dipped under the hem of her T-shirt, feeling her warm, soft skin. My hand strayed farther north and I paused. Normally, I didn't go from first kiss to *possibly* fucking in twenty-four hours . . . Normally, I had more time to know what someone liked and didn't like with an abundance of communication and consent in between. I was definitely not the sort of person to grind on a staff member against the door to an aviary, but somehow here I was, tumbling into this whirlwind headfirst.

I didn't have time to question it, not with that lust-filled look in Hannah's hooded eyes.

Hannah seemed to sense my hesitation and murmured, "Touch me," against my lips as she rode the seam of my pants, and fuck, it was so good, I thought I might come undone.

I let out another groan as I dove my hand into the cup of her bra, rolling her hardened nipple in my fingers and pulling a delicious moan out of her mouth. Maybe we could get away with it. Maybe I could grab those condoms burning a hole in my wallet. I was so fucking desperate to feel her, to take all of her. Maybe . . .

A shrill squawk broke our kiss, and we turned to see two Indian ringnecks against the aviary mesh watching us, their heads cocked in curiosity.

We both chuckled as Hannah pulled back just an inch and asked, "Do you think we'll be caught by anyone other than our feathered friends here if we . . . ?"

Her eyes danced with fire, and my whole body pulsed at that insinuation.

I shook my head. "This is the only way in," I said. "Everyone else will be finishing their jobs for the day anyway."

She kissed me again, a long, leisurely kiss, before pulling back and saying, "I would just like to make it clear that I don't normally do this sort of thing."

"You don't normally sleep with someone against an aviary wall in front of tiger spectators?" I asked, tipping my head to where Ptolemy stood atop his log and rope den, sniffing the air, trying to figure out what the fuck we were doing.

"Oh my god," Hannah said with a surprised laugh. "Nope, this would be a first."

I released my tight grip on her, holding her more gently to me now as I met her eyes. "We should probably slow down?" I asked it more like a question.

Her eyes dropped to where our hips joined and she arched a brow. "Do you want to slow down?" She let out a mischievous chuckle. "Because *despite* this being something I don't normally do, I would very much rather speed up than slow down."

"Oh, thank God," I said, grabbing her by the back of the neck and pulling her into another feverish kiss.

I rocked into her, eliciting another moan from her swollen lips. What I would give to make her unravel at my touch. I wanted her to completely lose herself in me, in this moment, wanted to be the one who made her come undone. The birds started squawking louder and louder as I kissed Hannah fiercely, devouring her.

When her hands dropped to my belt, my bruised lips parted on a groan. I couldn't believe we were doing this—here, now—the way I'd fantasized about having her every day since we'd watched the sunrise . . .

My mom's voice came over the radio, instantly dousing arctic ice water on my libido. "What's going on at the tiger aviary? I can hear the birds all the way in my office."

"I'll go check on them," Dove answered instantly. "I'm right around the corner."

Hannah and I shot apart.

"Shit," she hissed, frantically searching around for a place to hide. Her hands were splayed wide, her head swinging side to side in a half crouch like she was about to tackle someone.

I let out a surprised laugh. "What are you . . . ?"

She darted behind a bronze sculpture of a tiger as I adjusted myself and unlocked the aviary door.

"You're seriously hiding in the bushes?"

Hannah's head peeked up above the statue, her too-wide eyes glaring at me. "Would you like to announce what was just happening here to your *sister*?" she hissed, ducking back down.

"Good point," I said right as the door on the opposite side of the aviary screeched open.

Dove spotted me instantly through the mesh, a confused look on her face.

"What's going on in here?" she asked her birds, putting her hands on her hips and glaring at the female ringneck. "You can't possibly have another egg in there." She looked over at me. "What happened?"

"I was just closing up." I shrugged. "I think some weird noise must've set them off."

Dove rolled her eyes. "You weren't playing country music, were you? That croony, moaning stuff always gets them going."

I heard a snort from behind the tiger sculpture and coughed quickly, trying to cover it.

"Maybe it came from a boat," I said, nodding to the water just beyond the zoo gates. "You know how loud those party boats can get."

"Maybe," Dove said, seemingly unfazed. "Hey, can I run a couple zoo event ideas by you?"

I clenched my jaw. "Can it wait until later?"

Dove furrowed her brow at me. "Do you need help finishing?"

Another snort from behind the sculpture.

I coughed louder, more pointedly. We were both going to hell for this.

The radio beeped, and then Heron's voice said, "Hey, Hawk, can you grab my buckets at the giraffes on your way down?"

I let out a string of curses and picked up my radio. "Roger," I said, knowing that meant I'd have to wash their buckets too.

"I'll help you with the buckets while I tell you my ideas," Dove offered, which would've been a really nice thing to do any other time.

Finally, I relented, knowing that any opportunity to be with Hannah had vanished the second those traitorous birds started squawking. Besides, if we stayed any longer, I was pretty sure Hannah would erupt into laughter and then we'd have revealed we were sleeping together—or at least *attempting* to—to my entire family. There was no way Dove would keep that a secret from the rest of my siblings.

I clenched my hands into fists as I grabbed my buckets and headed with Dove to the giraffes, wishing to myself all the way that I didn't have so many siblings.

I patted the sticker in my pocket, a smile tugging at my mouth. I couldn't wait to plaster it across the bumper of the Jeep, claiming it once and for all as mine. My family never knew what to get me as gifts—I was notoriously impossible to buy for—but this little sticker had easily become my favorite present. It made me feel seen in a way that no one really did —the younger me, the playful one—I swore Hannah was unspooling him out of me. I'd already started plotting how I would return the favor even as I tried very hard not to think about everything that had just happened with Hannah . . . and how I could get it to happen again as soon as possible.

Whale hello there

Chapter Thirty

Hannah

"No sitting on the couches!" I commanded as Tessa ventured dangerously toward the all-white sitting area with a slice of pizza in her hand. "Maybe I should just move the furniture out of here."

"Calm down, Marie Kondo," Tessa said, wandering back over to the kitchen and sitting atop the spongy, chef-quality floor mat. "Stop killing the joy."

I rubbed a hand across my forehead. "I *really* am not cut out for fancy things."

We sat on the floor in the kitchen, eating our pizza after we decided that we couldn't be trusted to not stain any of the expensive furniture. We each had a flute of dessert wine, which we had decided had made us classy, pizza be damned.

Walter slept in a heap on my lap, drooling onto my work shorts.

I looked between Tessa and Mae. The three of us had turned into an unlikely trio over the past few weeks. It was the closest I'd ever felt to having sisters—this strange overprotective feeling toward them, this feeling like they understood me in a way most didn't.

"The dating pool is really slim this year," Tessa bemoaned as she took a sip of wine. "Maybe I should give Hans—"

"Anyone but Hans," I insisted.

"Agreed," Mae chimed in.

"That's easy for you to say," Tessa said, waving at me. "You've got the hottest guy in the zoo chasing your tail, you whimsical little bunny rabbit."

My wine blush intensified tenfold. I hadn't been able to keep what had happened between Hawk and me from my friends. They'd found me wandering through the Prickle Island shops like a horny deer in the headlights and it had all immediately spilled out of me.

I continued to scratch Walter behind the ear as I smiled smugly. Hawk *was* the hottest guy, full stop. Not just in the zoo or on the island. He was hot before, but when he kissed me in the Jeep, it was like every other person just faded into the background and I got Hawk tunnel vision. And then what happened by the tigers . . . Knowing how good someone would be in bed and not getting to have sex with them was its own circle of hell. I wondered how I could remedy that as soon as possible.

Tessa cleared her throat and I blinked, realizing I'd been daydreaming.

I deflated against the cream-colored cabinet behind me. "I have no idea what he sees in me," I grumbled.

Mae scoffed. "Um, hello? You're a catch! You're gorgeous and funny *and* smart," she said, waggling a finger at me.

"Thank you, Wellesley," I said, toasting the ceiling.

"What?"

"What?" I knit my brows in confusion. "Wellesley? My college?"

"I thought you went to Wesleyan?" Mae asked, exchanging glances with Tessa.

My pulse started hammering as my eyes flew wide. "Oh. Yeah. That's what I meant . . . All the Ws." I took another quick swig from my flute. "Too much wine."

Tessa's eyes narrowed at me. "What are you studying at Wesleyan again?"

"Biology."

"What *kind* of biology? What classes?"

It felt like my stomach was going to drop out of my ass. There was more than one kind of biology? The only thing that came to my mind was Bio 101 . . . What else was there? *Think, Hannah!* But Mae interrupted my swirling mind before I could think of an answer.

"What year did you graduate high school? Answer quickly."

My gaze darted to hers and my mouth fell open.

Mae snapped her fingers and pointed to Tessa. "I knew it! I knew she wasn't twenty-two," she said. "Are you in witness protection? Are you an undercover cop?" She looked down to the wine in her hand and quickly tucked it behind her back, as if I were about to bust her for underage drinking.

"I'm not a cop."

"That's what a cop would say."

I rolled my eyes, scrubbing a hand down my face. "You knew I was lying?"

"You were being super cagey about some things," Tessa said with a shrug.

"I didn't expect you two to ask so many questions!" I fired back.

They both started laughing at that.

"We were curious about you! Can you blame us?" Mae chuckled. "So who are you really?"

My gut plummeted again. Here it was, no turning back now. I didn't know how I'd managed to fail upward this long without being caught in a lie. I was terrible at keeping secrets. "I'm a journalist. I was hired to spy on the zoo for someone interested in buying it—" They erupted at that. I had to shout to be heard over their screeches of protest and litany of questions. "But I haven't told them anything."

"Are you going to?" Tessa hissed.

"No, I . . ." I pinched my eyes. "It's complicated."

"Explain," Mae demanded.

I let out a long sigh and then a rapid-fire stream of word salad flew from my mouth. I explained what happened with Dawn and my mom's retirement and the mysterious man named Rick. I was practically on the verge of tears by the time all the words had tumbled out.

"Please don't hate me," I said, dropping my face into my hands.

Tessa and Mae immediately shot forward, wrapping me up in a hug.

"We could never hate you," Tessa said. "You are going through *a lot*. That stuff with your mom? That's really heavy! But you can't do anything to hurt the zoo, banana."

"I know," I said. "I don't want to hurt the zoo. I just, I don't know how to dig myself out of this and I really, really need that money and . . ."

"Maybe you could just keep stringing Dawn along and not give her anything newsworthy?" Mae suggested. "Get the money. Protect the zoo. Win-win."

"But she'd still be lying to Hawk," Tessa cut in. She pinned me with a look. "You can't fuck him until you tell him the truth."

"That's going to be really hard." Mae feigned a swoon. "The pussy wants what the pussy wants."

"No, you're right," I said, rubbing my forehead. My brain felt like it was being squeezed in a vice. "I need to tell him. I just don't want to ruin something that could've been so good. I don't want to disappoint him like that." My voice cracked. "I don't want him to hate me."

"I don't know if he'll be as forgiving as us." Tessa grimaced at me. "But you've got to tell him, Hannah. The longer you leave it, the worse it'll be and the less likely he'll forgive you."

"I know," I groaned.

"Or . . . ," Mae said, looking between us. "You could have a fun summer fling that was destined to end in a couple months anyway. It's not like you're staying on Prickle Island forever. Why not be the wild mystery girl that rocked his world for the summer? Get your money without hurting the zoo," she added hastily. "And go on your merry way, having the best summer of your life."

I perked up at that.

"No," Tessa snapped, and I instantly deflated again. "You've got to tell him."

"After you have lots and lots of great sex," Mae sang.

I stared up at the ceiling and let out a long, grumbling string of curses. "You two are like the worst angel and devil on my shoulders right now."

They closed in on me, hugging me from either side. "You love it."

I tried to rehearse how I was going to confess to Hawk over and over in my mind, but I couldn't think of one single scenario where he still cared about me at the end of it.

HAWK'S JEEP

Chapter Thirty-One

Hawk

A long cold shower hadn't helped me last night and neither had jerking off the following morning. Nothing would satisfy me except for her now. I felt rabid. She was all I could think about. I was packing a semi half the day, trying to think of the least sexy things, but little echoes of Hannah's moans and soft lips kept playing on repeat in my mind. Imagining what would've happened with a little more time reignited my desire over and over again. I needed to see her, needed to finish what we started, and I hoped like hell she was struggling to function today as much as I was.

Somehow, I found myself volunteering in the vet hospital to help Finch and Crane do a health check of our albino ball python, Daisy. The day had gone by in a blur. I went through my morning routines, finding excuses to stop down at the front practically every hour, but whenever I did, Hannah was either not there or deeply engrossed in whatever work she was doing. The weather gods had blessed us with another stunning sunshine day. I swore Hannah brought the sunshine with her wherever she went.

I rubbed my hand across my forehead, half of my mind somewhere else instead of wrangling the six-foot ball python in front of me. I already knew this thing with Hannah was going to end badly. I knew she'd leave at the end of the summer and I'd spend the next several months pretending it didn't bother me until I eventually got over myself and moved on like a grown-ass adult . . .

"Hawk." Finch barked out my name in a way that I knew meant it wasn't the first time she'd called it.

I cleared my throat, refocusing on the task at hand. This was not the sort of job you could daydream through. I needed to put the Hannah stuff to the side for now.

I passed Finch the syringe I'd assumed she was asking for and tried to tune back in.

"So you seeing that Sunflower girl again?" I asked, trying to weasel my way back into conversation.

Finch and Crane exchanged bemused glances.

"Nah," Finch said, holding the syringe cap around her teeth as she drew Daisy's blood.

Daisy seemed entirely unbothered by the procedure as Crane stroked a finger down her triangular head.

"That was not a repeat sort of thing," Finch said, capping the syringe again. "I got the number of a Colombian masseuse at the Salty Dog last night, so I think I'll see what she's up to. Or maybe I'll just go hang with the lighthouse-ers. Otherwise, I've got a bottle of tequila and Netflix."

Crane moved Daisy back into her kennel as Finch removed her blue rubber gloves and tossed them in the trash. We'd all anticipated the blood draw to go smoothly, but you didn't want to take chances with a snake as big as Daisy. Finch and Crane would've probably been fine on their own, but I needed to feel busy today.

"I can help with the tequila," Crane offered.

"Not happening, wrecking ball," Finch said, grabbing the bottle of disinfectant and beginning to spray down the floors.

"I need a new nickname," he muttered

I leapt up and shifted over to one of the steel examination tables, knowing my sister wouldn't wait for me to get out of the spray.

"You're too young," Finch continued.

"I'm the same age as half the lighthouse staff!" Crane protested.

"It's not the same." Finch coated the floor in the soapy spray. "Everyone on this island knows you and knows how old you are. It would look bad for all of us if you get caught shit-faced at a party around here."

"Oh, but it's fine for you to supply the drinks to underage staff and fuck half the women on the island?" Crane sniped, jabbing an accusatory finger at Finch. "That's a pretty bad look for the family too."

"They're all from countries where the drinking age is eighteen. You're going to tell a bunch of French nannies and British golf instructors and Italian baristas that they have to stop drinking even though they've been legally doing it for years? I'm providing them with a safe space and adult supervision, and it saves the Salty Dog calling us because someone is passed out in the parking lot *again*."

I winced, remembering the incident. Everyone saw this summer job as one big party. We had a lot of problems with intoxicated staff members. Of course, my sister wasn't doing anything to help quell that problem.

"Crane, you take Daisy back and I'll help Finch squeegee down the floors in here," I said, putting on my authoritative eldest-brother voice.

Crane looked between Finch and me, seemingly understanding that I wanted to talk to our sister alone. Finch continued mopping as Crane wheeled Daisy's kennel out the door. Our radios crackled as Crane called to Heron to help him with the crate, but we all knew it was just his way of telling Heron where he'd be so they could hang out . . . and probably get up to mischief.

I folded my arms and watched Finch mop aggressively and methodically across the tiles as I calculated my words.

"You're going to tell me I need to stop," she said to the floor.

"Yep," I said. "There's too much heat on us this year. We've got the gala in less than a week and then the Westworths' financial report after that. We can't give them any more reasons not to sell us the zoo. Everyone used to turn a blind eye to your . . . shenanigans." I wheeled my hand in the air. "But too much is at stake right now, just as you said to Crane."

"I know it was hypocritical," Finch muttered. "I just can't believe he's twenty."

I chuckled. It really did feel like all of my younger siblings were frozen in time in my mind. Wren should be eight and still carrying her stuffed red panda around with her everywhere in a little plastic backpack. Heron should be thirteen with braces and greasy hair and sparkly nail polish. Where had the last decade of our lives gone?

"Look," I said to Finch as I grabbed the second giant floor squeegee and started pulling the water down toward the drain. Last task for the afternoon and then we could get dinner. Although, Finch would probably come back and do one last check on all of her patients who currently resided in the hospital. "I get the whole work hard, play hard thing. *Believe me*, I do," I said. "But not with staff. Not anymore."

"That's rich coming from you," Finch said. "Aren't you fucking that pink-haired girl with the bisexual art teacher vibes?"

"*We are not* talking about Hannah right now," I growled.

Of course, that accusation made me think about how badly I *did* want to fuck her. I balled my hands into fists.

Finch chuckled and shook her head. "Oh, Hawky Hawky Hawkerson, you've got it bad for the cute, little artsy chick."

"I do not *have it bad*." I spoke slowly and carefully, anger rising in me. "Also, it's different. Also, nothing's happened between us yet."

"Ah, hence the fact you're two seconds from pounding on your chest and stampeding around here like a puffed-up gorilla, hm?"

"And even if something were to happen," I continued. "We'd be discreet, unlike you."

She held her hand to her chest in mock offense. "You wound me."

"Seriously, Finch," I pushed. "It was all fun and games when you were twenty-three, bringing homemade moonshine to the lighthouse. You're going to be thirty this year." She winced at the number. "At some point, something's gotta give."

"I know," she groaned. "I told myself by thirty, I'd cool it a little." She glanced at me. "I mean, I still plan on having a robust sex life—"

I immediately plugged my ears with my fingers and started shout-singing the theme tune to *Friends* at the top of my lungs. Finch waved her finger across her neck in a "cut it" sign, and I dropped my hands.

"Do you have any acid I can pour in my ears?" I asked, turning to the floor-to-ceiling wall of medicine cabinets behind me.

"I'm just saying, I'll quit it with the lighthouse stuff," she said. "I'll do more dating on the mainland. I'll be more discreet, like you and . . ." She clearly was debating another funny moniker but then thought better of it. "Hannah," she said carefully. "She seems really cool, by the way. Dove's completely obsessed with her."

"She is certainly chaotic enough to fit in with the rest of us," I said and then immediately regretted it. Why was I thinking about Hannah fitting in with my family? She wasn't going to be here in another few months.

Finch hummed. "She certainly is," she said with a shake of her head as she mounted the hose back on the wall and started walking around the room, switching off lights. "She gets my seal of approval, anyway, not that you want or need it."

"She's going to be gone in two months," I said.

"Oh, boy," she said, folding her arms and studying my face. "This is like feelings-level serious."

"It's not serious," I said too quickly. "We've only just kissed and . . . things." I wasn't about to elaborate to my little sister. "Haze is a walking accident waiting to happen and . . ." Finch arched her brow at me, and I finally relented. "And I already know I'm going to be all sorts of fucked up when she leaves at the end of the summer."

"Why not ask her to stay?"

"What?"

"Ask her to stay?" Finch waved around the room. "This is the perfect place to study biology! She'd fit right in here. You can finish your 'cabin'"—she used air quotes and rolled her eyes at the word "cabin"—"and she can live here at the zoo with you and work and study. It'd be great."

"I can't just ask her to stay."

"Why not?"

"Because who would want to stay here in a place like this?"

The lemurs used that opportune moment to start chorusing.

"Literally everyone." Finch balked. "Everyone wants this! Well, at least, all the cool people do. Live at a zoo? Come on, this life is exhausting and intense and emotional, yes, but it's also fucking awesome, and Hannah seems like the sort of person who would love it."

"You've only met her once."

Finch shut off the last light, only the sun lighting the room now as she held open the weighted door with her hip. "Do you just want to fight me on this? Because as the oldest girl in the family, I hate to tell you, I can outlast you in any argument."

My shoulders slumped. "Let me just spend more time with her," I said. "That's all I want right now. Just to be with her. Whatever that means."

"Oh, sweet, sweet, foolish Hawk," Finch said delightedly. "I like seeing you all flustered and heart-eyed."

"Shut up," I gritted out, moving to push past her.

Finch followed after me, singing, "Hawk and Hannah sitting in a tree . . ."

"What are you, ten?" I grumbled, but my sister wasn't dissuaded, taunting me out the front door of the hospital. "And I meant what I said about the lighthouse stuff," I called over my shoulder, but my sister was lost in her teasing song.

Leaving through the back entrance, I cut up toward the

prep kitchens. I tried to stay behind the scenes wherever possible so I didn't have to smile and point visitors toward the toilets. I found a stray bucket that had probably fallen off the golf cart and carried it with me, swinging it mindlessly. But when I turned the corner, I froze, spying a pink-haired siren coming from the other direction.

Whale hello there

Chapter Thirty-Two

Hannah

My heart thundered in my chest when I saw him. Jesus, had he gotten hotter since I'd last seen him? Suddenly, I was wildly aware of the honeyed amber to his brown eyes, the smell of earthy musk that was so fucking manly. Most of the guys I'd dated were coated in body sprays to hide their funky smell. . . but not Hawk. He was naturally gorgeous too, muscled from hard work and tanned by his outdoor job. I bet that hard-muscled torso under that uniform was glorious. I needed a plan to get him shirtless STAT.

The entire pep talk from Tessa and Mae tumbled from my mind at that look in Hawk's eyes, like he was seeing straight through my uniform. I wondered if he was also thinking about getting my clothes off. Despite everything we did up at the Tiger hut, we'd both been woefully dressed.

He set his bucket against the wall and dusted his hands down his shirt. "Hi."

I shifted nervously as I smiled back. Why was I acting like a teenager being asked to prom? We were both adults. It didn't mean anything—couldn't mean anything other than wanting that physical connection to continue. I was investigating his family for crying out loud, and he was never leaving this island . . . There could be no future between us.

Still, I wandered over to him like I was caught in his tractor beam.

"Hi," I said back, tucking a stray wisp of hair behind my ear and taking another tentative step forward.

My shirt brushed against his, the proximity making my head spin. It was hopeless to fight against this pull now that I knew how good he kissed. I looked up into his eyes, and he was smirking down at me as if I had my desire written all over my face. I was about to lift up on my toes when he cleared his throat. I lowered back down, giving him a questioning look.

"Cameras," he murmured, looking at me like it was taking all of his strength not to touch me. "One on the shed and one on the gate."

"Shit," I whispered, staggering backward. "I didn't even think about the cameras." A sudden realization doused me in ice. "Were there cameras up by the tigers?"

"No," Hawk quickly reassured me. "Not in the hut."

"Good, that could've been a disaster," I said, imagining his family catching us grinding on each other like horny honey badgers.

Hawk shrugged. "Hazards of the job. I doubt anyone is watching, but . . ."

"Yeah, no, good call." I sighed, folding my arms in frustration. Dammit. I really, *really* wanted to kiss him again.

The way Hawk's laughing breath danced across my cheek made the hairs on my arm stand on end. "Same," he murmured, seemingly understanding. He pivoted toward the back of the barn and called over his shoulder, "Follow me."

My heart drummed against my sternum as I scanned around the empty back lot before following after him. I turned the corner, down the long stretch of ground that circled the perimeter, but Hawk had disappeared. I was about to stop when a hand reached out from the alley and pulled me to the side.

I yelped and Hawk chuckled as he yanked me into an alcove at the back of the barn. A steel workbench and wash-basin were built into the back wall, stacks of dusty, broken crates beside it. It was clearly not an active working space, but rather a space to gather clutter and broken things that some-body had probably overoptimistically planned on fixing.

Hawk pinned me against the wall, his arms on either side of my head. He smiled, lowering his mouth slowly to mine and whispering across my lips, "No cameras here."

I grinned up at him breathlessly. "Good."

Something in my eagerness gave him pause. He took a step away from me, his hands dropping to his sides. My brows knit in confusion and I wondered if I'd done something wrong.

"I'm not like Finch." Hawk searched my expression. "I don't normally do this. I can't have one casual night and act like nothing happened in the morning." He shook his head. "But this can't be anything . . . lasting either, and . . . I need to be here, and unless you want to extend your trip, which I'm not saying you'd want," he added way too quickly. "This is going to end badly for both of us."

"I know," I said. "But I can't stop thinking about you either."

Hawk's eyes turned to flame, his eyes dropping to my mouth again. "I missed you today."

Heat bloomed in my belly at that confession. I knew then for certain we were both falling hard. We couldn't even go one day without each other.

I shook my head and swallowed. "Why do you have to be . . ." I waved my hand up and down. "You?"

"This is going to hurt, isn't it?" Hawk chuckled and folded his arms in the way that made his biceps bulge, and I bit down on a groan. God, he was so gorgeous, I thought I might combust. "There's no way I'm saying goodbye to you in two months unscathed."

"Ditto," I said, practically panting. It was all I could think to say.

"Every time I see you, it gets harder to keep away," Hawk murmured.

"Then don't keep away."

Hawk tilted his head. "I don't want to hurt you."

"I can handle it," I promised as my chest heaved.

The air between us built with electricity, the magnetic pull so strong, the reasons holding me back growing smaller with every breath. There were a million reasons why this was a bad idea, not the least because I was supposed to be secretly investigating his family. But if I was going to burn every bridge by the end of the summer, I might as well set my heart ablaze too.

"Hannah," Hawk whispered, and the sound from his heavy breath snapped my tether to good sense and I shot forward, wrapping my arms around his neck.

Hawk met me halfway, his mouth landing on mine as his hands dropped to my thighs, and in one smooth movement, he hoisted me up and placed me on the steel workbench. My thighs gripped him tighter as my fingers threaded through his hair. I moaned and his tongue dove into my mouth, tasting me as I rocked my hips against him.

My frenzied hands explored his hard arms, chest, torso, dipping down to his belt buckle. With a groan, Hawk yanked up my tucked-in shirt and dipped his fingers under the hem. Skimming over the cup of my bra, he freed my breast and circled my peaked nipple in the same way he'd done the day before—his hands more confident and possessive now. I let out a sharp breath, frantically trying to free him from his belt.

"I want you so bad." I moaned, his corresponding growl making me slick with wet heat.

"I want to take my time with you first," he said, teasing my nipple as he kissed up my neck.

"Take your time later."

"I'm going to explore every inch of your sweet body." Hawk's hands dropped to my belt, his eyes filled with burning desire. "Pull every little moan out of you until you're begging."

"Begging for?"

"For me to fuck you so hard you won't remember your name."

My core clenched, that lust mounting so swiftly, I thought I might climax from the thought alone.

Hawk's hands dropped to my buckle, quickly loosening it and opening the top button of my pants. I could feel the fiery blush creep up my neck and cheeks as his hand dipped into the waistband of my underwear. His fingers stroked down my sex and I moaned, pushing myself into his touch.

"You're so wet for me," he murmured against my lips.

"Yes," I panted. "Always."

His fingers stroked me up and down, slicking my wet heat over me and circling my clit. My head fell back against the brick wall, the sensation already overpowering me. He'd been working me into this frenzy for days, and I had no control over how swiftly he was pulling this pleasure from me. His deft hands worked over me as he nibbled up my neck, his mouth poised at the shell of my ear as he dipped two fingers inside of me.

"Do you like that, Hannah?" Hawk purred as he massaged my inner walls.

The deep rumble of his voice pushed me higher, and I tilted my hips so he hit that perfect spot that made another breathy moan escape my lips. My hand fisted in his shirt, desperately hanging on as he thrust his fingers in and out. I rode his hand, chasing my pleasure until each breath was a gasp. When the heel of his palm landed on my clit again, I whimpered his name. So close.

Hawk's mouth found mine, devouring my moans, working me higher and higher until I shattered. My climax blasted through me, my pussy clenching around his fingers over and over again as he hummed against my lips, clearly enjoying every little sound he was pulling from me.

When he finally released me, I was breathless and tingling all over. "Please tell me you have a condom," I asked, my chest heaving.

A wicked grin curved his lips as he reached for his pocket. "You want more, haze?"

"I want you inside of me," I pleaded, fumbling with his belt buckle. "Now."

Hawk's eyes hooded with lust. "So desperate for my cock?"

"Yes," I moaned, reaching a hand into his pants and wrapping my fingers around his silken length. His eyes hooded as I stroked him.

"Hawk!" Finch shouted, her voice shredded, as if she'd been running.

"Oh for fuck's sake," Hawk snarled, pulling away and hastily buckling his belt. He whirled in the direction of his sister's shout. "What?"

"Your radio is on!"

Blood drained from my face in horror as I looked down to where my radio was pinned between my hip and the sink. Sure enough, the button was pushed in and the red light was on.

"Oh my god." I twisted the dial on the top, clicking it off.

Hawk's radio beeped and crackled to life, a lone wolf whistle ringing out over the radio followed by rowdy cheers and chuckles, which I could only guess were from the twins.

"Fuck." Hawk wiped a frustrated hand down his face as his sister came barreling around the corner.

I hastily buttoned up my shorts, my whole body drumming with my ratcheting pulse.

Finch bent over, resting her hands on her knees, chest heaving as she panted deep breaths. "Holy shit."

White-hot fear gripped me. I adjusted my clothes and slid off the bench top, my body numb with shock.

"Hannah," Hawk said, reaching for me, but I kept gliding past him, mortified. Everyone must've heard.

Everyone would know.

"Hannah," Hawk called after me, but I didn't stop.

They all would know I was sleeping with the boss's son before I even got to actually sleep with him.

I thought I might throw up. They'd all heard me say things that I normally would never say out loud.

Tears pricked at my eyes as my cheeks burned. I threw open the back gate and barreled toward the front building to hide in the nearest broom cupboard.

One of the Peckish Peacock staff walked past me and said with a snicker, "Where do I sign up for one of those private tours? Is the sex included, or do I have to pay extra?"

I swallowed, trying to keep my tears from falling. I tucked my head down as I crossed the stretch of lawn and headed back toward the front building. First, I needed to panic alone, then I needed to pack my bags and get the hell off this island. I couldn't do this. I couldn't be his mystery dream girl for the summer. We'd almost fucked and that would've destroyed me.

HAWK'S JEEP

Chapter Thirty-Three

Hawk

Finch folded her arms across her chest. "You want to talk to me about discretion again, bro?"

I dropped my head into my hands. "What the fuck was I thinking?"

"Sometimes the hormones just take over." Finch shrugged. "You've seen what hoops our animals will jump through to seize a mating opportunity. Dusty almost gnawed off his leg to get laid that one time."

"Comparing me to an ocelot, great." I groaned.

"Mistakes happen," Finch said, trying and failing to keep her lips from curving into a smile. "Yours just happened in front of the entire zoo."

"Ugh."

"I suppose now's not the best time to point out you won

251

our bet?" Finch chuckled. "The pink-haired one is the first incident report of the summer . . . Well, technically, the two of you are together. That's going to be a fun one for you to write up."

I scrubbed my hands up and down my face, trying to shove the embarrassment back into my pores. "It's a complete disaster."

"Silver lining—I'll be washing your buckets for the next week?" Finch suggested, but when I scowled at her, she only laughed. "It'll be fine," she said with a wave of her hand. "Would you like me to bring Party Animal Finch out of retirement for one more night?" she offered with a mischievous smirk. "Give the staff something else to gossip about?"

"That is oddly very kind of you," I said, looking at my sister.

She shrugged. "Lark would've given you a ten-step strategy. Dove would've shown you a billion YouTube tutorials about how to fix a PR crisis. The twins would've just set a fire to distract everyone. And Wren and Mom would've both told you just suck it up, buttercup, and face your mistakes head-on . . . and maybe stop seeing her."

"I don't know if I *can* stop," I said. "I've never felt so . . ." I shook my head. "I don't know, addicted? To another person. Is that a thing?"

"I'm not going to comment on what I think that means because I don't want you to punch me." Finch grinned. "There's probably a healthier option amongst our siblings, but mine's more fun. Let me have just one more flashlight party? Please?"

"Fine," I said. "I appreciate it." Finch pumped her fist in the air. "It's just a physical thing," I said as she turned away. "We are just, um, physically compatible, that's it. It's nothing serious."

I was scrambling now, trying to say all of the words to make my brain believe them.

"Uh-huh," she said as she wandered back along the building. "Of course it is."

I pushed off the concrete wall. "I should go talk to her."

"That's a good idea," she said. "She's probably freaking out right now."

I clenched and unclenched my hands as I walked, storming down toward the front and not making eye contact with a single staff member I passed. They were wise enough to give me a wide berth. I was sure I looked like I wanted to murder someone.

When I got to the front, Mateo popped his head out of his office. "Hey, Hawk, I think maybe we should talk about—"

"Later," I snapped, holding up a hand to him and scanning the gift shop. "Where is she?"

I knew I didn't need to say who. I knew he—along with everyone else—had heard us both say words that were only ever meant for the other to hear. My stomach plummeted. My mom was probably going to have my head for this. I could already imagine her scheduling a meeting in the boardroom and everything. This was probably even worse than that time Crane accidentally ripped his pants while going commando in front of a group of senior citizens.

"I think they're in the supply closet," Mateo offered. "But maybe it's not a good idea to—"

I wasn't listening. This was my mistake and I needed to make it right. I beelined through the break room and to the supply closet, pausing when I heard harried voices inside.

"I can't believe you're fucking him," one voice cheered.

"I thought we agreed you wouldn't?" another voice countered.

"You have to tell me, how big is he?"

"Mae, she's freaking out," the first one—Tessa, I was guessing—said. "Now is not the time! Deep breaths, banana. But you do have to tell us later. We want all the details."

"Tell me when the next ferry is," Hannah's voice sobbed between hyperventilating breaths, and my chest cracked. "I need to get the fuck off this island."

I couldn't take it.

I opened the door, finding the three of them huddled on the floor, Hannah in the middle with her head in her hands, taking panicked breaths as her friends rubbed soothing circles down her back. Hannah looked up at me with bleary, tear-streaked eyes, and it took everything in me to not instantly drop to my knees and wrap her up in my arms.

"Could I please have a moment alone with Hannah?" I asked tightly to her two friends.

"I think that's what got you two into this mess," Tessa said. I shot her a look, and she flashed me a fear grimace. "Okay. Come on, Mae, let's go."

Mae leaned into Hannah. "Are you okay if we go?"

Hannah nodded, her breathing still all shaky. Her two friends rose, eyeing me like they were imagining burying me as they walked past.

I crouched down, soothing hands up her arms. I cupped her cheeks and pressed my forehead to hers, anchoring us together. Everything felt like it was going to be alright when I touched her. I hoped more than anything she felt the same way.

"Haze, I—"

Hannah shot to her feet, suddenly a ball of energy. "Not here," she said, grabbing me by the hand and heading out the back door. We walked down the road and into a grove of trees, bushwhacking to the center before she stopped.

"Why are we here?" I asked her.

"I wanted to make sure no one overheard," she squeaked, taking sharp, panicked breaths between each word. She grabbed my radio off my belt and threw it into the bushes like it was on fire. "Seeing as that is such a common thing here."

"Take a deep breath for me. Please. Breathe," I commanded, balling my hands at my sides so I didn't touch her. If I touched her, I'd want to kiss her, and then we'd be right back in the mess we'd created. The last thing I needed was some volunteer finding us making out in the woods.

Hannah took a shuddering breath, then one a little slower. "Good," I said, waiting until those watery blue eyes finally met mine before I spoke again. "I'm so sorry for what happened. It's my fault. I should've known better." My frown deepened. "I should've had more restraint. It was unprofessional of me, and I just . . . I just couldn't wait, couldn't stay away from you."

"I know the feeling." She sniffed, wiping her shirt sleeves over her eyes.

I reached out and wiped her cheeks, catching the stray tears. "I'm glad I'm not alone in that."

"Everyone heard us," she said, folding her arms tighter around herself again. "I can't show my face here ever again. I . . . What do I do now?"

"I know it seems like it won't," I said. "But I promise you, this *will* blow over."

"I don't know. This is a big story."

"Clearly, you've never worked at a zoo before." I gently gripped her chin and lifted those beautiful eyes to meet mine. "Gossip around this place is fast normally, but when my sister gets involved, it's faster than the speed of light." I stole a quick glance at her before looking back to the road. "Finch is on it."

"What exactly does that mean?"

"It means, she's throwing a flashlight party down at the dorms tonight," I said. "And I promise you by morning, half the staff will have a story to rival ours."

"I've never been so relieved about excessive drinking," she said with a forced laugh. "That's actually really nice of her."

I grinned. "Sometimes having a party animal sister is a blessing."

"Three cheers for Finch," she said with a chuckle, a little less forced this time.

I pulled her into me then, feeling like I'd regained enough self-control to handle it. God, I loved the way she fit in my arms. I dropped a kiss to the top of her head. "It's all going to be okay," I said again, but I didn't know if it was for her benefit or mine.

Whale hello
there

Chapter Thirty-Four

Hannah

I didn't know when I became such a scent whore, but I slept that night with Hawk's jacket covering me like a blanket. I imagined his warm arms wrapped around me, his hands roving my body as I gave myself one entirely disappointing orgasm to take the edge off and go to sleep.

I woke up to a stream of texts from Dawn and my heart sank. I knew then for certain that I couldn't keep doing this, couldn't keep lying to Hawk, couldn't keep snooping for secrets for whoever this Rick guy was.

I groaned, rubbing the sleep from my eyes. I couldn't hurt Hawk. I had to tell him . . . but he would never forgive me, so maybe we could just be together a little longer and forget everything except him and me?

Guilt swirled like a hot poker in my gut.

Karma was coming for me. I braced for Taylor Swift's lightning bolt to smite me down.

Our burst of passion from the day before played over and over on a highlight reel in my mind. Maybe I could become a permanent dog sitter for the Holloways. Maybe they could use an off-season staff member at the zoo. Maybe I could piece together enough money that Mom could still have her city apartment and happy retirement. Maybe . . .

Or maybe that moment meant way more to me than it did Hawk and he would hate me when he learned I was lying to him and he'd make me walk the plank—*okay, maybe walking the plank was a tad overdramatic*. But it wasn't overdramatic to think I'd be left with no money *and* heartbroken.

Shit. How did we get into heartbreak territory already?

I thought this guy was an asshole a few weeks ago. I still did sometimes! No, not really. He was just misunderstood. *Goddammit, Hannah! Why? Why must you do this to yourself?*

I stumbled out of bed, each horrific future exploding out of me. I had already lived through eighteen different scenarios, each one more terrible than the next, by the time I pushed the button to turn on the fancy automatic espresso machine in the cottage kitchen.

Walter waggled over to me, and I stooped to smush his jowls together and give him a kiss on his adorable gray head. It was going to be okay. I needed coffee, a brisk walk with Walter along the beach . . . and probably a psychologist, but one thing at a time.

We could figure this out, and by *we*, I meant me and the ten different scenario versions of myself who were all equally freaking out right now.

I'd kissed him. I'd. Kissed. Him. And he'd kissed me and then did ungodly things to me that I wanted to happen more than I wanted oxygen in my lungs. And now I couldn't lie to myself about these happy butterfly feelings in my belly anymore.

My phone buzzed again in a relentless, annoying stream of notifications. I finally hit pause on my panic spiral to check my messages.

DAWN

Hello?

Earth to Hannah.

Do I need to call the Coast Guard? What is happening?

Why aren't you checking your messages?

ME

It is 6 a.m.

DAWN

And?

ME

I just woke up.

DAWN

This isn't a vacation. You're not getting paid to sip daiquiris on the beach!

ME

I'm still working on getting more information.

As soon as I hit send, I hated myself for it. I needed to end this. I needed to tell Dawn once and for all I wasn't doing this. But even when it was so undeniably the right thing to do, I hated saying no and disappointing people. Dawn was a super pushy, aggressive boss who knew how to use those insecurities to get what she wanted from me. My rejection sensitivity was really rearing its ugly head right now.

But if I didn't tell her to fuck off, I would be disappointing the super-hot zookeeper I was developing feelings for, so . . . ugh, there was no winning here. Something had to give.

I needed to brain dump all of these thoughts on someone, verbally express them until I could make sense of everything. I decided there was only one person I knew who could talk me through this: my mom.

I got Walter breakfast and took him on a walk down to the quiet end of the eastern beaches where I was certain no one would overhear me before dialing.

Mom picked up on the first ring. "Hi, Secret Agent Murphy!"

"Hi," I croaked.

"Oh no," Mom said, and I could hear rustling like she was sitting down, bracing for whatever I was about to say. "That's not a good hi. What's up, honey?"

I immediately burst into tears, because *of course* I did. Crying was pretty much a daily occurrence in my life. Most of the time, it was because something was really beautiful or moving or one of those animal adoption commercials came on TV or families reuniting at the airport videos, but I also cried when I was sad or angry or just needed to let off some steam. There were different kinds of tears, and right now, I was crying a dozen different kinds of them.

Luckily, Mom was fluent in the rare dialect of sobbing Hannah, and she listened to me as I relayed all of my churning thoughts to her.

She coached me through a few deep breaths before replying, "This is so much for anyone to take on, hon. I'm both happy for you and sorry for you at the same time."

"Yeah." I sniffed. "Same."

"Maybe you can try and slow things down with Hawk until you know what you're feeling and how much," she said.

"I think it would weigh on you to continue something with him before you tell Dawn definitively to go to hell . . . which you should've done ages ago, by the way."

"I know I should just tell her now." I moaned. "I just . . . I just . . . There's a lot of good reasons to see this through too."

"I know this feels really big," Mom said. "But it's not something that actually needs to be decided on right this very second." I opened my mouth to speak, but Mom pushed on. "I know you hate when I say that." I laughed as I wiped my tears. "Give yourself today to just be. Sit with these feelings. Lightly, don't stew."

"Easier said than done," I muttered.

"Oh, I know," Mom said. "Just take it easy on yourself today. Give yourself a little breathing time for the answer to come to you."

"I know what I want. I know what I *should* do. But I just . . . can't do this. I can't tell him. I'm not ready for him to hate me." As I started spiraling again, Mom started taking deep breaths on the other end again.

"I'm happy to stay at this house if—"

"No," I cut in.

"I'll be okay." She sounded so resigned, it made me ache.

It broke me—the thought of her pretending to be happy in that house, alone and sad. I couldn't do that to her, not when a solution was right in my hands, but I couldn't keep lying either. I was torn between two opposing loyalties. The pressure built and built and built inside me and I knew I was about to combust.

"I know it's going to be tough, but you're stronger than you know." Mom's voice was warm and gentle. "Call me tomorrow and we'll make a game plan, okay?"

"Okay."

"I love you, honey," she said. "One way or another, it's going to be okay."

"Love you too, Mom. Bye," I said, battling the knot that was forming in my throat.

Curse my mother and her knowing the perfect thing to say to make me burst into tears again. I sat down on the old stone wall that cut through the sand and dropped my head in my hands and cried.

Walter just plopped down on top of my feet and waited while I tried to ebb the flow of tears. I knew I was being ridiculous. Maybe I could just stay away from Hawk until I could figure out a solution that wouldn't hurt anyone.

I nodded. Perfect plan: delay the problem.

Whale hello there

Chapter Thirty-Five

Hannah

I spent the next few days playing the worst game of hide and go seek ever. Every time I saw anything in khaki or remotely Hawk-shaped, I'd duck into the toilets or flee into the break room. At one point, I resorted to hiding behind a frickin' bush. But I didn't know what to do. What did I say to him? How did I explain? How should I confess or apologize for everything I'd done? A tiny, *tiny* part of me was still wondering if I could get that money from Dawn and rescue my mother from her disappointing retirement . . . How could I still be a good daughter without ruining the zoo *and* breaking my own heart?

"Another week down," Mae said from the front desk where she was scanning the barcodes of giraffe-print slime. "How are you feeling?"

"Tired and sweaty," I said from where I was cutting out little zebra stickers.

"I bet you'll feel better tomorrow," Tessa sang, dancing over to us.

"The zoo gala," Mae said, waving her jazz hands at me for emphasis.

I had memorized enough of the staff handbook by now to be familiar with the gala. It was apparently an annual summer event hosted by the Westworths, an exclusive black-tie, invite-only event for the rich elite that happened after hours. Mateo was already working out where to station each of us throughout the zoo so that the attendees always had someone on hand to offer animal fun facts . . . and subtly mention why they should donate to the zoo. Baby animal stories were highly encouraged.

The zoo earned a huge chunk of money through gala donations, and the event made up a substantial part of the zoo annual revenue, which meant it had to go well. Now more than ever. If they made enough money, all of my plotting and scheming wouldn't matter anyway and they'd be able to keep the zoo and everything would be fine. Maybe then I could pass on any damning information with immunity and still see Hawk . . .

I didn't know what kind of Cinderella fairytale that was, but I had to hold out hope. Maybe I could seduce some rich lord into donating a boatload of money? Ew, okay, I needed a better plan.

"My dress is blue velvet with rhinestones," Tessa said, twirling as if she were already wearing it. "I found it at this thrift shop, and it is disgustingly gorgeous."

"I'm going with simple black slacks, jacket, and a sequin top for a little pizazz," Mae said, doing her jazz hands again —a move I thought she was having a little too much fun with. "What does your outfit look like, Hannah Banana-fana?"

"I . . . I didn't bring a dress," I said with a shrug.

"It was in the welcome email!" Tessa said. "You are really hopeless, bonanza, but we love you anyway. I'm sure one of these bougie shops will have something perfect for you. Mrs. Holloway would probably even buy it for you if you threatened to stop taking care of Walter."

I chuckled. "Probably."

The front desk phone rang, and Mae answered it while Tessa wandered back into the café, where she was stationed for the day. I squatted down behind the front desk to grab another stack of stickers, and a little knock sounded on the desk above me.

"Be right with you," I said in my best customer service voice. But when I popped up from behind the desk, I came face-to-face with Hawk. Startled, I threw the sticker sheets into the air and they rained down over us like confetti.

I wondered if I could successfully cover for myself by shouting "surprise?"

Instead, I stood there. Immobilized. Frozen to the spot.

A little voice nagged in my ear on repeat: *You need to tell him. You need to tell him. You need to tell him.*

Hawk's normally surly face broke a little at the sight of me, his cheeks dimpling, and it made my stomach do all the happy, flippy things that were so problematic right now. He stooped and collected the sticker sheets, tapping them together into a neat stack and passing them back to me.

"Hi," he said, and that single syllable made me tingle all the way to my toes.

"Hi," I squeaked back.

"I, um . . ." He tapped his fingers across the desk, looking at Mae who was turned away from us, talking on the phone.

The day was drizzly and quiet, and no visitors lingered around the shop. "I was wondering if maybe you wanted to get a coffee during your lunch break?"

No! Why? Why did he have to sound so sweet and hopeful? This wasn't the Hawk I knew; he was still a little rough around the edges, but that was actually a really nice question and he seemed legitimately nervous about asking it.

Fuck me. I couldn't spill everything to him over coffee, could I?

All the sirens went off in my brain: Abort! Abort!

"I already had my lunch break," I said breathlessly. "Sorry."

"Okay," he said, narrowing his eyes at me. "Maybe this afternoon—"

"I have to give a tour this afternoon," I said, feeling like a grade A asshole. The phone at the welcome kiosk behind me started ringing. "I should get that. See you later!" I chirped in a voice two octaves too high for me.

I didn't look over my shoulder to see Hawk's expression. But I caught a flash of his khakis as he exited the automatic doors behind us, and there might as well have been a cartoon storm cloud drawn over his head. I crumpled forward. I just needed to put on my big girl pants and just fucking tell him . . . after I told Dawn I was done . . . or I could wait until after the gala and hope they earned a shit ton of money. Just one more day. I could dodge him for one more day, right?

I tried to focus on my work for the next few hours, reorganizing the shelves, cleaning the giant glass windows and aquarium of all the finger smudges, making cute little swirl designs out of the magnets on the magnet board . . .

The radio on my hip scratched.

"Carnivores to Lima Three."

It was Hawk calling Mateo. My stupid heart picked up speed at the sound of his voice.

"Lima Three, go ahead."

"Hey, can you send Hannah up to my office, please?"

My mouth fell open and I dropped the stack of lanyards in my grip. I quickly scrambled to pick them up, feeling like I might pass out or throw up.

Mateo poked his head out of his office. "Hannah, did you copy that?"

"Roger," I said to Mateo, giving him a thumbs-up. My hands were shaking so badly, I had to shove them in my pockets. "You know, I was kind of busy organizing things here. Maybe you could send Mae up instead?"

Mateo shook his head. "He requested you by name; there might be something he needs to do with your paperwork."

"Or something else," Mae taunted as she gave me a wink.

Great, did everyone think this was a booty call? Or was it an actual legitimate paperwork question?

Bile rose up my throat. Did he dig into my paperwork? Did he already know? This was the problem with keeping secrets: the fear of always being caught. I hung my head, feeling like I was being marched to the principal's office, and braced myself to face Hawk and my lies head-on.

Whale hello there
RINCKLE ISLAND ZOO
Shop
EF

Chapter Thirty-Six

Hannah

I rapped on the door so lightly, I hoped no one would hear, but a second later, Hawk's voice called, "Come in."

I walked into the tight windowless room, lit by a flickering fluorescent lightbulb and Hawk's computer screen. The whole place looked like something out of an episode of *Stranger Things*, but I didn't take any time lingering on the messy decor, not when Hawk was staring daggers into me.

I shifted under the weight of his stare, clasping my hands together in front of me. I didn't dare speak and damn myself further, just waited while he watched me.

"You've been avoiding me," he said, tilting his head slightly to consider me as I nibbled my lip.

"I've, um, just been, um, busy?" I said the last word like a question, my words breathy and quavering.

Hawk let out a long sigh and rubbed his eyes. "This is my fault," he said. "I knew I was pushing things too far too fast. That moment with the radio—"

"I don't regret that moment," I said quickly, cutting off his self-doubt tirade. "Except for the part where everyone heard. That wasn't so great." I couldn't bear him thinking this had anything to do with him or how much I wanted to actualize all those promises. "I mean . . . I think it was pretty clear I was enjoying myself." I felt the fiery burn of a blush spreading across my cheeks.

"Then what's going on?" he asked, rising from his chair.

All of the breath was stolen out of me as he stood. He was so close to me now, those beautiful brown eyes scanning my face. I dropped my eyes to his mouth, already knowing exactly the way it would feel. I suddenly had visions of him scooping me up and sitting me atop the boxes behind me and taking me right then and there.

He let out a little grumble, as if he were thinking the same thing, but he pressed his lips together and took a breath.

"There's something I need to tell you," I said.

This was it. Time to bite the bullet.

"Can you tell me over lunch?" he asked eagerly. "Grab a bite to eat with me. Please, don't say no."

I instantly flung all my resolve out the window. I'd tell him later. After lunch. Everyone handled bad news better if they weren't hangry . . . although I doubted how much a full stomach would fix this.

He waited for my answer, my mouth opening and closing twice before I said, "Okay."

"Thank God," he said with that sexy grin that made me melt. "Because I have a surprise for you."

He took my hand and led me out of his office and down toward the Peckish Peacock.

"I think they're closed for the bad weather," I said, pointing to the latched shutters and the darkened windows.

Hawk pulled a key from the dozens on a chain on his belt and waved it at me. "One of the many perks of living at a zoo," he said.

I giggled as he pulled me inside and flicked on the lights.

"You, sit," he said as we walked into the restaurant's kitchen.

I perched on the countertop beside the stove as he rifled through the pantry.

"You had the sudden urge to cook?" I asked skeptically.

"Aha!" he said as he pulled out a bowl and a bag of flour. He snagged an apron off the long row of black ones hanging on the far wall and then opened the fridge to grab out a giant pallet of eggs. I watched him in delighted wonder for a few minutes as he set to work. I liked the way he used his hands: strong, confident. Cooking shouldn't be such a turn-on but, right now, it absolutely was.

I kept considering butting in, taking this opportunity to finally confess everything, but this moment was so perfect. I didn't want to ruin it. After we ate, I'd tell him.

"Okay, I give," I said, swinging my legs. "What are you making?"

He dusted a floured hand down his apron. "It's Friday."

"Okay." I strung out the word as I darted looks around the room, trying to figure out what that meant.

Hawk shrugged and pulled a bowl of blueberries out of the fridge. "I'm making pancakes."

I just stared at him, unblinking for a second before my mind finally came back online.

He remembered.

He remembered what I'd told him on that night when he'd walked me home. He remembered my mom and I made pancakes for dinner every Friday and that my favorite were blueberry. It made me homesick and heartbroken and grateful and guilty all at once.

My eyes misted. "You're making Friday Pancakes for me?" My voice wobbled.

"Baby," he said with a smile, gravitating over to me, "I wasn't trying to make you cry."

He'd just called me baby like it was nothing, like he called me baby all the time, like I was someone special to him, and it only made my eyes well more.

"I cry when I'm happy." I sniffed. "You're just going to have to deal with it. You did something really nice, and now I'm crying."

He nestled himself between my legs, leaning in as his hands reached up to wipe my tears. From this high counter-top, our faces were exactly parallel. He didn't have to lean down to kiss me. He barely needed to move at all. My breath hitched as he bridged the distance.

He hummed as his lips worked over mine, like he was savoring a delicious meal. My hands lifted from the metal table and threaded into his short hair, pulling him closer as I breathed him in.

Oh sweet baby Jesus. This was everything. There was kissing and there was *kissing*, and this was definitely the fire-works-exploding kind. Something about the way he moved, the way we joined, it was unlike any other relationship I'd ever had before. His taste, his sounds, his *tongue* . . . every little movement sent lightning bolts of pleasure zipping around my body. My hammering heartbeat lodged in my throat as I let go and free-fell into his lips.

My fingertips pressed into his warm skin as if he weren't close enough even flush against me, as if I could fuse the two of us together into one. It would never be enough. Not with him.

Hawk broke our kiss to rest his forehead against mine. "You're distracting me with this sweet mouth, haze, but I don't want to burn the place down."

I pulled away, a satisfied smile on my lips. "I guess that's a worthy reason," I teased, willing myself to slow down. He and I were always going feral for each other.

Let him make you pancakes first, Hannah! But when Hawk's lips were on mine, nothing else existed. No amount of delicious food would satisfy compared to the taste of him. I was ravenous, but only for him.

With a groan, I finally released him, and Hawk seemed perfectly smug with my reluctance to let him go. He went back to mixing the batter, and I swung my legs as I watched him confidently navigate the kitchen.

"Is this a Lachlan family pancake recipe?" I asked.

Hawk grinned. "It's my grandpa's actually. My dad's dad. He was the one who taught me to make them . . . although I'm pretty sure he just wrote down the recipe on the back of a syrup bottle."

I chuckled. "That is very much my brand of cooking. What was your grandpa's name?"

"Simon," Hawk said. "It was my dad's name too."

I hated the way he hung on the word "was" for a split second too long. My fingers clung to the countertop tighter, and I wished I were hugging him to me.

"I'm surprised his name wasn't Tiger or Dragon or something," I lightly teased, earning the slightest dimpling of Hawk's cheek.

He shook his head. "No, I was meant to be Simon too, but, well, my dad wasn't exactly one for tradition. They settled on giving it to me as a middle name, but I could see myself naming a son Simon someday, carrying on the tradition."

"Hawk Simon Lachlan," I mused. "I like it." Hawk grabbed a whisk and started mixing the batter. "What was your dad like?" Hawk's whisking paused. "Sorry. If you don't want to talk about him——"

"No," Hawk cut in. "I like talking about my dad," he assured me. "It was just a nice question, that's all. Some people feel too uncomfortable asking me about him, like they're afraid it'll upset me, but it feels like I'm honoring him when I talk about him. It's like it keeps him fresh in my mind or something, dusts the cobwebs off the memories. I don't know if that makes sense."

"I think that makes perfect sense." I nodded and he grinned down at the batter. "Tell me about him."

Hawk fished a pan out from a drawer and set it on the burner. "Dad was a lot like me," he said as he started searching for butter in the fridge. "People who didn't know him well thought he was a bit rough around the edges, hard-working, a man of few words." He shook his head. "But that wasn't him at all. He was actually pretty funny, always had a bad dad joke on hand for any occasion." He laughed lightly to himself. "He hated small talk but could talk about animals for hours. He always made time for each of us even with his crazy schedule. He was the kind of father I hope to be one day." Hawk stared at the pancakes sizzling in the pan, his face pinched. "I wish the younger ones had more time with him. I wish we all did."

I couldn't contain myself at that. I slid off the countertop and hugged him from behind as he flipped the pancakes. He twisted to the side, wrapping an arm around my shoulders and pulling me into him as he continued to flip.

"I'm so sorry," I whispered into his chest, squeezing him

tighter, wishing I could pull all of his sorrows out of his body and carry them for him. I'd heard from Tessa and Mae about how Simon Lachlan had died—how Hawk was the one to find him. It made tears well in my eyes again. I couldn't imagine that kind of pain. "If ever you remember something about him, if ever you need someone to help you dust the cobwebs off those memories, I'm here for you."

When I sniffed, Hawk set the spatula down and lifted a flour-covered hand to cup my cheek. "Don't cry, haze," he murmured, dropping a kiss to my lips.

"I warned you about me and crying."

"You can cry for the both of us, then," Hawk said with a laugh as he wiped my tears. "I haven't cried since the day my dad died."

I reared back at that, my eyes widening. "Really?"

"Really," he said as if that were no big deal.

That just made me want to cry even harder. "You should probably talk to a therapist about that or—" He cut me off with another kiss and I lifted onto my tiptoes, my hands roving up his sides. "I know you're trying to distract me," I murmured against his mouth, "but I promise we're going to come back to this therapy thing."

Hawk's arms banded around my waist and he pulled me in tighter, deepening our kiss. I could lose myself in his lips, in his arms, his scent and warmth wrapping around me and making me dizzy.

But as my tongue brushed the seam on his lips, I smelled smoke. We shot apart as Hawk took the pan off the burner, rescuing the pancakes that were now charred on one side.

"Did I mention I love slightly burnt pancakes?" I laughed and hooked my thumb back to the countertop. "I'm just going to sit over there. No more distractions."

Hawk laughed and shook his head. "I think you're turning me into a hazard right along with you, haze."

HAWK'S JEEP

Chapter Thirty-Seven

Hawk

Charred pancakes were my new favorite flavor. I still had a little burn on the edge of my tongue from where a nuclear blueberry burst on it, but now it just reminded me of Hannah and her little, happy hums she made with every syrupy bite. She'd kept trying to tell me something, but I'd been too distracted by her presence and that perfect moment between us. I had interrupted our lunch several times to kiss her, like I couldn't help but go three bites without her sticky, sweet lips on mine. After lunch, I vowed I'd take her to dinner after the gala and she could tell me everything. I *really* needed to focus all of my energy on the gala, but I didn't know if I'd survive a whole twenty-four hours without her.

What was happening to me? I felt so unlike myself . . . . Well, that wasn't true. I felt like a version of me before: before life caught up with me, before all of my responsibilities started to weigh me down. I felt oddly giddy, like Hannah spiked the air I breathed.

We'd spent our lunch talking about our families, our childhoods, the oddest memories popping up into my mind. She helped me dust the cobwebs off so many of them. It was like she dug up this part of me long buried. We could've talked for another ten hours straight and not run out of things to talk about.

I didn't want her to go back to work, but I'd already eaten up a good chunk of both of our workdays and knew it'd be time to start the afternoon feeds soon. Couldn't keep the animals waiting. There would probably already be a crowd of visitors waiting for the Tiger Talk, and if I didn't want a bunch of family members hunting me down, I knew we'd have to end this burnt pancake lunch eventually.

Still, I didn't want it to end, wished we could just steal a little more time together. I hoped Hannah felt that way too. She was an enigma, impossible to pin down, and I was afraid every time we parted that she'd go back to this hot-and-cold dance between us. She'd been avoiding me, and I still didn't really know why. I assumed that was what she was trying to tell me, but maybe I kept interrupting her because I didn't want to hear it. If she had reasons why the two of us couldn't be together, I didn't want to know about them. Not when she lit up all my senses and made everything brighter.

Not when I was falling in love with her . . .

That was what this feeling was, wasn't it? I knew any last attempts to push this away were long gone now. Nothing left to grab onto. I was free-falling.

But Hannah was probably right to set some distance right now, especially with the gala. Every time we were together, it felt like a tornado, like a kind of desperate magnetism I didn't think existed outside of movies. I just needed to figure out how to keep her in my orbit.

My feet paused halfway to the tigers at that thought.

Did I want to keep her in my orbit? Did I want her to stay? My mind answered yes before I could even give it a second thought. I didn't know what that meant, didn't know how to pick it apart, but there had to be some way to keep this thing between us. The end of summer didn't have to loom over us like a ticking time bomb, did it?

"I didn't know the hedges were so fascinating to you," Mom said.

I twisted and realized she was standing right beside me. How long had I been staring at a hedge, daydreaming about Hannah?

I swore Mom had cursed us all that day when she'd said, "Lachlans fall hard and they fall fast." Judging by the look on her face, she seemed to know exactly why I was stalled out here.

I cleared my throat. "I was just thinking."

"About the girl with pink hair wearing your jacket?" Mom asked. I shot her a skeptical look, and she threw her head back and laughed. "You seriously underestimate me," she said. "For one thing, that jacket is way too big for her."

"She could've borrowed it from someone else."

Mom arched her brow in a way that would make The Rock jealous. "The zipper is bronze," she said. "An error in my order from that year. The rest of the jackets have silver zippers." She gave me a gotcha smile. "I suppose I could always go and ask her to read the tag? I suspect a very thoughtful mother has sewn a name onto it. I wonder whose name that could be?"

"Okay, fine, you win," I said. "Are you sure you've never been a detective?"

"She's cute," Mom replied, ignoring me. "And seems just crazy enough to be able to handle you."

"Hey," I said, elbowing her playfully.

She chuckled, waving her hand up and down. "I like this," she said. "You seem happy, getting lost staring at the bushes and all."

"I should be focused on the zoo," I said. "Especially this year of all years. Look what happened when Lark got distracted with Logan."

Mom folded her arms. "She met the love of her life and is living her dream happily ever after?" she asked incredulously.

She and I both knew that wasn't what I meant, but I'd let her have it.

"Don't worry so much about this year." Mom gave my shoulder a squeeze. "If the Westworths sell the zoo, then they sell the zoo."

My eyes bugged out of my head. "*How* can you say that?"

"Trust me." Mom squeezed my shoulder again. "If they sell, I have a horse in that race. We'll be able to keep the zoo."

My eyebrows shot up in my hairline. "What are you talking about? Who?"

Mom pressed her lips together, and I knew she wasn't going to tell me. "Just enjoy your time with Hannah."

"No," I said. "Whatever you're thinking is a backup plan. We deserve this zoo. This is our home and I'm going to secure this future for us," I insisted.

Mom sighed, clearly knowing I wouldn't let this go. "This zoo is my life, Hawk," Mom said, her lip sticking out to one side in the way it always did when she was concerned for me. "But this isn't my whole life. It's the people in it that give it meaning."

I narrowed my eyes at her. "Okay?"

Mom threw her hands up like I was hopeless. I knew she wanted to say more, smother me in her Evelyn Lachlan wisdom, but when her watch buzzed and she looked down at the screen, she frowned.

"Aren't you late for the Tiger Talk?" she asked.

"Shit." I took off at a sprint, leaving Mom laughing behind me.

Whale hello there

Chapter Thirty-Eight

Hannah

I walked down Prickle Island's main road, peering into each boutique window but not entering. I stalled out in front of a pin-striped awning, the glass window emblazoned in gold letters: Johnny's Rockin' Candy Emporium. A root beer float *would* be an excellent way to take my mind off my wardrobe woes, but I forbade myself to enter. The last thing I needed was to form an attachment to overpriced, vintage sodas.

I bounced on my toes, humming a little whining song to myself as I searched the shops for anything that looked like it sold dresses for less than one thousand dollars. There was no way in hell I could afford one of those for the gala. I turned in a circle, anxiety rising with each spin. What were the chances there was a quaint little nautical-themed Target hiding amongst this row of designer shops?

Tessa and Mae had gone back to the lighthouse to get ready for the gala, leaving me to hunt for a dress alone. I wondered if I could pull a *Sound of Music* and turn some of the fancy curtains from the cottage into a dress?

No. I knew better than to listen to that optimistic voice in my head that said, "I could probably make that myself."

I'd had a brief hyperfocus with sewing—watched every video and tutorial, hours of researching the best materials, bought a sewing machine that cost an entire paycheck, sewed one wonky pillow, and then lost interest. So, the DIY dress option was out.

On a scale of one to stalker, how inappropriate would it be to just ask one of these preppy tennis girls walking past if I could borrow one of their dresses?

I was seriously considering just calling in sick when the door to the store across the street opened. The ostentatious bell clanged as Alfred stepped out, his nose instantly scrunching when he saw me, as if I were covered in monkey feces. He paused, taking in my work boots and wool socks, khaki shorts, and sweat-stained T-shirt. His lips curled.

We did this every time we saw each other—I'd be my warm, friendly self, and he'd look like I'd just thrown up a hairball in front of him. I was starting to just take it as his version of "hello," like when someone in Boston gave you the middle finger.

"Window-shopping?" he asked, his voice dripping with sarcasm as he adjusted the three heavy bags in his hands.

"I need a dress for the zoo gala tonight," I said.

He released a sharp, honking laugh that made him sound like a posh, drunken goose. "You can't be serious."

"I forgot to bring one," I muttered, crossing my arms. When Alfred laughed again, I snapped. "Hey! Have you enjoyed having your fingers intact these last few weeks?" My gaze dropped to his hands. "Because I'm starting to think about moving back to the lighthouse, so . . ."

"Oh, please." Alfred let out a long, sarcastic sigh, trying to stop his mocking laughter. "You are a rookie at this manipulation thing. You have no idea the kind of sharks I deal with all day long." He looked me up and down again. "But I do like a project." He cocked his head. "Okay, fine, I'll help you."

"Just like that?" My eyebrows shot up. "Why?"

"Why not?"

"Because you look like you have food poisoning whenever you see me?"

Alfred squared his shoulders. "What is the name of the gatekeeper?"

"Who, Daryl or Sean?" I asked, confused. "Daryl is the one who's married to a pastry chef, has three grown kids, and he and his wife spend a good chunk of their year working on private yachts. Sean is one of the golf instructor's kids and is obsessed with *Fortnite* and futsal, which I thought was just him mispronouncing football at first, but *actually* it's a real sport where—"

"Exactly," Alfred cut in with a nod of his chin. "That's why I'll help you." I had no idea what that meant, but he didn't give me time to process as he said, "Go back to the cottage. I'll organize to send someone over with dresses in your size."

I crossed my arms and popped my hip out. "How do you know my size?"

He scoffed. "I know a lot more than that, Hannah Murphy."

My jaw fell open, and Alfred reached out with a single finger like he was touching a gaping fish and shut it.

"You think I didn't vet you the second I offered you the job?" he mused. "Hannah Murphy, twenty-eight, daughter of

Rebecca Murphy, journalist at the *Shoreline Gazette*—of course, I use the word journalist very loosely. Would you like to know your credit score?" He cocked his head. "I can assure you it's not good."

My face heated as I stole glances up and down the street. "Are you going to tell anyone?"

Alfred weighed his head from side to side. "There's really no one to tell. I don't hang around with zookeepers like you do," he said. "Don't worry, I don't find your secrets all that intriguing anyway."

"Great." I didn't know why I found that offensive. Alfred had a way of making everything he said sound like an insult.

"Go take a shower," he said, proving my point once again. "I'll get Chloe to head over after she's done with Mrs. Holloway."

I'd bumped into Chloe a few times on my way in and out of the property. She was a perky stylist with a chic bob and makeup skills that made it look photoshopped onto her. I wasn't sure what wardrobe an octogenarian's stylist could pull for me, but I accepted the offer without complaint.

"This is really nice of you," I said, shooting forward before he could stop me.

I gave Alfred a swift, tight hug, making his shoulders bunch up around his ears. He peeled me off him and smoothed down his jacket.

"Not a hugger," I said. "Got it." He started walking away with a roll of his eyes. "Thanks, Alfie!"

"Alfred," he called over his shoulder then fled into Johnny's Rockin' Candy Emporium.

"We'll work on it!" I called back as the door shut behind him.

HAWK'S JEEP

Chapter Thirty-Nine

Hawk

I paced back and forth in the kitchen, checking my watch for the hundredth time. "Guests will be arriving soon!" I shouted up the stairs. "Staff are already in welcome positions!"

Finch stumbled down the metal stairs. She wore an all-black tuxedo, her hair slicked back like a forties gangster. She adjusted her skinny black tie and winked at me as if she, too, knew that she looked better in her suit than I did in mine.

Dove's tan leather boots clanged down the grating and she appeared beside Finch. She wore a sage-green linen dress with a white corset-looking bodice thing that made her look like she should be serving mead in a tavern and not welcoming visitors to a zoo. Her hair was pinned back off her face by two floral silver clips, and she'd painted white freckles around her rouged cheeks.

"Well, hello there, Galadriel," Finch said. "Point me to the Shire."

Dove gave her an exasperated look. "There are so many things wrong with that sentence, and I don't have time to correct you."

"I look forward to your nerdy rant later," Finch said with a wink. "Let's go dazzle some old, rich people."

We wandered over toward the Peckish Peacock, where the space had been converted into a glittering wonderland—crystal chandeliers, twinkling Christmas lights, bar tables with elaborate floral centerpieces. The trees surrounding the Peckish Peacock had been dramatically lit with pink and purple floodlights, and a string quartet was tuning their instruments on a silver dais right beside the bar. A photographer wandered around snapping photos of the decor in between the drifts of well-dressed guests arriving from the front entrance. Volunteers and summer staff members milled about in their finest attire, holding trays of Champagne and hors d'oeuvres.

I found myself scanning through the crowd for Hannah even though I'd been telling myself all day that I needed to focus on the gala. I'd take her to dinner afterward. It would be my reward for getting through this event, as I knew her presence would soothe all of the nerves building inside of me. We needed to raise an impossible amount of money to ensure the zoo passed to us. Our meeting with Mrs. Westworth was in two days. This was it.

Still, as my eyes snagged on the animal photos projected onto the side of the Peckish Peacock, all I could think about was what happened inside that kitchen—Hannah's eyes misting when she realized I was making her pancakes, the way her smile widened when I told her stories about my childhood, the way she hummed a little tune after every bite of burnt pancake . . . Nope, I was definitely not thinking about her until after the event. But even my professional level of dogged determination was nothing compared to the hypnotic pull of Hannah Newton.

My phone buzzed and when I saw it was Lark again, it was like the universe had bitch-slapped me and told me to focus. Lark had been pestering me all day with questions about the gala. The only person more freaked out about the success of tonight than me was Lark.

LARK

Will you please just double-check all the locks for me??

ME

You're being insane. Everything is fine.

LARK

Tonight needs to be perfect.

ME

I KNOW ALREADY.

LARK

Keep me updated.

ME

No.

LARK

Hawk, seriously.

ME

Stop texting me and calm down. I'm not replying until the event is over.

LARK

Text me right after.

When I didn't reply, she added:

Okay, fine. Good luck!

ME

Don't harass any of our siblings either.

LARK

I can't promise that.

ME

eyeball emoji

LARK

winky face emoji

Lark's badgering had once again reminded me of what had happened last year. Lark was so busy fucking Logan, she'd left a door unlocked and some drunk asshole broke in and tried to steal a monkey. It had been a disaster. We had an official zoo inquiry and had to file a million statements to the police. The Westworths had helped us settle the lawsuit the asshole tried to file against us, and they helped us mostly keep the story out of the news headlines. I didn't want to know what kind of intimidation tactics they used to do it. But perfect, pedantic Lark had felt terrible, of course, which was all the more reason I couldn't follow in her footsteps and let sex distract me.

But when I looked up and saw Hannah milling through the crowd, I knew this was so much more than sex. She looked like a goddess, sauntering in a white satin dress with sparkling silver accents that hugged all her curves and accentuated her perky, round ass. The dress was cut high in the front and low in the back, and I had the desperate urge to run my hand down all that exposed skin. Her pink hair had been pinned up in curls, and she wore a matching shade of lipstick that I was determined to kiss off by the night's end. Silver teardrop earrings shimmered with each move of her head, her whole outfit catching the light like every single one was pointed toward her.

She laughed at something one of the patrons said, and my heart might've stopped beating altogether. Fuck the gala. All I knew was I needed to be next to her. I drifted through the crowd, ignoring half the people who were trying to get my attention, and headed straight as an arrow toward her. But all of that excitement drained away when I saw the woman Hannah was turned toward. My gut plummeted and I picked up my pace, forgetting all decorum as I shoved through the crowd and toward that traitorous face.

What was Beverly fucking Madigan doing here?

Whale hello there
SHACKLE ISLAND ZOO
t Shop

Chapter Forty

Hannah

I offered Kevin, the blue-tongued skink, out like a platter of food, letting all the rich patrons give him a stroke down the back. I still couldn't believe I'd been entrusted with holding a live animal, albeit a very relaxed, nearly comatose one. He almost looked fake, apart from his probing blue tongue that lazily tasted the air every few minutes.

I was about to offer him up to an older woman with platinum-blond highlights wearing a purple leopard print dress when I recognized her face and my mouth dropped open.

Beverly Madigan—Australian reality TV queen and co-owner of the Madigan Mountain Wildlife Park stood there in front of me. How did no one tell me she was coming to this event? Did Hawk know? Was he freaking out? She looked like a caricature of a real person, exactly like she appeared on her hit reality show. Her divorce drama had even been picked up in the US tabloids, and the *Shoreline Gazette* had printed a fluff piece titled "Name your kids like the Madigans," with a list of fifty animal-inspired baby names.

Beverly lifted her thin penciled eyebrow at Kevin. "We've got plenty of these in my backyard," she said. Her voice was surprisingly warm and her smile genuine. I understood a little more of the appeal. "It would be like me bringing around a squirrel."

"Right, sorry." I winced, trying to inch away when a deep voice at my back made me stop.

"Beverly."

I looked over my shoulder to see Hawk and I nearly dropped Kevin at the sight of him. Hawk wore a navy jacket and matching pants, a white shirt, and a thin gray tie. He hadn't shaved, his jaw still stubbled, his wet hair combed to the side as if he just got out of the shower.

Hawk winked at me and I shut my mouth, realizing I was gawking at him. He'd caught me staring at him like he was the last slice of pie. Was I drooling? Right, well, time to go jump into the sea.

Hawk gave Beverly a tight smile. "I didn't know you'd be here." He said it almost like it was a pleasant surprise, but he couldn't quite pull it off.

"I'm a guest of Ethel Holloway," Beverly said with a smile. Not a single line appeared on her overly Botoxed face as she moved it. "It's so nice to see you again, Hawk. You were so little the last time."

Hawk's expression was pinched, an undercurrent of tension to his tone as he said, "Yes, it's been a while."

Either Beverly was very good at hiding her disdain or this

rift seemed kind of one-sided. Maybe the reason she was divorcing Gaz was because he was the problematic one, not her . . .

I took a step back, trying to bow out of the conversation, when Hawk put a gentle hand on my bare back. The contact of his warm, calloused palm made my skin buzz. I swallowed the lump in my throat as I tried to maintain a pleasantly neutral expression.

"Beverly, this is Hannah Newton, one of our front staff," Hawk said, and I felt the sudden urge to curtsy like I was meeting the queen or something. Instead, I settled on a super awkward half-smile.

Beverly gave me a warm smile back, looking between Hawk and me with intrigue. Was it really that obvious? Did I have a neon sign flashing the words "Daddy Hawk" over my head or something?

Hawk looked back at Beverly with a predatory stare that perfectly fit his raptor name. Hawk's pinky dipped beneath the fabric of my dress, and I nearly choked as he slid it down to the top of my butt crack. The tension in Hawk's expression eased a fraction at the strangled sound I made as his fingers traced over my ass.

He retracted his hand as an elderly woman sidled up beside Beverly—one of the other wealthy patrons from the gala. She dripped in crystals and wore an amorphous dress and silver, embroidered shawl. Ethel Holloway, I was guessing. I wondered if I should introduce myself to her, considering I'd been staying on her property for weeks and we'd never met.

"How's it going this summer . . . ?" The woman dragged out her vowels, narrowing her eyes at Hawk until he finally relented and gave her his name.

"Hawk," he supplied through clenched teeth.

"Ah!" She tittered. "I was going to say Crane."

"That's my younger brother," he said.

"Well, there's a lot of you to keep straight." She chuckled, elbowing Beverly, who gave the two of us an apologetic look. "You should know. You have quite the brood yourself."

"A zoo owner with eight kids, all with animal names, wherever did you get that idea?" Hawk asked Beverly, his voice dropping an octave.

"Great minds," Beverly said with an uncomfortable smile.

Hawk didn't make any further comment, but I could read the disgust all over his face.

I started to inch away again, but Hawk's hand found the small of my back, and he rubbed his thumb rhythmically across my bare skin in a way that made my knees weak. I shot him a "not cool" look. I didn't want to be the buffer in this unwieldy conversation, but the way he touched me made it so damn hard to step away. Even Kevin was getting annoyed, his tail starting to move and his tongue flicking faster.

Beverly quickly changed tack, gesturing to the decor. "This is lovely, by the way. Your sister has a knack for event planning. I do hope this fundraiser will cover the costs needed for you to buy this place from the Westworths."

Hawk folded his arms. "I don't know what you mean by that."

"Don't you?" Beverly pursed her pink, overdrawn lips. "Oh, look, Fox! Come over here."

A dapper, young blond man in a flinty gray suit walked over, offering me a wicked smile—one I'd seen once before.

My heart exploded from my chest.

No. No. No. No.

I'd met this man before, except last time we met . . . he'd called himself Rick.

Rick was Fox fucking Madigan?

Beverly's clumpy black eyelashes flicked toward me and then back to Hawk. It was such a quick movement, barely a glance, that to anyone else it wouldn't have meant anything. But in that moment, I knew. It was the Madigans who'd hired me to get the dirt on the Prickle Island Zoo. The reality show stars were certainly wealthy enough to be throwing careless amounts of money around. And it would make sense they'd be trying to buy the zoo from their rivals too.

These petty motherfuckers.

My stomach turned into a tight knot, and I thought I might double over and vomit on Beverly Madigan's stilettos. Fox just winked at me like he knew I wouldn't reveal our secret. The smug bastard.

I couldn't look at Hawk, couldn't *breathe*.

Where was a good Rapturing when you needed it?

"I think it's time to swap out the reptiles," I said, my voice trembling as I definitively stepped away from the hand Hawk tried to place behind me again.

"Pleasure to meet you," Fox called and flashed a toothless grin.

"You too," I murmured before hastily retreating.

"Some people get so shy around celebrities," Beverly said loud enough for everyone to hear. "We're just normal people!" She said it in a way that made it clear that she didn't want anyone to think of her as a normal person.

I shuffled quickly back to the enclosure. "Shit. Shit. Shit," I muttered, placing Kevin back at the entrance to his tunnel.

This was so much worse than just some random land developer. I grimaced as I filled in the handling form on the old computer in the corner with trembling hands. I should've said no to this harebrained job . . . or at least demanded to know who I was working for. How could I have been so thick? Of course the person who wanted those details was someone who wanted to own the zoo, and now I was giving the one and only Beverly Madigan enough information to destroy the guy I was falling for.

When I exited the skink service area, I ran smack into a tall chest and bounced backward. The floodlights went off at the movement, illuminating the person standing in front of me who didn't deign to catch my fall. I clung to the chain-link and righted myself as a grating laugh sounded beside me. I looked up to see that weaselly face backlit by the blinding white lights.

Fox Madigan.

"Hello again, Hannah," he said, a cruel curve to his lips.

"*Rick*," I said tightly, and he laughed. My vision spotted as my eyes adjusted to the sudden brightness. "If you think I'm going to do anything to help you and your family—"

"You already have, sweetheart, just by existing," he crooned, his eyes scanning me from head to toe. "You've been the exact sort of disaster this place needed."

"Excuse me?"

He cocked his head at me, his smile not meeting his eyes. "You didn't think we picked you for your investigative prowess, did you?" The sound of his laughter made my skin itch as I folded my arms. "Someone who didn't think me walking in and introducing myself as *Rick* was suspicious?" He threw his head back and laughed. "Someone whose biggest article was about goat yoga? You think we hired you because you were good at your job?"

"Then why?" I spat. "Why, if I'm so inept, did you hire me?"

His eyes twinkled with wicked delight. "So we'd have someone to pin it on when the findings of our own investigation are brought to light."

I felt like the floor opened right under me. "What investigation?"

"I've had my eyes on this zoo for some time," he said. "And this year was the perfect year to finally put the nail in the coffin of this disaster of a zoo, finally put the *perfect* Lachlans in their place. I am my father's son, after all. Of course, my mother will be furious about what I've been doing, after all she's done to keep this place afloat."

My eyes flared. "What?"

"I trust you'll keep that little secret too." He winked. "I needed to convince her this place wasn't worth saving, give her all the evidence she'd need to know that this place is a complete money pit, though my methods for obtaining said information weren't necessarily legal," he added. "And I didn't want the Lachlans finding out and having any of this coming back on my family. So, naturally, I needed to find a stupid little scapegoat, and here you are."

My mouth fell open. I really wanted to punch this guy right in that smirking mouth. "So you were going to ruin the zoo and let me be the fall guy?"

He weighed his head back and forth. "More or less."

"You can't—you can't do that!"

"Don't worry," he said. "I've called off my dogs. There's no way they'll have enough money to keep this place. The Lachlans didn't even need me after all. They're already crumbling under the weight of their own ineptitude."

"I'm going to tell them what you're doing," I hissed.

"You think anyone will believe you?" he asked with a chuckle. "You think *Hawk* will believe you? After you've lied to him about who you are?"

I took another step back at that, shaking my head. "I'm going to tell him."

"If you were going to tell him the truth, you would've

done it already," Fox mused. "But you haven't told him, have you, Hannah? I see the way you two look at each other. You love him, don't you?" My stomach lurched, eyes welling as Fox scoffed. "Well, you're at least fucking him, right?"

Before I could think, I swung my hand out and slapped him hard on the cheek with a satisfying *thwack*.

Fox stumbled backward, clutching his face with a laugh right as Hawk turned the corner. "What's going on?" Hawk growled, not waiting to make heads or tails of the situation before grabbing Fox by the lapels and shoving him backward.

"Hawk, wait!" I called as Fox took a swing at him.

Hawk ducked under his fist and jabbed Fox right in the ribs. Fox let out a grunt as the air whooshed out of his lungs, but his mouth was still twisted into a smile.

"You've been blinded by her pussy, Hawk." Fox's laugh was cut short as Hawk landed an uppercut right to the center of his jaw. Fox fell hard but quickly scrambled up and tackled Hawk backward into the hedges. I screamed as the two grappled, landing blow after blow on each other.

"Don't you *dare* talk about her," Hawk seethed as he pummeled Fox. "She's not a part of this."

Fox caught him on the cheek and rolled out of Hawk's next blow. His eyes found mine and dread spiderwebbed through my veins. "Oh, but she is, Hawk. I'm the one——"

"Hawk Simon Lachlan!" Evelyn Lachlan shrieked as she came careening around the corner with Beverly hot on her heels.

"Fox Madigan, what the hell do you think you're doing?" Beverly shouted, letting her real Aussie twang out. "Let him go, you fucking idiot. We're leaving. Now."

Beverly yanked her son up to a stand as Hawk's mom stood in front of him, glowering at him with a lethal death stare that had even me quivering. But when Fox caught my eyes again and winked, I knew my time was up.

I turned in the opposite direction and fled toward the front entrance. I couldn't face Hawk now. Not after this. I'd been unwittingly working for his *sworn enemy*.

Shit. Shit. Shit.

What had I done?

ISLAND ZOO
HAWK'S JEEP

Chapter Forty-One

Hawk

My chest rose and fell in heaving breaths as Mom grabbed my chin and turned my head to inspect the bruise on my cheek. She'd triaged enough wounds in her life to know it was nothing serious. Still, she clicked her tongue in disappointment.

"I turned the corner and Hannah slapped him," I said by way of explanation. "I swear to God, if he even so much as looked at her wrong, I'm going to fucking kill him."

I tried to turn to look in the direction of Fox and Beverly's hasty exit, but Mom's grip on my chin tightened. "This is not how we handle things," she said, putting on that too-calm voice she did when she was trying to contain her anger. "This is unacceptable behavior at any time, let alone when you're working. You're not a little boy, for crying out loud." She paused and considered the bruise again. "Though, luckily for you, it seems like Fox still hits like one."

I chuckled and she released me. With as many kids as Mom had, she was a hard woman to startle, though it had been a long, long time since she'd broken up a fight that I was involved in. Still, I felt justified in Fox's pummeling. It was long overdue.

A thought caught in my mind as I swept my hair back. "Why were you and Beverly coming from that direction?" I tipped my head toward the vet hospital.

"I was showing Bev some spreadsheets," Mom said a little too mildly.

"Spreadsheets?"

Mom hummed in response, and I groaned. "Mom, *please* tell me this backup plan you had for the zoo doesn't involve *Beverly Madigan.*"

Mom crossed her arms. "It is none of your business."

"It is *literally* my business," I pushed. "And that's not a no."

"Don't ask questions you don't want the answers to," she replied, pinning me with a look.

"You can't be serious. You're trusting a Madigan?" I threw my hands up. "Jesus, Mom. What would Dad do if he knew—"

"Enough!" Mom barked. "I knew Simon a lot longer than you, Hawk, and for all of your sakes, I like to focus on remembering the good things about him. But he wasn't a saint; he had his grudges and petty feuds and his way of dealing with things, and I had my own." She pointed a finger at me. "You know *nothing* about this, and you can hate me all you want for it, but maybe one day you'll be ready to hear the whole story and not the candy-coated one." She looked me up and down and shook her head. "But not today. Now, why don't you trust me to handle this, and you go check on Hannah."

I stared at her for a long time, looking at my mom in a new light. Fear dropped in me like a stone in deep water, and I knew she was right—I didn't want these answers. There'd never been a clear answer as to why my dad and Gaz Madigan had a falling out, and I'd always carried a lurking suspicion that it wouldn't be a simple reason. If it had been something easily explained, they would have, but I knew whatever this was about was something that would probably change the way I viewed my dad. I knew in my heart that no one was perfect, but to me, my dad always was. I didn't want to let that go. Not yet.

Even in a family as close as ours, there were secrets.

I let out a long, frustrated sigh and turned back toward the reptile service area. "Hannah?"

"She went that way," Mom said, hooking her thumb away from the party.

I reached for my radio and missed, remembering I was wearing a suit and had hung it from my pocket. I grabbed it successfully on the second try. "Carnivores to Delta Seven."

It wasn't Hannah who answered, but rather Mateo's voice. "She's left early for the night, said she's feeling sick."

I looked at my mom, who was frowning at me. "Roger, thanks."

"Maybe she was a little freaked out by you brawling like a teenager," Mom said pointedly.

"I need to go find her." I took two steps down the path before pausing. Turning swiftly, I closed the distance to Mom and pulled her into a fierce hug. Her arms wrapped around me in that familiar, comforting way as I said, "I could never hate you." Then I turned and ran after Hannah.

Whale hello there
PORCUPINE ISLAND ZOO
shop

Chapter Forty-Two

Hannah

I fled the gala after telling Mateo I was sick. I was never returning to the zoo. The Madigans' appearance made that much clear. I needed to get out of this place and run from all of my mistakes before I destroyed myself and everyone around me.

My bare feet slapped against the rough asphalt, the wind whipping my hair into my eyes. I'd thrown my very expensive heels into my work locker and stormed through the night, wishing I were wearing anything other than white satin. I wrapped my arms tighter around me, dropping my chin to my chest to keep the pinpricks of rain out of my eyes. I needed to call Dawn and do what I should've done from the start.

I stormed down the old wharf, the gray boards undulating

under my feet. The bright lights from the mansions along the shoreline cast just enough light to navigate. Careful to avoid the broken edges of the wood, I walked all the way to the end before turning back to shore and pulling out my phone. No one could eavesdrop on this conversation . . . unless there were scuba divers in the water or . . . I leaned over the edge and saw nothing but black, choppy water. I knew I was being ridiculous but, after what had happened with the radio, I wouldn't be taking any chances.

Dawn answered on the third ring. "You shouldn't be calling me."

"Because that's more suspicious than you texting me a hundred times a day?"

There was the sound of clinking glasses and jazz music in the background as she spoke. "What if someone is listening?"

I rolled my eyes. "I'm alone."

"You sound like you're in the middle of a hurricane."

"Island life," I said. "A storm is rolling in. Listen, I'm leaving today."

"You already got what you need? Do tell."

"I'm done, Dawn," I said, trying to hide the wobble in my voice. Tears were already welling again, and I was sure I had two black lines of mascara streaking down my cheeks.

"So you're giving up?"

"I'm not giving up. There's just no story here, okay?" I needed her to leave these people alone. I couldn't be responsible for her putting any more information in the Madigans' hands.

I could hear her lighting her cigarette on the other end. "No story means no money, you realize?"

"Yes," I muttered, even though that was never what we agreed.

"What happened to make you lose your fire?" Dawn

asked, and I knew *logically* that she was trying to manipulate me into staying, but it still stung.

"Oh, the fire is the reason I'm in this mess," I snapped.

The sound of a lighter clicked through the phone, Dawn's voice muffled as she took a drag of her cigarette. "You've got a story there, I'm sure of it. Seven kids. Wild animals. The richest of rich . . . There's something to make us go viral in there. Tell me and I'll pay you ten grand whether it's the dirt our backer wanted or not."

I scoffed. There was no way in hell I was taking that money, especially not when I knew it came from the Madigans. "No."

"No?"

"I said I'm done and I mean it," I pushed. "I'm not going to hurt these people."

A red truck pulled around the bend and my stomach dropped. I watched as Hawk parked at the start of the wharf, effectively blocking me in. My heart hammered in my ears as he watched me through the wet glass, his face lit up in the eerie orange glow of his dashboard. The windshield wipers slowly swished back and forth, and it was only then that I realized it had started raining in earnest. My beautifully styled curls had all schlumped down and were falling haphazardly over my shoulders. I bet I looked like a clown with this much makeup streaking down my face. Alfred was going to kill me for ruining the dress he'd organized for me.

"You've gotten too close to your subjects, Hannah," Dawn said. "You need to be impartial here. You're a journalist."

I guffawed at the word "journalist" because we both knew that was never what I was. "Not anymore I'm not."

"Excuse me?"

"Consider this my resignation," I said quickly as Hawk opened his door. "Goodbye, Dawn."

I shoved my phone back into the cleavage pocket created by my backless bra, my shoulders bunching around my ears as the rain coated my skin. The waves roiled higher, splashing up the sides of the wharf as the wind picked up speed.

Hawk seemed immune to the rain. He stood tall, shoulders back, head high, as he prowled toward me. I couldn't read his expression. Was he angry? Did he know?

He'd changed out of his suit and was back in his khakis. I wondered if the second the event was over, he'd fled back to his house to change, as if he were allergic to formal wear. Shame. He looked heartbreakingly sexy in that suit. But now, he looked the most like himself: a hot zookeeper with a pissed-off look in his eyes—one I *really* hoped I hadn't been responsible for putting there.

I shifted my eyes from one side to the other, debating if I could battle the stormy waves and swim back to the mainland. Had Fox found him and told him everything? Was this it? I'd cornered myself with nowhere to go, and now the last person in the world I wanted to talk to was stalking toward me with heat in his eyes.

HAWK'S JEEP

Chapter Forty-Three

Hawk

I'd captured enough skittish animals in my life to know how to spot one, and right then, Hannah looked more startled than a hopped-up antelope. I walked slowly. No sudden movements. Not when she looked like she might jump into the ocean rather than speak to me. I wouldn't put it past her. When she got nervous, it was like her body just involuntarily flung her off things . . . I decided I should be in grabbing distance just in case.

"Are you okay?" I inched forward, holding up my hands as if calming a spooked zebra. I wouldn't be surprised if she kicked me in the nuts and bolted just like our zebra, Tony, had. "What are you doing out here? I thought you were sick? I came to check on you, but the guy at the gate said you weren't there."

"Making a phone call," she said, fishing her phone out of her bra like a magician and flashing me her blue case as if in evidence. "A private one."

"Well, you picked a good spot for private, not so much for sheltered." I huffed, looking at her through the water dripping off my brow. "This couldn't wait until daylight? Or at least after the storm passed? I'd give it a handful of hours and it'll blow over."

"I needed to make this call," she muttered, her shoulders lifting higher as the rain fell heavier.

I was certain now that she wasn't sick at all. "What happened with Fox?"

"Nothing," she said too quickly.

"Hannah."

"Seriously." She folded her arms tight across her chest, her wet dress becoming sheer as it clung to her body. "Nothing happened."

"Then why did you slap him?" I should turn back right now and rip that bastard's head off. A few punches was wholly unsatisfying. The way he wheezed after I hit him . . . I prayed he cracked a rib.

"I slapped him because he deserves it," she said tightly. "And because he has a very slapable face."

"I can't argue with that." I let out a surprised laugh, swiping away the rain beading down my face. "So you're okay?"

"I'm fine."

Fine never meant fine. Nerves filled my body. Something wasn't adding up, and I couldn't figure out what.

"Let me drive you home." I had to shout over the downpour of rain.

"I can walk," she said. "It's not that far, and I'm already drenched anyway."

"Hannah." When I said her name, her nose wrinkled like she was holding back tears, and it made my chest crack open. "Please, let me take you home. I won't be okay until I know you are."

"Fine," she muttered, not meeting my eyes.

She hopped over the splintering bits of board, and I stared down at her bare feet.

"Where are your shoes?" I asked.

"Back at the gift shop."

"You must have feet of steel."

She grimaced. "No, but plenty of splinters."

"Come here," I said, and before she could protest, I bent down and threw her over my shoulder. I raced toward my truck through the deluge, trying not to think about her perfect ass pressed beneath my fingertips.

She grunted as her diaphragm hit my shoulder. In a few long strides, I ate up the distance to my truck, opened the side door, and plopped her onto the worn passenger seat.

Hannah wiped her wet hair out of her face, panting at the break from the storm. She looked like a half-drowned squirrel monkey, her too-wide eyes staring fixedly out the window instead of at me.

"Sorry I'm ruining your truck," she said as I climbed in the driver's seat.

"This truck has seen everything," I said. "You have no idea. Pretty sure every possible bodily fluid from every animal in the zoo has been washed out of it at some point or another. A little water will probably make it cleaner."

That was, apparently, not a comforting sentiment to her, judging by the way her nostrils flared.

I shifted into gear and took off around the narrow path that hugged the edge of the peninsula. The road here didn't even have a railing before crumbling off into the sea. Sprays of salt air splashed onto the windshield, and I switched the wipers up faster. Waves slammed into the side of the truck and Hannah gasped.

"Is this safe?"

"Safer than you standing out on a decaying wharf in a fucking storm," I growled, my pulse racing as I pictured her getting swept out to sea. "Seeing you out there like that." I shook my head. "I think my heart stopped beating."

"I was making a call."

I kept my gaze trained on the road, droplets of water falling off my furrowed brow. I definitely, *definitely* wasn't looking at the slit of her dress that had ridden up to the top of her thigh. "And you couldn't find a single 'private' spot in the entire house that the Holloways gave you—a spot where, bonus points, you wouldn't get knocked over by a rogue wave?"

She swallowed thickly as another blast of water crashed into the truck. We needed to get inland, quick. The roar of the ocean made us have to shout to be heard even from inside.

"I was about to head back to the house," she added defensively. "I was just overwhelmed from the busy evening and needed to make a call."

"Those fancy iron gates might not have opened for you if the storm cut off the power. And I don't suppose you have anyone's number to come manually open them for you, do you?"

"No," she muttered, folding her wet arms around herself. "What happens at the zoo when the power goes out? What about the animals?"

"We have generators," I said. "For the animals and the electric fencing, but it's expensive. We don't have it installed for nonessential spaces."

"Like for the humans," Hannah said, finally a little laughter in her voice. That lightness made something in me ease.

I reached over and squeezed her knee, her cold skin pebbled with goose bumps. "They'll be fine. Trust me."

"I want to. I want to be worthy of it," Hannah said and then pressed her lips closed.

I quirked my brow at her. I didn't know what that meant.

We turned inland, back toward the main road that cut down the spine of the island. Rolling into the drive of the guest cottage, I was relieved when the buzzer to the gate worked. The main house in the distance was still all lit up, but I noticed the normal evening lights in the gardens and cottage were out.

"Guess only the main house has a generator," I said, looking out at that duck-egg blue door of the mansion on the hill.

When we reached her door and I cut the engine, we sat in silence for a while before Hannah finally said, "Thanks for the ride."

I nodded at her bare feet. "How are you holding up?"

She lifted one foot up and cringed. The whole pad of her foot was covered in tiny black splinters. "Well, this is going to be a fun night."

I unbuckled my seat belt. "Let me help you."

She was all too quick to say, "I can handle it."

"I don't think I've ever met someone more stubborn than myself, but you might just win yourself a gold medal, haze."

"Yeah, well . . ." She didn't have a comeback and my grin made her scowl. "Bye," she said, clumsily opening the truck and letting the downpour of rain into the cabin.

She winced as she looked at the cottage door. The short

sprint was probably going to be torture, along with the night of tweezing pieces of wood from her feet.

"Yeah, right," I muttered, and before I could think better of it, I opened my door and dashed around to the other side. This wasn't how our night together would end—me running off with my tail between my legs, wondering if she was in pain from all those splinters—not when I knew I could help, not when I *needed* to help. I had to figure out what was going on with her, to find a way back to the look in her eyes while I made her pancakes.

Before Hannah's feet could hit the ground, I scooped her up into my arms, shutting the truck door with my hip and carrying her to the cottage. I thought way too much about the proximity of her soft, wet body against mine as I opened the unlocked door, carried her over the threshold, and sat her on the countertop. That slit in her dress rode dangerously higher, the satin clinging to her body now, leaving nothing to the imagination.

"Stay put," I said, giving her a knowing look. She rolled her eyes in confirmation of my suspicion.

Turning on my phone's flashlight, I set it on the counter and went searching through the kitchen. I fished out my headlamp from my pocket, and Hannah snorted.

"You just happen to have that on you?"

"Always be prepared," I said with a wink.

"Such a good Boy Scout," she quipped.

I grabbed an embroidered dishtowel from the oven and tossed it to her, so she could dry herself, and grabbed its companion to blot the beads of rain still clinging to my face.

I turned the tap on, running the hot water, and went scavenging through the pantry. I returned with a saltshaker and a bucket from under the sink.

"What are you . . . ?" Hannah watched me in amusement

as I grabbed the Rolls Royce of dining room chairs and placed it below her feet. I emptied the saltshaker into the bucket and filled it with hot water. Carrying it to the chair, I placed it between Hannah's feet.

"Soak," I instructed.

She cocked her brow at me.

I grinned at her as she put her feet into the hot water and moaned at the sensation, then she clenched her teeth as if to quiet herself.

A whining sound accompanied scratching at the back door, and I leaned back to spy an elderly black cocker spaniel waggling at the doorway.

"I need to let Walter out." Hannah started to lift her feet out of the water, but I rested my hand on her dangerously bare knee. I couldn't help but notice the goose bumps that reappeared up her leg with my light touch. The way I wanted to trace those bumps with my tongue . . . At the sound of Walter's continued whining, I cleared my throat and stood.

"He's a bit temperamental," she warned. "Don't try to pet him. He's a biter." I took another step. "Seriously, be careful!"

I gave her an incredulous look. "I hope all of the lions and tigers have trained me for this moment," I said with a chuckle. "You stay here. Twenty minutes and most of the splinters will have pulled themselves out, and then we can get to work on the deeper ones."

Her eyes tracked me around the room as she instructed me on Walter's many extensive needs. I nodded and obeyed, doing exactly as she said. Walter waggled over to me, and I tentatively crouched, reading his body language. He didn't seem to be concerned with my proximity. I reached a hand out and he danced into it, letting me give the base of his tail a thorough scratching.

"Well, I'll be damned," Hannah said.

When I glanced over my shoulder, she had her chin in her hands, watching me in a way that made goose bumps trail down my arms. There it was—that Friday Pancakes, watching the sunrise together look in her big blue eyes.

With that look, I knew there was no more falling. I'd already fallen. I loved her.

Whale hello there

Chapter Forty-Four

Hannah

I hissed through my teeth as Hawk pulled a splinter from my heel. His fingers pressed in tighter on my ankle, holding my foot on his knee.

"One more and we're done," he said softly.

"I'm not a wild animal," I groused. "You don't have to use that gentle voice with me."

"But it works so well," he purred.

My insides clenched at that deep, smooth tone. Damn, he was right.

I could just make out his dimples in the shadows of his headlamp, beaming down at the pad of my foot. The power still hadn't come back on, and now our only light was the headlamp and the lone candle beside us.

Hawk nodded to the glass of wine clenched in my hands. "Wine helps."

I chuckled, swirling the dregs of my glass. "Are you trying to get me drunk?"

Hawk let out a little laugh that had no right to be so sexy and shook his head. "Yeah, half a glass of fancy pinot grigio will definitely do that."

Walter sat across my lap, happily snuggled against my belly like a hot water bottle. I stroked him with one hand and tipped more wine to my lips with the other. I was going to need something harder than vintage wine if I was going to survive potential death by a thousand splinters.

Hawk moved his thumb up the arch of my foot to the last splinter and I braced. The hot salt water had nearly gotten them out, but a few sneaky bastards had plunged too far under my skin.

The headlamp flicked up to me, and I squinted against the sudden light. "Ready?"

"Yes," I gritted out, taking another long sip of wine and holding Walter tighter to me.

Hawk lowered the tweezers, making one attempt and not quite grabbing it; the sting made me flinch, and Hawk flinched right along with me. His thumb swept over my ankle bone and I shuddered, the soothing sensation distracting me from the prodding tweezers. Hawk paused, waiting for me to give the go-ahead.

"I'm okay," I said a little too breathlessly. His thumb swept over my ankle again, and he grinned as he grabbed the splinter and successfully extracted it this time.

"Done," he said triumphantly and placed a kiss where his thumb had been. My core tightened at the movement, butterflies fluttering low in my belly as I wished those lips would trail higher up my leg. Hawk didn't seem to read those signals though. Instead, he took off his headlamp and got up. He moved the chair back to the dining room and then set about washing the bucket.

"Thank you." My shoulders sagged in relief that it was over. "I've literally had a hot yoga instructor tell me to give up because I was so un-bendy, so I have no idea how I would've done that on my own."

"But you still tried to," Hawk pointed out with a smirk.

"Stubbornness is a Murphy curse," I said. "I-I mean Newton," I quickly amended. Fuck. "Murphy's my middle name."

Hawk didn't seem too suspicious of my blunder. "It's a Lachlan family curse too."

I hated that I was still lying to him. I needed to come clean. I started hyping myself up for it as he moved around the kitchen.

He placed the cleaned bucket and tweezers on a dish towel to dry beside the sink and then turned back to me. Walter let out an indignant huff, peeking one eye open, as Hawk lifted him off my lap and placed him on his luxurious wool bed by the back door.

"Poor Walter," I said, but the spaniel was already snoring again, his third eyelids peeking over his rolled-back eyes.

The storm raged outside, and the windows rattled, pelted by gusts of salty wind. Hawk peeked out of one, pressing his face to the glass.

"Are we still in Kansas?" I called.

We had our fair share of thunderstorms back home, but they felt extra nerve-wracking on an island, like one rogue wave could wipe us all out. Lightning flashed outside, illuminating the storming sky. Trees bent at sharp angles, and a multitude of leafy debris flew past the trembling panes.

Hawk merely laughed. "We'll need to check the fences in

the morning before the animals go out in their enclosures for the day, but it doesn't look any worse than any other storm. We Prickle Island folk build our homes to withstand the weather."

"But driving in this would surely be unsafe," I said, letting the thought linger for a moment before adding, "You really should stay the night."

I meant it so that we could talk and I could confess to all my secrets, but when Hawk's eyes danced with mischief, I quickly abandoned my plans. I wondered if he was thinking about our shared moment behind the vet hospital. I certainly was. The things he said he wanted to do to me . . . I licked my lips.

Maybe I should tell him after we had sex. Everyone was more open to hearing the person you're sleeping with is a liar after a good orgasm, right?

Hawk returned to where I sat, walking until his hips pushed open my knees. I scooched forward, the slit of my dress rising to my hip as he stood between my legs. "Let's get to bed, then."

He tugged on my knees, making me wrap my legs around him as he lifted me up by my ass. His hand grazed across my ass cheeks and he groaned. My stomach fluttered as I circled my arms around his neck. He carried me up the stairs as if I weighed nothing. All that lifting grain bags had turned this man into an Adonis.

I leaned in and planted a kiss on Hawk's neck, sliding my lips up to his ear. "Bed or *bed*?" Pulling away, I searched his expression.

Hawk's lips brushed over my bare shoulder and I trembled. "Which were you hoping for, gorgeous?" His husky breath danced across my bare skin.

"I mean, I *am* injured," I said, his deep laugh making my

pussy flutter. "But I think I can survive." I paused, nerves overriding my lust. "There's something we should really talk about first though."

"Tell me tomorrow," he said, clearly not wanting to ruin this moment.

I really didn't want to ruin this moment either. "Okay," I said breathlessly.

His lips found the shell of my ear. "Do you still want me so badly?"

My whole body trembled as he reached the top step and paused at the door to my bedroom. He didn't release me, only lingered as my legs and arms held his torso to mine. Hawk searched my eyes, waiting for my reply.

"Yes," I breathed, eyes dropping to his parted lips.

"Thank God," he said as he kicked open my bedroom door.

HAWK'S JEEP

Chapter Forty-Five

Hawk

My mouth crashed into Hannah's as we stumbled toward the bed. She kissed me with the same desperation that I'd felt from the moment I spotted her standing out in the rainstorm. My tongue dove into her mouth, searching, tasting. Her hands roved up my sides, exploring every muscled curve as my eyes hooded. I needed her, needed her skin, needed her mouth, needed all of these anxious thoughts to finally be sated as our bodies intertwined.

I dropped her onto the plush bed, my body immediately covering hers and pressing her down into the mattress. Her still-damp hair splayed out across the pillow, and I took her in for one glorious second before it was too much. My lips needed to be on hers. I didn't know how to exist without touching her.

She'd said she needed to talk to me and I had told her to wait. For the second time today, I wasn't ready to face whatever truths the people in my life had in store for me. I just wanted this one perfect moment with her. It was probably selfish, but I didn't want this feeling to end, and I was afraid whatever she had to tell me would change things between us.

I debated stopping, slowing down to let her tell me whatever was on her mind, but when she murmured against my lips, "Take your clothes off," I knew all bets were off.

"Yes, ma'am." My voice was muffled against her mouth as I began unbuttoning my shirt. I loved how eager she was for me, how her desperation seemed to match my own. I unbuttoned my shirt halfway and then hauled it over my head.

When I looked back at Hannah, she let out a choked sound at the sight of me.

"Please tell me you're a gym rat and this isn't all from working at the zoo?" She waved her hand down my torso, her finger tracing from my dusting of chest hair *all* the way down to my happy trail. My cock strained in my pants at her touch.

"I'm constantly lifting weights," I said. "Just the fur and feathered kind. Do you know how heavy a wombat is?"

Her lust-filled grin made my veins fill with molten heat.

"You should start offering fitness memberships. You could be the poster child. I can picture it now—you shirtless, shoulder-pressing a porcupine or something. Happy to volunteer to oil you up and take your photo." I could tell the moment her brain caught up to her mouth as her words fell off into silence. She looked side to side and then settled on winking at me.

"Did you just wink at me?" I chuckled, dropping my head into her shoulder and kissing her warm skin. The feeling of her soft figure under mine made my body ignite like a thousand Pop Rocks tingling below my skin.

"Maybe."

"Maybe," I said, my voice growing husky. "Maybe I'm starting to rub off on you."

She spread her legs wider, rocking her hips against the hardening seam of my pants. "That's what I'm hoping for."

I snarled, nipping at her earlobe before stepping away and unbuckling my belt. Fuck, I wanted her so badly. Finally, in a cottage behind a fenced gate in the middle of a storm, we could take our time without being interrupted.

Hannah propped up on her elbow to admire my hasty striptease. "Do you have a condom?"

My wolfish smile widened. I reached into the pocket of my work pants and pulled out my wallet. Flipping open the fold, I placed three silver packets on the nightstand. "I lifted some from Finch's stash."

"Umm." She furrowed her brow in confusion. "Forgive me for my ignorance here, but I thought dental dams were more her jam?"

"You're not wrong." I snorted. "But she keeps the volunteer house and all the parties well-stocked. Pretty sure she has an industrial-sized shoebox of safe sex supplies."

"We love a responsible partier," she said with a nod. "Goldfinch Goodall Lachlan—what an enigma."

"Someone's memorized their welcome packet," I said with a surprised laugh. "Now, can we please for the love of God stop talking about my sister?"

"Right. Sorry."

I unbuckled my belt and let the weight drag my pants down until I stood in only my fitted black boxer briefs. Hannah swallowed as her eyes dipped to my erection straining against my undershorts. I couldn't help but smile at the impressed, hungry look in her eyes.

"Do . . ." She bit her lip, clearly embarrassed for asking but unable to stop herself. "Do you need to replenish this stash often, or . . ." She dropped her head into her hands. "Sorry."

"It's okay." I paused, kneeling back on the bed to kiss her again. "Are you nervous?"

"No," she said. "Maybe. A little."

I threaded my fingers through hers and kissed her more gently. I gathered her into my arms. "We can go slow, haze."

She shook her head, looking up into my eyes. "I don't want to go slow. I just need to turn my brain off."

I chuckled, searching her face. "I need you to be honest with me," I murmured, and her eyes guttered at that, something like sadness streaking across her expression. There and gone. "If you want to slow this thing down, tell me. I don't want to mess this up." I brushed another featherlight kiss to her lips. "You're too important to me."

Her finger traced up my jaw and over my lips. I playfully nibbled one and she laughed.

"You're important to me too," she whispered. She rolled farther into my arms until she was flush against me again. "But I don't want to go slow." She rocked her hips against me. "If I don't have you tonight, Hawk, I'm going to combust."

Those words reignited our frenzy. I rolled her back under me, grabbing the hem of her still-damp dress and tugging it over her head. She ripped off whatever contraption was holding her boobs up and threw it on the floor.

I took in her delicious, soft curves, her full breasts rising and falling with her panting breaths. She was so stunningly beautiful, it made me ache.

"I've wanted you for so long," I murmured, fingers trailing from her pebbled nipples to the lace of her underwear. I needed to know every inch of this body. My cock was painfully hard as I kept moving my fingers in featherlight touches, needing her to be just as ready as I was. "I remember the day. This gorgeous woman wearing a purple pullover fleece and ripped jeans was sitting in the back of my truck, staring at me like she hated me."

"*That's* the moment you wanted me? The day we met?" she asked incredulously as I dropped a kiss to her belly and tugged on her panties. She lifted her hips, allowing me to pull them down and unceremoniously drop them to the floor. I hungrily stared at her glistening core. "I didn't hate you, by the way. You were just . . . distracting."

"Distracting?" I smiled against the flesh of her thigh, my lips trailing tauntingly close to where I knew she needed them.

"And then you caught me," she whispered, her fingers threading into my hair as I kissed my way up the inside of her thigh.

"I'll always catch you, haze," I murmured, my mouth hovering just above her wet core.

"Hawk," she panted.

"Yes?" My voice was taunting as I lowered another inch and blew across her sensitive sex.

Her voice was thick and raspy as she said, "If you don't start touching me, I think I might die—"

Her words ended on a sharp moan as I dropped my mouth to her swollen clit, licking up her wet pussy in one long, lascivious sweep. Her hips bucked into my mouth as I circled her clit again, lapping up her tangy sweetness. Her fingers dug in tighter to my hair, her hips lifting, urging me faster. Oh, she was definitely as desperate as I was. My forearm covered her lower belly, pinning her hips to the bed and holding her still as I repeated my strokes.

The sounds she made almost had me spilling into my boxers. She was the most glorious symphony, and I was the one ringing each sweet note from her body. I loved the way she was losing herself in this, lost to my touch. I loved that I was the one who knew how to quiet her mind.

She groaned, her free hand fisting into the bedsheets as she writhed against my mouth, but I kept her pinned to the mattress. My fingers circled her dripping entrance before dipping inside her tight core. Hannah's back arched as I filled her, my cock twitching as I imagined her wet pussy wrapped around it. My fingers massaged her inner walls, my tongue moving faster.

I could hear in her voice the moment it was too much. I was pushing her higher and higher, like the undertow of the biggest wave.

I hummed against her wet sex, the vibrations seeming to unleash her further until she was screaming.

"Come for me, haze," I commanded against her throbbing clit.

She stopped fighting me, her orgasm already peaking. My tongue and fingers worked her to that point beyond her control. She rode my mouth with wild abandon as she shattered.

"Hawk," she moaned again, making me echo a groan against her. The rumble of my lips sent her shattering over the cliff of another orgasm. Hannah let out a sharp cry as she jerked beneath me.

I licked her through each wave until her pussy stopped clenching around my fingers and her body collapsed into the mattress. Something prideful and victorious blazed through me. I always wanted to be the one to make her come like that. I wanted to be the one to bring her so much pleasure she was screaming out my name.

Wet heat slid down her thighs as I removed my fingers. I trailed kisses up her hip and circled her navel.

When Hannah propped up on her elbows to look at me, though, I knew we weren't done.

"Get a condom," she panted, pushing me roughly toward the side table, making us both laugh with her eagerness. "Now."

SNORKLE ISLAND ZOO
Whale hello there
Gift Shop

Chapter Forty-Six

Hannah

Hawk scrambled across the bed, a cheeky grin on his face. "I like it when you get bossy."

Before he could turn toward the nightstand, I hooked my finger into the waistband of his boxers. He stilled, his lips parting as I pulled them down, freeing his sizable erection.

His eyes hooded as he looked down at me. I stroked him once, loving the way his breath caught in his throat. His lips parted as I licked that glistening bead at the head of his cock before taking him into my mouth.

He let out a hissing sound through his teeth as I sucked, laving my tongue along his shaft and taking him deeper.

"Fuck," he panted, his head falling back.

One hand found my hair, fisting it in his grip, and the other desperately grabbed for purchase behind him. I hummed, sucking him down until he hit the back of my throat. My eyes watered but I kept going, spurred on by the sounds he was making.

"Hannah, shit." Hawk groaned, rocking his hips into my mouth.

I worked him up and down, his sounds making me even wetter.

"It's too good," Hawk panted, pushing back on my shoulder.

I released him, my wet lashes lifting to look up at him.

"Get back on the bed," he rumbled, turning toward the nightstand. He ripped open the condom packet with his teeth and stared at me with scorching desire as he rolled it on. "I promised to fuck you so hard you couldn't remember your name, didn't I?"

"Yes," I whispered.

His eyes darkened. "Do you still want that?"

"Yes." I could barely form the word, I was so desperate for him. I spread my legs wide, giving him a full view of my wet core, and he groaned at the sight.

"You are so fucking beautiful, you make it hard to breathe," he said, crawling up the bed. He settled his hips between my legs, stilling as he looked into my eyes. "I don't want you to leave at the end of the summer."

I paused, pulling back to stare into his eyes. "What?"

"I know we just met, but . . . I don't want you to go," he murmured, his eyes imploring mine. "There's something here. I don't want it to end."

"I . . ."

"We have a biology internship program here," he offered. "You could keep studying and—and be with me." His hair fell into his eyes, and I instinctively brushed it away. My heart cracked a little at the pleading I saw there. I was lying to him.

There could be no future between us, but with his cock poised at my entrance, I didn't have the strength to slow down this train. He told me to wait, to not tell him everything yet, and I was more than happy to oblige. "You don't have to say yes now. Just . . . will you think about it?"

I lifted my hips, grinding against him. "If I say yes, will you fuck me?"

"I'll fuck you either way," he promised with a dark laugh. "But if you say yes, you'll get a lot *more* of me fucking you."

I writhed beneath him. "You better make it good, then."

"Is that a challenge?"

"It—"

He pushed in, making my words die off, my lips forming into an O as he pushed another inch, and then another. He worked his way in with light, rolling pulses, stretching me until he filled me to the hilt. I tilted my hips, trying to make him move faster, desperate for the friction.

Hawk let out a throaty chuckle and obliged, pulling out and slamming back into me. I cried out, the feeling so delicious, it stole my breath. My body arched off the bed as he pulled back and did it again, hooking my knee over his hip.

"That's how you like it, baby?"

I swallowed, barely able to rasp out the words, "God, yes," as he rewarded me with another rock of his hips that made the headboard bang against the wall.

Again and again, he hit that perfect spot inside me that made my eyes roll back. This was so much better than I'd fantasized about, so all-consuming that nothing else existed except where we joined.

"Fuck, Hawk," I cried out.

His hips moved in deep thrusts, some torturously slow, some fast and wicked, keeping me on the edge. My hands clawed down his back, and my ankles locked around his ass as he played my body like a fucking musician. He lifted onto one arm and grabbed the headboard, the whole bed rocking with each strong piston of his hips.

I felt drunk, so filled with sensation that every thought fell out of my mind except for where he ended and I began. It overpowered me in every way, and I had no choice but to surrender to the pleasure. Each moan from my lips seemed to push Hawk higher, faster. Was this what sex was meant to be like? Fuck, it had never felt this good before. Usually, I had to concentrate, my mind wandering, but this . . . It was utterly mind-blowing, and I knew all future trysts had been ruined by this glorious sex god of a man.

"You feel so good, haze." Hawk groaned as his hips moved in sharper, jerkier motions. "So, so good."

Wet heat slicked my thighs as my hips tilted to each of his deep thrusts. "Yes, yes, YES." I whimpered, each breath ratcheting me higher toward my release. "I'm so close."

Hawk pounded into my wet core now, chasing me toward another orgasm.

"Hannah," he purred into my ear, and I realized I was moaning his name over and over like a chant. "I love the way you sound with my cock inside you."

I shattered, a scream cutting off into a deep, primal moan. I raked my fingernails down Hawk's back, holding on for dear life as my orgasm roared through me. Waves of ecstasy crashed over me, so much louder and brighter than the first. My muscles clenched around Hawk until he barked out a cry, jerking as his climax erupted through him. We came together—each of his sounds wrung out the pleasure in me, more and more, until I collapsed back down into my pillow, boneless and ecstatic.

Hawk rolled to the side of me, gathering me into his

sweat-slicked chest. I listened to the sharp rise and fall of his breath as he kissed the top of my head.

I sounded like I'd just crossed the finish line of a marathon as I said, "That was . . ."

Hawk pressed his cheek to the crown of my head. "Enough to convince you to stay?"

I chuckled as he swept his fingers idly up and down my spine. "Maybe," I panted.

"If you need more convincing," he goaded, his calloused hand trailing down my side to cup my ass, "I'm happy to oblige."

Whale hello
there
PORCUPINE ISLAND ZOO
t Shop

Chapter Forty-Seven

Hannah

The buzzing alarm made me grunt into my pillow, and I folded it in half to cover my ears. Hawk quickly grabbed his phone and switched it off, kissing my shoulder and moving to roll away. I grabbed his arm like a pouncing cat and folded his muscled forearm around my side. Wiggling my ass back into the perfect nook he made around me, I felt his morning erection pressed hard against my backside, ready for another round.

I didn't know if I'd ever have enough of this. Hawk wasn't going to be someone who I could sleep with until I got bored of him. This whole life actually, I realized all at once, was an ADHD wonderland of constant novelty. New animals, new staff, new visitors, the island shops changing pretty much every season, new, unexpected adventures, new stories to tell .

. . And at the center of all of it was this sexy, big-hearted grump of a keeper and a ginormous family filled with so much love, it made me ache and wish it were my own.

Gibbons whooped in the distance, the post-storm stillness making their calls carry all the way to the Holloways'. Or maybe it was just because I knew what to listen for now. Hawk let out a little disgruntled sound, and I felt the weight of his responsibilities like someone had just placed a dozen kettlebells on top of him.

"All of my siblings will be up early because of the storm," he murmured into my hair, slowly moving his arm away as if it pained him. "I need to be conducting this orchestra of crabby, under-caffeinated keepers I call a family or it will be pandemonium."

"I really wish you didn't have to go," I whined even as I released him. "I was hoping we could talk about some things. But maybe on your lunch break?"

It was long overdue. I needed to tell the guy I-I *liked* the truth. Jesus, I almost said loved. I'd fucked the guy once and the L-word was just tap-dancing around in my brain on a loop now. *Get a frickin' grip, Hannah!*

"Lunch date sounds good," Hawk said with a sleepy smile. "I wish I could stay. God, do I wish I could, but we've got to check the fences before we let the animals out." He rolled to the side of the bed and jumped into his boxer briefs, hiding his gorgeous posterior from me. I had the sudden urge to roll over and bite his glorious ass, but I shoved that intrusive thought away. There was weird Hannah, and there was ass-bitingly weird Hannah . . .

"Can't the animals have a sleep-in today?" I grumbled into my pillow.

"They've got to be out and fed before we open," he said as he wandered over to the bathroom.

"Who visits a zoo the day after a hurricane?"

"If the sun's out, people come." Hawk shrugged and, honestly, it was the sexiest, sleepiest shrug ever, and I wanted to walk over and slide my hands over all that bare skin and kiss him until he relented and came back to bed. He hooked his thumb at the bathroom behind him. "Is it okay if I grab a quick shower?"

"Fine." I wished more than anything that I could watch said shower. "I'll go make coffee."

"Thank you," he said, his eyes lingering on me for another second, and I wondered if all the same thoughts were tap-dancing around in his mind too. Or maybe I was misreading that expression . . .

He let out a sigh and scrubbed his hand down his face, commanding himself to turn away from me.

When the bathroom door clicked shut, I hopped out of bed and immediately stubbed my toe on the bed frame. At least my naked clumsiness wasn't witnessed by Hawk.

I waited until I heard the shower turn on and grabbed Hawk's khaki shirt, doing up just the bottom two buttons to keep it closed. It hung all the way down to mid-thigh and smelled gloriously like musk and earth. My pussy clenched from Hawk's scent alone as vivid flashbacks from the night before rocked through me.

My stomach dropped. I knew today *had* to be the day I finally came clean. I couldn't let him tell me "later" one more time, not when the feelings swirling through my mind were so much greater than a summer fling.

"First, coffee," I muttered to myself, stumbling down the steps.

Even Walter wasn't amused by my early arrival, giving me the barest of tail thumps before falling back asleep. Sweet old man. Guessed it was my lot in life to fall for grumpy, misunderstood guys.

I turned on the coffee maker and checked my phone that I'd discarded on the countertop from the night before. I had five emails and *twenty-seven* texts from Dawn asking about Finch. My boss seemed convinced that the tattooed veterinarian was the best story to run with . . . considering it was the only story I'd given her.

Pulse quickening, I hastily typed back:

ME

I told you, Dawn. I'm done. You need to let this go.

I hated confrontation. It made my heart lodge in my throat and my stomach drop every single time. My eyes misted and I suddenly wanted to either cry or throw up. Curse Dawn for how many times she was making me say no. I swore she knew she was fucking with my rejection sensitivity!

I could've elaborated to Dawn about Finch's flashlight party and the copious amount of drinks she brought to it. Underage drinking, supplied by the boss no less. That oughta do it. Finch's revolving door of lovers would probably be a fireable offense to the Westworths too. Every workplace had its fair share of sleeping around, but Finch Lachlan made it an art form.

My phone buzzed.

DAWN

Why do I get the feeling you're not telling me everything? Why quit out of the blue?

What's really going on?

> We've got a story with this Finch Lachlan
> now whether you have your name attached
> to it or not. If you don't want the money, then
> fine.

And there was the ultimatum again. Dawn's message was loud and clear: *Last chance. Either play ball or be cut out. Decide.*

I'd have to tell my mom I was moving back in. I'd have to watch her try to pretend that she didn't mind. I'd have to see the disappointment she did such a good job hiding. Once again, I'd managed to fail everyone who was important to me.

The pipes silenced as the shower shut off overhead. I'd figure out how to stop whatever story Dawn was planning on printing about Finch later. I hastily poured two mugs of coffee, one black, one with cream and sugar, hedging my bets as to which Hawk liked. He'd had black coffee when we watched the sunrise, but maybe he was just in a rush that day. I was definitely overthinking this. Having his coffee order right wasn't going to soften the blow.

Coffee first.

Then I'd figure out how I was going to tell him.

I tiptoed back up the steps, careful not to spill the life-giving liquid, and pushed open the door with my hip. When Hawk walked out of the bathroom with nothing but a fluffy white towel wrapped low around his waist, I almost dropped both mugs. His hair was mussed to the side, wet and clinging to his forehead. He paused when he spotted me, his lips curving up with lust-laden desire.

Okay, maybe coffee second.

HAWK'S JEEP

Chapter Forty-Eight

Hawk

The sight of her in just my shirt made my knees shaky. The way her breasts and lower belly peeked from the deep V of parted fabric undid all of my efforts to quell my libido in a cold shower. Now that I knew what she felt like, what she tasted like, it had made my desire for her a million times worse. Maybe it was time to finally take a day off like my family was always pushing me to, like I had *demanded* everyone else do.

"Cream and sugar or black?" she squeaked, holding out both mugs as her eyes lingered on my happy trail.

I stalked over to her and selected the black one. Watching her over the ceramic rim, I took a long, fortifying sip.

"Good," she said, swigging back her milky coffee. "I'd have to go add it to mine otherwise."

I took another sip and then set my mug on the dresser and grabbed Hannah's mug out of her grip and set it aside too. I could be late one time. Just this once. This burning inferno inside of me wouldn't let me do anything else.

I grabbed the two clasped buttons on my shirt, Hannah's peaked nipples flashing as I pulled on the fabric.

"You knew exactly what it would do to me to see you in my shirt, didn't you?" My voice was scratchy and deep as I unbuttoned the shirt and let the fabric fall open, baring her to me.

She trailed her finger along my waist before hooking into my towel. "And you knew exactly what this towel would do to me."

I smirked. "I guess we're even, then."

"No," she whispered, lifting on her tiptoes and brushing a kiss to my lips. "Not yet."

I nipped at her bottom lip, catching it between my teeth and tugging as she lifted up higher on her toes with a moan.

"You want to play?" I asked, my hand running up the bare skin of her thigh and drifting over her backside. Her breath smelled of coffee, her skin branded with my scent.

"I do." Her fingers roved up my muscled chest and into my wet hair.

My tongue licked into her mouth, tasting her as she yanked my towel and let it pool around our feet. My hand cupped her sex, and she leaned into my palm as I delighted in the feel of her bare skin against mine. Her hard nipples rubbed against my chest, and she moaned again as I pressed one finger in, rubbing her already swollen nub.

"You better fuck me fast if you don't want to be late," she whispered against my mouth, taunting me.

I let out a groan at that tempting command, the sound coming from somewhere deep within me as I flipped her around so her chest was against the tall dresser. I grabbed the third and final condom from my wallet. I should've already known I'd use it. There was no leaving here, this room, her body, until I had to restock. I hastily opened it, my hand clenching her hip as I rolled it on.

"Hold on tight, haze," I said—my only warning as I lined myself up and slammed into her. This wouldn't be a long, leisurely bout of lovemaking like our second round had been last night. There'd be no slow or gentle. This was desperate, needing to be buried in her, giving her exactly what she wanted, and fucking her hard until nothing else existed except her sweet moans.

She cried out, rocking into the dresser as I drove into her again, all the way to the hilt, the slick, carnal sound of our skin slapping filling the room. Coffee sloshed from the mugs onto the wood, but neither Hannah nor I could summon a single fuck to give, not as I reached around and began rubbing her clit as I took her from behind. My other hand fisted in her hair and pulled her back against me as I licked up her neck and nibbled her earlobe.

"Fuck," she hissed, my cock taking her deeper from this angle. She was wetter than a fucking rainstorm for me. "Hawk. Yes."

How was it this good? Her rhythm, her height, her sounds, it was all like she was perfectly designed for me, like she was an instrument only I knew how to play—and fuck did I know how to play her. Normally, it took a bit of messing around to know what another person liked, but Hannah was always an open book. I knew exactly how to read her, exactly when to apply a little more pressure and make her unravel.

"You walking in here in nothing but my shirt . . ." I groaned, pumping into her again and again. "I hope you smell like me all day long." I drove into her harder. "I hope you remember this moment every time you sit down." I rubbed her faster. "I'm yours, haze."

Hannah gripped the back of the dresser tighter, her fingers turning white as she clenched her eyes shut and cried out so loudly, I was certain they could hear us all the way across the island, but I didn't care one bit. Nothing existed except that explosion building between us, like we were making our own sort of magic, the alchemy of her and me greater than the sum of our parts.

"I'm so close," Hannah mewled, pushing back against my thrusts to take me deeper. "I-I'm . . ."

Her climax exploded from her, her cry cutting off as she keeled forward and clenched around my cock. I battled her tight core, finally releasing that control as I roared her name. My orgasm made me fold over her until my chest pinned her against the wood as she milked my cock with her own release. My fingers kept circling her, her muscles pulsing again and again, wrapping around my shaft and drawing out our plea-sure, until finally her pussy stopped fluttering.

I rested my sweaty forehead against her back. "I knew it. You are a fucking siren," I whispered, kissing up her spine. "I'm sure of it now. You walked straight out of the sea to ensnare my heart."

Had I really just said that aloud? Everything in me felt so raw, like all of the many barriers between my brain and my mouth had fallen down and my thoughts were just spilling out of me.

I slowly pulled out of her, and Hannah winced.

"Shit, are you okay?" I asked, spinning her in my arms to search her face. I'd been too rough, too careless, too overcome.

But Hannah only laughed. "I'm more than okay," she said, smoothing the worry lines from my face and using her thumb and forefinger to force my lips into a smile. "I might be walking funny all day, but that doesn't mean I won't be begging for a repeat tonight."

The things the word "begging" did to my dick . . . I gave her a warning look. "If it's too much, you'll tell me, right?"

She flashed that mischievous grin. "It will never be too much."

I grabbed her chin and lifted her face to meet my eyes. "Hannah," I warned.

She rolled her eyes. "Of course I'd tell you." She pushed me lightly on the chest and passed me my discarded shirt. "Here. May you forever think of this moment when you wear it."

I chuckled. "I'm going to be hard all day thinking about you, you know that?"

"I know," she said breezily, giving me a smile.

My phone buzzed on the dresser. Probably my siblings wondering where the fuck I was.

Her phone buzzed too, and she straightened like an arrow, suddenly all of the playful warmth disappearing with the sound. "I should get ready for work too," she said, hastily grabbing some clothes out of the middle drawer. "I'll see you at the zoo."

"Still on for that lunch date?" She made to move past me, but I caught her elbow in my grip. "Why do I feel like you're pulling away from me again?"

"I'm not," she said, but her eyes didn't lift to meet mine and anxiety started clouding my thoughts all over again. "I just need to shower."

I released her elbow and reached for her face instead, cupping her cheeks in both hands and kissing her. I knew I shouldn't push her. This was all still so delicate, but I couldn't walk out of here without saying it. "Will you think about stay-ing? Please?"

Hannah's eyes flared with surprise. "We can talk more about it at lunch, okay?" She gave me one last kiss and pulled away. "There are some things I need to tell you first, and if you still feel that way, then we'll see."

Fuck, it was too much too soon. I was going to scare her away if I didn't slow down. The word "love" was already on the tip of my tongue after only a few, short weeks together. She was trying to warn me, and I just wasn't listening.

I rubbed the back of my neck, concern still marring my expression. "Okay," I said tentatively. "I'll see you at the zoo."

She paused at the threshold to the bathroom and shot over her shoulder, "You better keep your distance from me this morning or I'll likely pull you into the nearest broom closet, even if my radio is on full blast."

Whale hello there

Chapter Forty-Nine

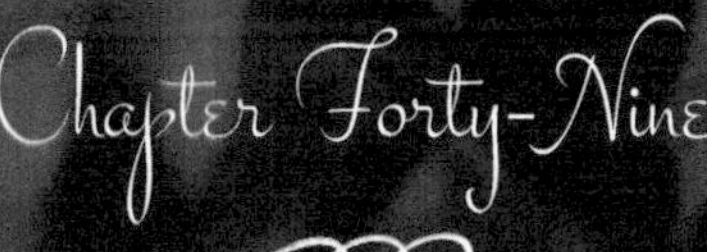

Hannah

I took my time in the shower, vivid sex flashbacks slowing me down as I tested my way through the basket of fancy sampler soaps and shampoos. By the time I got out, I smelled like a French perfumery. I leisurely dried my hair, having another hour before I needed to get to work. My sore body echoed in the wake of Hawk's touch. All I could see when I closed my eyes was his face, like the rest of the world was a blurry fuzz and only he existed in perfect focus.

I decided to take Walter for a walk before Mrs. Holloway came to get him for the day . . . which I knew would probably entail carrying him because he was not a morning walk kind of guy.

As we wandered along the sidewalk that hugged our end of the island, the aftermath of the storm was evident all across the seaside. Seaweed and driftwood were scattered across the road, sand burying our steps as we curved toward the park.

My mind churned over all of the ways I could break the news to Hawk. Did I just rip it off like a Band-Aid? Did I warm him up to it first? Did I explain I was trying to help my mom, or would that be a cop-out? I played a million scenarios over in my head, but not in a single one could I imagine him forgiving me. All of that fear didn't matter anymore though, not now that I understood how I truly felt about him. He deserved so much more. He deserved someone who never lied to him, and I was determined from that heartbeat onward to be that person, fear be damned. Acknowledging it gave me my own kind of courage.

I had to do it. Today.

My phone buzzed in my pocket, and I picked it up, readying for another one of Dawn's texts and to remind her *once again* that I had quit.

My brow furrowed at the name "FINCH" above the message.

FINCH

I've got the bloods back on Sammy. Call me.

I flipped the innocuous blue phone case over in my hand, and my stomach sank as I narrowed my eyes at the lion photo lock screen.

This wasn't my phone.

THIS WASN'T MY PHONE!

My eyes shot up toward the zoo as if I could see all the way to Hawk in the distance. He must've grabbed my phone by mistake. Nausea roiled in my stomach. Would he be able to see my texts from Dawn? All the blood drained from my face. She wouldn't say anything too incriminating in a text, would she?

I already knew the answer: Yes. Yes, she absolutely fucking would.

I scooped up Walter by his belly and darted down the sandy road, praying every step that my mom had flooded my messages with random life updates and photos of the neighbor's cat. My heart thundered with each bounding leap, and I could feel that happiness pulling away from me like the sharp pull of the tides.

This was my fault. Here we were, once again, with me fucking up my entire life.

I had waited too long. I had so many opportunities to tell him the truth and I didn't take them, and now I was reaping what I'd sown.

I called upon any deity that would listen, begging that Hawk wouldn't see anything else. But I already knew the truth in the pit of my stomach: time was up.

This was it. This was how it would end.

HAWK'S JEEP

Chapter Fifty

Hawk

I pulled into the vet hospital and popped in to see Finch at her desk, wondering why she hadn't messaged me about Sammy's blood test results yet. Dove sat at her chair beside Finch, looking bored at her computer monitor as Finch regaled her with a long-winded diatribe about accounts payable and how they needed a full-time vet nurse.

"You look way too happy and it's making me uncomfortable," Dove murmured.

Finch's eyebrows shot up when she saw me walk in. "Hey, didn't you see my message?"

I paused, brows furrowing as I felt for my phone in my pocket. "No, I . . ."

I picked it up and spotted a line of texts from "Mom" and "Dawn."

"Shit, this is Hannah's," I grumbled, looking at the wall and out toward the direction of the cottage.

"Spending the night together. So things are getting serious between you two?" Finch prodded, her eyebrows dancing as she leaned back in her chair.

"Maybe," I said. *Hopefully*. If I could convince her to stay. I was about to put my phone—Hannah's phone—back in my pocket when my eyes snagged on one text. I couldn't help myself. I touched it, and it expanded.

DAWN

Okay, listen, I'll still cut you into the deal if you just help me out here. A lot of money is at stake. Give me the zoo dirt, Murphy.

"What the fuck?" I murmured, scrolling back through her unread text messages that filled her lock screen. She'd received a dozen from this Dawn person in the last hour. I found another from Dawn.

DAWN

We need to know how far off they are after the gala. If they're getting close to buying the zoo, we need that info STAT.

"What?" Dove asked, spinning around in her chair.

My limbs went numb as dread burned through my gut. "Can you pull up Hannah's application?"

Dove furrowed her brow but did as I asked. Hannah's file popped up on the screen.

"What's going on? You think she's lying about who she is?" Finch asked, grabbing the phone from my shaking hands and flicking through the texts. "What sort of James Bond espionage bullshit is this? Who would spy on this place?"

"Someone who wanted to buy it for themselves," Dove

hissed as Finch picked up the landline next to her computer. "Who are you call—"

Finch held up a finger and Dove shut up.

"Oh, hi, Debra," Finch said, putting on her airy feminine voice that made Dove and me exchange confused glances. "It's Susan from accounting. I have a discrepancy in my file for one of your students." She paused, laughing in a way that made my skin itch. "Yeah, they're going to have my head for it. You know how they are." Dove shot me an impressed look. "Yes, her name is Hannah Newton. She's a master's student in the biology department?" Finch paused, listening. "No? Oh no, that must be my fault. Is it Hannah something else? A different year, maybe?" She waited, bouncing her knee and chewing on her lip ring. "No Hannahs. Any recollection of a girl with pink hair? Right, I'll check the other departments. Thank you for your help, Deb. Buh-bye."

She hung up the phone and turned to look at me, shaking her head as she shifted out of her flight attendant voice.

"Who the fuck is this bitch?" Finch whirled back to her computer, digging through searches of the name. "There are a bunch of Hannah Newtons, but none of them look like her."

"Try searching for Hannah . . . What did she call her? Murphy? And Dawn in New Haven," Dove said. "Try the word *news*."

"Holy fucking shit," Finch barked, clicking on a photo of Hannah on the screen.

My stomach was in white-hot knots at the smiling headshot that stared back at me. My sisters' words felt underwater as the rage rose higher. My heartbeat thundering against my eardrums was deafening.

"Hannah Murphy," Dove said, turning to look at us. "A journalist at the *Shoreline Gazette*."

I would've rather been sucker punched, rather been kicked right in the gut by a fucking giraffe, because this felt a million times worse.

She'd tricked me. She'd used me. She'd *fucked* me just to get close to my family.

The three of us jolted as someone pounded on the door. "Hawk?" It was Hannah's voice.

"Speak of the motherfucking devil," Finch said, rising out of her chair as if she were about to wrestle Hannah to the ground.

I held up my hand, stilling her. "Let me handle this."

"Are you sure?" Finch asked. "Because I've got dart guns that can take down a rhino and—"

"Yes." I turned and stepped out, shutting the door behind me. The last thing the zoo needed was my sisters to go apeshit on Hannah, even if she deserved it.

Hannah's cheeks were flushed and she panted as if she'd been running. Walter wagged his tail from where Hannah held him tucked under her arm. Her pink hair was windswept, her eyes wide with fear as she stumbled over her explanation. "I think you grabbed my phone by mistake and—"

"Who are you?"

Hannah's eyes widened and she took a tentative step back. "Hawk—"

"Who are you?" I growled, taking a step closer until I was towering over her.

"I . . ."

"Wait, I already know," I said. "Hannah Murphy, journalist at the *Shoreline Gazette*."

As if on cue, her eyes welled, but this time I felt no sympathy, no urge to comfort her, just a broken hollowness that she had made me fall in love with her only to manipulate and betray me.

"I can explain," she choked out.

"You came here to spy on me?"

"I was supposed to look into the zoo's finances and see if there was anything worth reporting to share it with the investor who hired me . . . I should've told you, but—"

"But? BUT?" I seethed. "You were too busy fucking me to tell me you were trying to ruin my life? My home? My *family*?"

"No, I—"

"What did you tell them, Hannah? What do they know?" She flinched at the way I shouted her name, and I didn't care. "Do you even know who this mystery employer is?"

"I didn't tell them everything," she said, her whole body shaking, and for the barest second, I still had the traitorous urge to gather her up in my arms. That just made my rage burn brighter. "I stopped reporting back to them after we kissed. I wasn't planning on this, us, or falling in love with this place." Her voice cracked. "I quit a-and I was going to tell you . . ."

I tossed her phone at her, and she caught it in one hand. "It sounds like this Dawn person already knows more than enough to shut us down." I scowled. "Let me guess. Some rich bastard wanted to buy the land for himself? Flatten the zoo?"

"I don't think so."

"What do you mean you don't think so?"

"The person who hired us to investigate, he said his name was Rick, but then . . . at the gala, I saw him again."

"Who?" Fear clawed its way up my throat. In the back of my mind, I already knew.

"Fox Madigan."

"The fucking Madigans!" Finch and Dove burst out the door behind me, clearly having been eavesdropping on the other side. "Are you fucking serious? The Madigans are trying to buy the zoo from us?"

Hannah stumbled back a step, her eyes darting between the three of us. "I was going to tell you . . ."

"But you didn't!" I shouted. I screwed my eyes shut and took a breath, trying to control my anger. "You had *every* opportunity to be honest with me and you didn't."

Dove, of all people, shot forward, and Finch had to grab her by both arms and wrangle her back. "Easy, tiger," she said, struggling to keep our little sister from throttling my ex-lover.

I shoved my hand in Hannah's jacket pocket and grabbed my phone out of it. Walter growled and snapped at me, his loyalties clear.

"There's a ferry leaving this afternoon," I said. "I suggest you be on it, unless you want us to call the cops on you for trespassing."

I watched the tears welling in her eyes finally spill over, and it was like a shot straight through my chest. Even if she deserved it, even if she was a lying piece of shit, I hated every single one of those tears, wished I could reach out and wipe them away. But the person I hated to see cry didn't exist. I didn't know this woman at all.

I gripped my phone tighter in my hand and turned up the path toward the African animals exhibit.

"Hawk," Hannah called. "Please."

"Walk away, Hannah," Finch commanded as she and Dove stepped between the two of us. "Walk. Away."

I gave Hannah one last look, the sight of her tear-streaked face permanently branding itself into my mind. The lions were already roaring their morning calls, and I had work to do. I could lose myself in the cleaning and sweeping, working until my body was exhausted enough that I could wrap my mind around all of this. Until I was tired enough that Hannah's tear-streaked face didn't flash behind my eyes. I strode up the hill, not turning back, every step feeling like a death sentence as a fresh set of storm clouds rolled overhead.

My body was numb. Not a single tear or the tiniest spark of hate, just utter numbness. My hand didn't feel the grip of the bucket, nor did my legs feel the scratch of the prickly bushes leading to the lion enclosure. I walked slowly, mind absent. Crane tried to talk to me at one point but left it when he saw the look in my eyes.

My hands went through the motions, even as my mind tried to disappear, tried to avoid all of those questions that were desperate to break free: Why had she done it? How could I have been so blind? Was she really that good of an actress? Was all of it a lie?

I unlocked the gate, re-latching it behind me and tugging on the lock out of habit. Lucy and Lilith's chuffs were eager from the echoing concrete enclosure. Sammy's were absent, the male lion probably still asleep. I trudged down the steps into the darkened tunnel before the next set of gates and locks. I went through them again, re-latching the door behind me. I'd focus on the work until I didn't feel like my heart was shattering.

But when I turned the corner, my heart stopped entirely.

Whale hello there

Chapter Fifty-One

Hannah

"So you're just leaving?" Mae asked, folding her arms and leaning against the doorframe to the break room. "What happened to fighting for him?"

"I'm sure he never wants to see me again." My voice wobbled as I took off my boots and chucked them onto the pile. I unhooked my keys from my belt and passed them to Mae to hang back up by the lockers.

Tessa slung her arm around my shoulders and hugged me into her. "You made a mistake in not telling him, Hannah, a big one," she said. "But you decided you weren't going to deliver this story ages ago. You quit your job. You turned down money you needed for him."

Mae craned her neck up to the ceiling. "I mean, you probably shouldn't have taken the job at all—"

"Not helping," Tessa snapped, glaring at Mae.

"No, she's right. It was a shitty, unforgivable thing to do." I wiped my tears with trembling hands, adrenaline and shock and shame coursing through me in equal measure. "I saw a big dollar sign, a way for my mom to finally see I was responsible enough for her to sell her house. I'm so fucking selfish. I saw it as an opportunity and I took it. I honestly didn't think anyone would get hurt by it until I got here, and then I just didn't know how to fix it, and I . . ."

"He loves you, Hannah," Tessa said, rubbing her hand down my back as I unclipped my radio.

"If he did, he doesn't anymore." I sniffed. "I'm a terrible person. I hurt him in the worst possible way."

"Maybe you can make it right," Mae said, taking the radio from me. "Maybe he just needs time."

"This is unfixable, Mae," I said, holding my hands to my eyes as if I could stymy the onslaught of tears, but now that they'd started, I didn't think they'd ever stop falling. "I appreciate all your optimism, you two, I really do. But this is broken beyond repair. I broke it."

The radio beeped to life and Hawk's voice crackled through, making my tears come thick and fast again. "Carnivores to vet team."

The radio fizzled with static as Finch replied, "Vet team. Go ahead."

"We've got a CB in the lions." His voice was too even, too calm, eerily steady. It was the voice of someone used to emergencies and trying not to cause a panic, but I could *feel* it coming over the radio. Hawk was in agony. "Resus in progress. It's Sammy."

Mae and Tessa gasped, shooting each other glances.

"No." I choked out the word.

The beep of his radio barely cut off before Finch's voice came through. "On my way."

My heart plummeted into my boots. This lion was not just any lion. Sammy was Hawk's last piece of his dad, his last special connection to him.

I leapt to my feet and barreled toward the door.

I didn't know what came over me. Hawk probably didn't want me there. But I couldn't just sit there and let him face the death of this animal alone, even if the only thing I could offer was to redirect his rage toward me. I refused to let the man I loved go through this alone.

And fuck, I loved him.

The words over the radio rang in my ears. Hawk's voice was an unsettling neutral, stripped of all emotion, and I knew he was probably trying his damndest not to fall apart.

I bolted, dropping my bag at the front entrance and shouting over my shoulder, "Watch that for me?"

"Hannah? Hannah, you're going to miss the ferry!" Mateo called after me, but I was already racing away.

How did someone safely resuscitate a lion? Another horrible thought pierced through me: Sammy was probably already dead, discovered by Hawk on his morning rounds. It was probably too late.

I sprinted past the early morning visitors, everyone slowly sweeping up through the zoo at the start of the day. My heart hammered in my chest as I reached the thin bamboo trail that disappeared behind the macaw aviary.

I darted down the twisting paths, vaulted over the gate, and unlatched the next. Finch was barreling toward the enclosure from the other direction, calling loudly on the radio for Dove to get the truck, her vet bag slung over her shoulder. Mrs. Lachlan's voice then took over like a quarterback calling a play as she instructed everyone from her children to the front staffers on where to be to keep visitors out of the way.

Finch ignored me as she ran, letting me follow her up the ramp and into the back of the lion enclosure. What we saw made my heart break.

The door to the first room was flung wide open, only the iron sliding doors keeping Hawk and Sammy from the rest of the pride. Hawk leaned over Sammy's lifeless body, pounding heavy compressions onto the lion's massive side.

I ran in, dropping to the other side of Sammy.

"Hawk!" Finch barked, but Hawk didn't respond.

He kept up the maddening compressions, his arms straining, his teeth gritted, and I suddenly remembered: this was how his father died. He'd been the one doing compressions while Finch raced them to the wharf. I could see it all on his face, him reliving that moment, trapped in the memory.

Finch cursed something and entered behind her brother, getting her stethoscope out and listening to the lion's chest. She did it steadily, not rushed or urgent, and I knew then that the lion was surely gone and Finch was performing this little act for her brother alone.

Tears streaming down my cheeks, I was so fucking grateful for Finch in that moment. That she could be the calm in this storm. That she knew how to switch into her professional brain and keep everyone calm when her brother was breaking apart. I loved that he had all these people who would put him back together, even as I wished desperately that I could still be one of them.

Finch hung her stethoscope back around her neck and placed her hand on her brother's back.

"No," Hawk gritted out. "Check again." He pumped

Sammy's chest faster, the veins on his arms and neck and forehead straining as his face went bright red.

"He's gone," Finch said gently.

"No." Hawk's voice broke. "He can't be. We still had years left."

"His bloodwork wasn't looking good. He would've been on a heavy cocktail of meds for the rest of his life, and even if we caught this sooner, that might've only given him a few more bad months. I was going to tell you today that I would advise euthanasia." Finch said all of the information slowly and carefully. "Let him rest, Hawk."

A tear slid down Hawk's face, and it was like a sledgehammer to my chest. The first time he'd cried since losing his dad.

"I can't," he said through gritted teeth. "I can't just let him go."

A sudden bang to the door behind us made us all jolt. One of the other lions had managed to shove a single claw under the slide door, wiggling it open an inch. I gasped as that paw slid the door another inch, a muzzle appearing and trying to work open the slide. Half a face poked through now, sniffing and pushing that creaking slide door upward.

"Shit."

Fear gripped me so tightly, I froze. In that split second, my first thought was being disappointed in myself at how I'd just rooted to the spot, directly in the line of danger. I thought I had good instincts in an emergency. Apparently, being potentially mauled to death by a lion didn't make the list. Staring at that giant animal tearing open the door, I just stood there, thinking for certain this was how I was going to die.

Well, this would make a better headline than "drowned by adorable penguins."

But then I caught sight of Hawk, who was just as frozen

beside me, seemingly so broken by sorrow that he couldn't move. That spurred me into action with a singular thought: get him out of here, make him safe.

I encircled my arms around his waist and hauled him backward. The heels of my boots skidded across the wet floor and I fell back, dragging Hawk down with me.

"She can't lift the slide," Finch said as she shut the door and bolted it, doing up the lock and yanking it twice in a swift, practiced motion. "It locks at three inches, so you were safe. But thanks for trying to save my brother's life, I guess," she added sarcastically.

My heart was pounding so fast, I didn't have time to feel embarrassed. How was I supposed to know that? It looked like something straight out of *Jurassic Park*.

Lucy toyed with the slider but couldn't lift it enough to pass through. A snarl escaped her maw as she attacked the door again, and Finch unlocked it to lift fully. Lucy prowled into the room and sniffed Sammy. Tears streamed heavier down my cheeks as I watched the lioness rub against Sammy's lifeless body.

My arms tightened around Hawk, and he turned into them. Dropping his head into my shoulder, he gripped me so fiercely, I thought he might break a bone. But I didn't care. Not in the slightest. Not as he sobbed into my hair, and I knew he wasn't just grieving the loss of Sammy but his father too.

I held him for what felt like hours, the sky darkening as another storm rolled in and the automatic lights flickering on. Finch called back to the keepers over the radio, informing them of what had happened and making plans for removing Sammy's body.

Even Finch's voice wobbled, as if seeing her brother so broken had broken her too. She checked the locks again and shifted the lions properly into place, securing them in another part of their enclosure.

It wasn't until Hawk's breathing steadied and his hands dropped their white-knuckle grip on my shirt that Finch said, "Hannah, you should go."

I could barely speak, my voice cracking. "I don't want to leave him like this."

"We'll take care of him," Finch said, like she knew I needed to hear it, but when I shook my head, any level of civility was immediately dropped. It was like she remembered all at once who I really was. Finch huffed a bitter laugh. "I'm sure you've already got one hell of a story for your headlines. I have a feeling you'll be hearing from the Westworths' lawyers. Now get the fuck out of here."

I pulled away from Hawk, and he dropped his head into his hands, not looking up at me.

"I'm so sorry," I whispered to him, my eyes dropping to where tears stained his shirt. "I'm so, so sorry. For every-thing." I swallowed back another bout of tears. "I know I fucked up so badly, but it wasn't all a lie. I really fell in love with you."

"Let's go, Hannah." Dove's voice sounded behind me now.

Hawk didn't look up. Didn't acknowledge my words.

Finch's hand landed on my shoulder, and I knew she'd drag me out of there if I didn't move.

I looked up at her through watery eyes. "I'm glad he has you," I said, wiping my nose with my sleeve. "I'm so sorry I hurt you too." Dove gave me the barest of nods. "I'll do everything I can to fix this." I stood and gave him one last look. "Goodbye, Hawk."

He didn't look up at me, and my world fell apart.

HAWK'S JEEP

Chapter Fifty-Two

Hawk

We all stood out on the wharf behind Kangaroo Point as the sun set.

I shook my head and pinched the tears out of my eyes. So many fucking tears. Maybe once every eleven years, I needed a good cry, but once I started, I couldn't seem to stop. I mourned Sammy, yes, but I mourned Hannah too. With Sammy, we'd grieve together and find a way to eventually move on, just like we did with all of our animals. But with Hannah, there would be no closure, only bitterness.

"Sammy was the runt of his litter," Mom said to the sunset, eulogizing him. "But your father always believed in him. I was a little less than thrilled when he brought a lion cub into the house when I was heavily pregnant with you—" Mom squeezed Wren's shoulder. "But Hawk volunteered to raise him alongside Simon." Her voice thickened. "Your dad was so proud, seeing you step up like that, seeing the adult you were growing into before his very eyes. He knew his mission would live on in you." She looked around at my siblings. "All of you."

"If I'd found him sooner—" I started.

My family all made noises and words of reassurance at once, silencing the thought. I didn't know who I was talking about, Sammy or my father, but I felt the guilt and weight of both. I kept playing those "what-ifs" over and over in my mind right along with all the ones about Hannah.

What if I hadn't invited her to feed the lions? What if I hadn't called her into my office? What if I hadn't found out before our lunch date and heard the truth directly from her? Would that have changed any of it?

"You did everything you could for him," Finch assured me. "Sammy had a great, long life. It's all we can hope for."

Finch had performed a necropsy on Sammy, confirming that his death was sudden and he wasn't in pain long. That was the hardest part. Some animals hid it too well and the guilt always stuck with you when they'd been living with injuries or diseases and probably should've been let go a long time before. Those decisions were some of the toughest parts of the job.

"To Sammy," Crane said, lifting his bottle of birch beer toward the sunset.

"To Sammy," the rest of my family echoed.

Dove scattered a handful of Sammy's ashes out across the water. The rest would be buried beneath the trees by the Jeep playground so that I could go visit him when I wanted some time just him and me.

"It never gets easier," I said as Heron came over to me

and slung their arm around my back, instigating the rest of my siblings to swarm around me in a giant group hug.

Working with animals was like a lesson in constant heartbreak. I'd never wanted to do anything else, but man did it hurt sometimes. There were some animals whose deaths were sad, and then there were those special ones that were just devastating—the ones that would keep popping up and making you break all over again for years to come. But the rest of the animals in my care needed me and I was grateful for that work. Nothing could break me badly enough that I wouldn't wake up the next morning and keep going, opening myself up for another animal like Sammy to break my heart all over again.

My family pressed in tighter around me and I felt grateful to be surrounded by so much love. They were overwhelming and annoying and chaotic, but we'd never let each other go through something like this alone.

I thought about Hannah again. Would anyone be there holding her together right now?

I shouldn't think about it, shouldn't care, but the idea of her being in pain didn't make mine any lesser. There would be no vengeance or retribution that would soothe what I felt. I'd fallen in love with her and she'd broken my heart, and I'd just have to find a way to keep going without her. Without her laugh, her warmth, her frenetic energy and goofy jokes, the way she helped me dust the cobwebs off all those memories that were too painful to look at alone. She'd made me feel seen and loved and whole in a way I didn't know could exist . . . Somewhere deep in my soul, I believed her. I knew it wasn't all a lie. The way she'd held me as I cried wasn't a lie. The way she told me she loved me wasn't a lie either.

And in some ways, that made every broken part of me hurt even more.

My siblings released me, all perching on the rocks and watching the sun set as the animals made their last noises before settling down to sleep.

"Family meeting tonight," I said, and a riot of groans and swears chorused back. "We need to debrief. After the sun goes down."

My siblings mumbled their agreement at that and went back to watching the sunset.

Mom squeezed my shoulder, and I knew she wanted to tell me she was proud of me.

We'd sat here countless times before, farewelling the most important and beloved members of the zoo family. We came down here on the anniversary of Dad's death too, and I hoped one day long, *long* into the future, my siblings and their children, and maybe some children and grandchildren of my own, would come down here and watch the sun set and say goodbye to me too.

Whale hello there

Chapter Fifty-Three

Hannah

I sobbed into my mother's lap through the first half of *Pitch Perfect*, our mother-daughter comfort movie that was brought out in the most dire of circumstances. It did nothing to ease the flow of tears. Now, I was half comatose on her lap, wrapped in a weighted blanket as she fed me popcorn one piece at a time and combed her fingers through my hair.

She knew I'd fucked up, even told me as much right to my face, and then she held me through the fallout like only a best friend could.

Half of Mom's stuff was in boxes now, a "For Sale" sign prominently displayed outside the house. She'd already put a down payment on an apartment in the city after I'd had a meltdown to her about how she had to move on with her life and not let me hold her back anymore. I'd convinced her that

I'd find another job, assured her I'd find a way forward and had no need for this house.

I'd managed to squirrel away a little bit between not having to pay rent for over a month and the stipends from the Holloways. I'd never gotten my zoo paychecks . . . probably because they were for a different name. Dawn probably had them, but there was no way I was returning to face her and demand them back. Leaving the *Shoreline Gazette* was like its own kind of messy breakup, but at least Finch's threat about the Westworths' lawyers wasn't true. There was no story about Finch anywhere, no story about the zoo at all in fact. And for that, at least, I was grateful. It wouldn't make up for what I'd done, but at least it wouldn't make it any worse.

When the movie ended, Mom clicked the remote and turned the TV off. "Right, we've wallowed," she said as if she were ticking something off her list. "Now we need to fix this."

"There's nothing I can do, Mom." I groaned, curling up into a ball on the couch as she stood.

"Oh, that's such BS," she said, swatting me with a pillow.

"I've tried to contact him, but he won't reply," I said. "His sister sent me one text saying that he was alive and to stop worrying about him and if I texted him again, she'd put me in their industrial composter."

"Well, that is a very interesting threat at least." Mom said like it was some sort of silver lining.

"Tessa and Mae think he looks sad," I said, burying my face in my hands. "I made him sad. I'm such an asshole."

"We're moving out of the self-loathing now," Mom said. "Believe me when I tell you, people have made bigger mistakes and been forgiven. I think you might need a bigger gesture than just texting him more apologies though."

"I don't know what to do," I said, getting all choked up

again. "Is there a guidebook to grand gestures? Are flash mobs still a thing?"

"Oh, honey. Here," Mom said, grabbing the pint of Ben & Jerry's and offering it to me.

"I love him, Mom," I cried.

"Then fight for him," she said, swatting my leg. "Don't give up."

I frowned at my giant spoonful of ice cream, not hungry anymore, but I ate it anyway. It did seem to magically make the crying lessen. "I wish I had ten million dollars to anonymously donate to save their zoo. That would be the biggest grand gesture."

"You really think they might lose the zoo?" Mom asked, perching beside me.

"I think it's a possibility," I said. "At least there's no news article kicking them when they're down."

"Maybe there needs to be one to build them back up?"

I paused, spoon poised halfway to my mouth, and considered my mom for a second. "Maybe there does . . ." I threw the weighted blanket off me and raced over to where my phone was plugged into the wall.

I dialed my first contact, bouncing my leg as Mom gave me a quizzical look.

He picked up on the second ring.

"Alfred, it's Hannah."

"This better be important," he muttered. "I have six Band-Aids on my fingers, Hannah. Six!"

I cringed. "Six is an improvement though, isn't it?"

I'd been working with Walter on warming up to people but had found that adage about old dogs and new tricks was mostly true. Alfred had looked like he wanted to strangle me with his pocket square when I told him I was leaving. I fought back the fresh wave of tears when I thought about sweet, shmoopy-faced Walter. I hadn't expected I'd fall in love with him either.

I made a little sniffle as I spooned more ice cream into my mouth.

"Six is still greater than zero," Alfred snapped, then he added quickly, "You sound absolutely dreadful."

"Thanks." I set the ice cream back down. "Hey, I was hoping you could do me a favor?"

Alfred guffawed. "You know I'm not your personal concierge, right?"

"I know." I groaned. "I'm sorry. I just . . . I'm trying to make things right with Hawk."

"I'm intrigued," Alfred said. "Especially if making things right involves you returning to the island and resuming your pet-sitting responsibilities at your nearest convenience. What do you need?"

I took a steeling breath and straightened my shoulders. "Do you happen to know anyone working at the *Holloway Times*?"

HAWK'S JEEP

Chapter Fifty-Four

Hawk

Mom, Finch, and I sat in three plush upholstered chairs in front of Mrs. Westworth's giant mahogany desk. The whole place was giving me flashbacks to last year, when she issued the ultimatum that we had one year before she sold the zoo.

I bounced my leg, holding our financial reports in my hand and trying not to sweat on the paper.

Mrs. Westworth's assistant, Katie, was a woman in her mid-thirties. She wore a fashionable white blouse and a tight gray pencil skirt. I surmised her high heels were also super painful judging by the way she kept shifting her weight from where she stood in the corner, typing on her phone and loudly chewing her gum. She glanced up, gave me a fake smile, and went back to typing.

When we'd arrived promptly at two p.m., Katie had told

us Mrs. Westworth was just finishing up her afternoon tea and would be with us shortly. That had been half an hour ago . . .

When Mrs. Westworth finally entered, she seemed more stooped than when I'd seen her at the gala. She leaned heavily on her cane and it took her twice as long as last year to walk around the desk to her chair.

Finch and I both immediately stood up, as if we were greeting a monarch or a president of something. Mom wrung her hands nervously from where she sat in the middle chair.

"Sit, sit," Mrs. Westworth said, surprising us both with her informality. "This won't take long."

I tenderly placed the financial report on Mrs. Westworth's desk, and she unceremoniously shoved it back at me.

"Unless this has entirely different figures than the one you sent me this morning, I'm not interested," she said.

"It does have an addendum," Finch offered. "Our sister, Lark, added some more potential revenue options. Also, have I told you how lovely you're looking today, Mrs. Westworth? That brooch is exquisite."

"Save your flattery, Goldfinch," she said. She clasped her hands together and leaned her forearms across the desk, her jewelry clanging with the motion. "I normally don't take this much vested interest in my holdings," she began. "My business manager handles these sorts of things. But my family has been supporting your family's strange little zoo for generations and I felt I owed it to my grandfather, who loved your zoo, to oversee this myself."

I noted how she implied that she didn't, in fact, love the zoo herself.

"You have been a most wonderful patron—"

Mrs. Westworth cut Finch a look at the same time I attempted to subtly kick her.

"As you know," Mrs. Westworth continued. "I am reducing the number of Westworth charities and patronages. Extended family members have been coming out of the woodwork offering to take over for me, but I know none of them would do a good job." She huffed bitterly, looking at me with rheumy eyes. "I want to leave the zoo in capable hands."

"We are more than capable, I assure you," Mom vowed, placing her hand on her chest.

Mrs. Westworth's eyes dropped to the sweaty financial report in front of me. "Apparently, you are not."

My heart sank. This was it. It was all over. I'd failed my animals, my family, my father.

The door burst open behind us.

"Wait!" Dove shouted, her face bright red as she waved her phone in the air like it was a golden ticket.

"What is the meaning of this?" Mrs. Westworth blustered.

"We've done it," Dove panted. "We've made the money."

My heart leapt into my throat, dangerous hope reigniting within me.

Mrs. Westworth narrowed her eyes at my sister. "How?"

"We've just secured a contract to be a filming location for the next Deacon Harrow movie," she said, shooting me an apologetic sideways glance before refocusing on Mrs. Westworth. "Look."

She passed the elderly woman her phone. Mrs. Westworth picked up her glasses and held the phone right up to her face. "Katie, how do I make this bigger?" Katie leapt to attention and helped Mrs. Westworth zoom in. Mrs. Westworth swatted her away when the font was the right size.

Everything was frozen and silent for several long seconds.

Finch stared at Dove until she looked up from where she was staring at her boots. "What the fuck did you do?" she mouthed as Mrs. Westworth continued to read, her thin lips silently moving with every word.

Dove shrugged and mouthed back, "I'm sorry. I had to do something."

My eyes darted back and forth between Mrs. Westworth and my sister, and I felt more guilty with every passing moment. I'd told Dove not to pursue this, and right now, I was incredibly grateful that my siblings never seemed to listen to me.

We waited for what felt like an eternity before Mrs. Westworth pulled her glasses down and returned Dove's phone.

"And this is just the beginning," Dove promised. "We have so many more plans and—"

Mrs. Westworth shot Dove a look, and Dove's words immediately died on her lips. It felt like we were waiting for our execution, my stomach in knots as we waited for the judge before us to dole out our sentence. She had the power to completely destroy our lives.

My heart was racing so loudly, it pounded against my eardrums. Everything hinged on this moment.

"I thought Prickle Island Zoo was stuck in the past," Mrs. Westworth said, giving Dove an approving once-over. "It pleases me to know I was wrong. Katie, call Baxter and have him draft up a new contract."

HAWK'S JEEP

Chapter Fifty-Five

Hawk

I raised my glass and shouted over the crowd, "To the official owner of the Prickle Island Zoo, Evie Lachlan!"

Our assortment of glasses clinked together as we cheersed each other. We'd decided to splash out for a celebratory dinner of pizza and fries from the Peckish Peacock. We gathered around the picnic tables, many of the summer staff in attendance—Aya, Mateo, and a smattering of zoo volunteers we'd invited to join us for an impromptu pizza party.

We'd really done it. The zoo was ours. A dream my father had his entire life was finally fulfilled. My mom gave me a watery-eyed look, and I knew she was thinking the same thing. He would be so proud—a home for his children and grandchildren to be passed down through the generations—a place where so many families had made memories, celebrated birthdays and proposals, so many children deciding they would be future conservationists, and just simply a bunch of people having one beautiful, happy day over summer.

Prickle Island Zoo mattered to a lot of people beyond our family, and now we'd be able to protect it forever. My smile faded as I stared over the crowd, my eyes falling to Tessa and Mae, who were entertaining the cockatoos with their little dances and laughing as the birds followed them across the aviary.

I'm not missing her, I told myself for what felt like the hundredth time.

I cleared my throat and focused back on other things, more important things, like the people who actually mattered to me.

I tapped a spoon to my beer bottle with a *cling, cling, cling* and the crowd quieted again.

"There's another person we should be celebrating tonight," I said. "A person I would like to personally apologize to." That made the crowd quiet further as everyone leaned in. "And that is my sister, Dove." Dove looked at me like I'd sprouted a second head as I turned to her. "Dove, I'm sorry I didn't listen to your plans to improve the zoo. It's because of *you* that we're celebrating today. You see a future for this place that I was too close-minded to see, and because of that, we were not only able to raise the funds we needed, we're also going to be a filming location for a new Deacon Harrow movie."

The crowd oohed and ahhed at that. "To Dove Lachlan." I raised my bottle again. "Hero of the Prickle Island Zoo."

"To Dove!" The crowd cheered, making my sister's cheeks flush a furious scarlet as she began to duck behind Finch. Finch grabbed Dove by the shoulders and paraded our sheepish sister through the crowd like a two-person conga line, doing a whole loop around the Peckish Peacock to receive the accolades of the rest of the staff.

Once Finch finally released her, the group went back to their individual chatter and I wandered over to Dove.

"Thank you for that," she said with a nod.

"Deacon Harrow," Finch said, shaking her head. "I can't believe you two still keep in touch."

Dove's blush brightened further. "We don't really."

"I remember him as this gangly kid who used to come to the zoo every day over that summer when you two were little," Mom said. "Who knew he'd become a movie star? I can't believe how buff he is now."

"Mom," Dove groaned, trying to hide behind her hands.

"I think I have a picture," Finch said, grabbing out her phone. Her face morphed from one of taunting laughter to one of confusion and then surprise as she opened her phone and frantically started scrolling. "Holy fucking shit."

"Language," Mom said through a tight, fake smile as she glanced around at the rest of the staff.

"Look at this!" Finch dropped her phone onto the picnic table, and all of my siblings gathered around it.

"Holy hagfish." Dove gaped at the screen. "How much is it?"

"How much is what?" Wren asked, lifting up on her tiptoes to try to see over the twins.

"The zoo donations page is being flooded," Dove said.

"Sixty thousand in the last three hours?" Finch exclaimed, her beer bottle still poised halfway to her lips. "They're all little donations—five dollars, ten."

"Where is this money coming from?" Mom asked, her eyes scanning the donations page wildly.

"What happened to—"

Finch's question was cut off by Mom's phone ringing.

She answered it. "Hello, Evelyn speaking. Yes. What? No." I turned just in time to see her eyes bugging out of her head. "Yes. Yes. The morning news?" She snapped at Finch for a pen, who scrambled in her pockets to pass her one, and then she started jotting notes furiously down on the back of her hand. "Yes. Absolutely. Yes. Uh-huh. Okay." She paused, whirling toward me. "What article?"

"I can't believe she really did it," Dove murmured to herself, shaking her head in disbelief.

"What? Who?" we all asked at once.

"I wasn't going to tell you," she hedged. "I didn't think it would be this massive. Though I guess Hannah was never one for subtlety."

I froze at the name as Dove pulled out her phone and placed it on the picnic table beside Finch's.

My heart pounded in my ears as I stared down at the title: "One in a Chameleon: Saving the Prickle Island Zoo by Hannah Murphy."

Whale hello
there

Chapter Fifty-Six

Hannah

I sat at my desk, typing away on my keyboard, as my coworker, Kevin, honked his nose loudly in his tissue in a way that made my skin crawl. I missed Kevin the blue-tongued skink, a much better co-worker. The fluorescent lights buzzed above my head, giving me a headache. I swore the lights in this place were so mind-bendingly loud.

My new office was some sort of purgatory—my punishment for everything I'd done. I deserved it, being wedged in the corner of a windowless room, transcribing forms from a stack that never seemed to end. I'd been here one week and already the monotony of it was driving me crazy.

Between hours spent at my soul-sucking job, I'd been fielding a lot of media inquiries as my article went viral. Dove had turned into a bit of a Prickle Island Zoo liaison—texting me screenshots of the donations page every few hours and keeping me updated. I told her to stop thanking me, and she told me to stop apologizing to her. We'd reached a friendly equilibrium, chatting most days on Morph. She seemed to be the only one who'd forgiven me. Maybe because we were the same brand of awkward, neurodivergent, and chaotic.

I missed her. I missed the animals. I missed Walter and Tessa and Mae and even Alfred.

And most of all, I missed *him*. His smile, his gruff laugh, the way his face scrunched when he was thinking, the golden rings in his eyes when he stared at the sunrise. . .

Hawk Lachlan was the best kind of man—smart, loyal, caring, hardworking, tough yet heart-meltingly thoughtful . . . and I'd stomped all over him like the careless whirlwind I always seemed to be. I ruined everything I touched eventually —every friendship, every job, hell, even every hobby as evidenced by my closet full of half-finished art projects that I messed up once and never touched again.

I was a quitter. A disaster. An epic disappointment even to myself.

I'd finally found a place where I felt excited to be every day, a job I was actually good at, a person I really loved, and then immediately went and fucked it all up like I always did.

The old printer beside me squealed to life, and I didn't even jump at the sound of it this time, too numb to it all. I was sure this place was making me even more depressed than I already was.

At least the article had been a success. At least the zoo had some extra funds. Maybe I could gently encourage Dove to redo the penguin enclosure and make it less of a death trap? Maybe Hawk could build that new bush hut by the tigers that he'd been dreaming of?

It gave me a little sense of closure at least, knowing the

zoo would be okay. They could all move on with their lives, even if I never would.

I sighed, staring at the yellowing white wallpaper in front of me. Mom's house had sold almost instantly and well above her asking price. I'd managed to find a rental down the road from her new place—granted, I'm pretty sure my apartment used to be a storage closet, but it was cheap and thus far, I hadn't seen any evidence of rats or roaches, so it was good enough for me. It wasn't a gorgeous cottage amongst a garden of white lilies, but it was better than a triple bunk bed or a hammock that people liked to have sex on so . . . I'd count it as a win.

I dropped my head into my hands, the memories of the island flooding back to me. Everything reminded me of him. It cropped up on me all of a sudden, like a wave of emotions I couldn't control. I tried not to cry too loudly, but three seconds later, Kevin shouted, "Hey, Tina! New girl's crying again."

HAWK'S JEEP

Hawk

I fell back into my routines, the rhythms of the day worn into the grooves of my soul. I kept working, focusing on caring for the animals and building my cabin now that I was certain we owned this property forever. Finch's apartment was almost done too, and the twins were clamoring for us to move out and for them to move in—their first time ever having their own rooms.

I sat on the lookout just beyond the parking lot, watching the sunrise. I wasn't usually sentimental. I shouldn't be thinking of her at all, but I woke up long before the sun and decided to wander down here, my feet steering me of their own volition.

The visitor numbers boomed after Hannah's article. The ferries were packed with people coming to Prickle Island just to see us and one unlikely animal in particular: Colin the cow.

In her article, Hannah had written:

"The zoo's most egregious offense is that they have a cow named Colin. Who names a cow Colin? Anyway, if you go to Prickle Island Zoo, please tell Colin I say hi."

And boy had people taken that to heart. Dove had even started a "Colin the Cow" TikTok account. He was a mini superstar.

I'd read and reread Hannah's article more times than I cared to admit. Her words were beautiful, funny, and poignant, capturing the spirit of the zoo more perfectly than I ever could myself. She really understood its value—that much was clear. And I was glad at least that the zoo worked its magic over her too. It was hard to hold as much anger after reading her beautiful words, especially now with the comfort of knowing the zoo was legally ours.

Emotions clogged my throat as the sun rose. I took out my phone and tossed it over and over in my hands. Even the sight of the blue case made my stomach clench. This was pathetic.

Hannah had texted me a few times, but I'd never replied. She'd messaged me a last apology and a final goodbye and that was that. I knew Dove was keeping in touch with her at least. A few times, I'd seen Hannah's name pop up on Dove's phone, and every time it made my stomach summersault. I didn't *want* to want to know how she was doing . . . but also, I really, really did.

In my periphery, I saw Finch appear on one side of me and then Dove on the other. Each of my siblings had been trying to look after me in their own misguided ways. Dove curated me a break-up playlist, Finch made sure to keep the fridge well-stocked with drinks, Lark sent me twenty articles about regulating my nervous system, Wren knit me a comfy beanie, and the twins mostly just worked harder so I didn't have to pick up their slack—never had their runs been finished faster, buckets always cleaned, nothing to ever pull them up about.

Finch and Dove stood there, staring out at the sunrise with me, and even though they didn't say a word, I knew their presence was because they were concerned for me.

"Is she okay?" I finally asked to the ocean. "Is she happy?"

Dove pursed her lips, debating if she should answer. "She's miserable, but other than that, she's okay," she said. "She's got a new job she hates and a shitty little apartment. She asks about the animals all the time. She asks about you."

"I don't know if that makes it easier or harder," I said, hanging my head at the first piece of news I'd heard about her in weeks.

"You should talk to her," Finch said, nodding at the phone in my hands.

"There's nothing to say." Finch snorted at my reply, and I glared at her before tucking my phone back in my pocket. "I thought you two were on my side. I thought you were even more furious at her than I am?"

"We're always on your side," Dove said diplomatically. "But we've forgiven Hannah. She messed up, badly, but she's tried really hard to make amends, and I really do think she's a good person who just made a mistake. It's kind of hard to stay mad at her."

I shook my head. "I can never forgive her for what she's done."

"Of course you can," Finch said, as if I were being

ridiculous. "If I can forgive you for that time you put blue hair dye in my shampoo when I was eleven, then you can forgive her for this."

"You ended up liking it and keeping your hair blue for a year," I said. "It's not the same."

"The time you locked me in Daisy's enclosure and told me you'd trained her to eat humans on command?" Dove suggested.

My lips traitorously curved into a smile at the memory. I'd forgotten about that. Maybe I was a little too hard on Heron and Crane for their antics. I'd been a hellion when I was younger too.

"That wasn't that bad," I said.

"I was seven!"

"You've kept plenty of secrets from us too. How often have we all fucked up and forgiven each other?" Dove asked pointedly, and I knew she was referring to how often I'd dismissed her ideas—the ideas that ultimately saved the zoo.

"That's different," I muttered.

"No, it's not," she pushed. "We forgive the people we love."

"I do *not* love her," I growled.

Finch and Dove burst out laughing—deep, mocking belly laughs like I'd just told the world's funniest joke.

Dove whipped out her phone. "I need to tell Lark you said that. She's going to die."

"You really are an idiot," Finch said, wiping tears of laughter from her eyes. "You're going to pass up on all this potential, future happiness because you can't forgive her?"

"She lied to me," I said.

"She was trying to take care of her mom," Dove said, and I hated the way that piqued my interest. "She was trying to do the right thing by her family, even if the way she went about it was wrong—something the two of you have in common, by the way."

"I don't care."

"She gave up a hundred thousand dollars because she couldn't bring herself to hurt you," Dove said emphatically. "*A hundred thousand dollars*, Hawk. That is fucking love."

"Love is not lying to each other."

"Why are you just dying to be righteous and alone? She screwed up," Finch said. "And you don't have to forgive her if you don't want to, but . . . you clearly don't want to let her go and move on either. You're pining."

"I am *not* pining," I spat.

"Hawk, you're sitting here alone, staring at a fucking sunrise." Finch guffawed. "That's pining!"

"Her mom has a charity exhibition in town tomorrow," Dove offered.

I folded my arms. "I don't need to know about that."

Dove shrugged. "Just putting it out there."

"You know that article was a love letter to you, right?" Finch asked.

I shook my head. "She was just feeling guilty."

"She literally wrote, 'Maybe you'll find someone you fall so deeply in love with, you will want to sing them love songs every morning like the gibbons,'" Dove said with a scoff. "You think she just made that up? She was obviously talking about you."

My shoulders bunched around my ears at the memory of that quote, of this place, of that sunrise. "She was asking her readers a hypothetical question."

"We both know that's not true." Finch clapped me on the shoulder, forcing it back down. "She loves you, bro. And you love her. And you can waste that because it hurts too much to fix it, but I think you're a stronger person than that."

That made the knot in my throat thicken. Maybe crying wasn't a once-in-eleven-years thing. Maybe this was just me now, my adult life split in two: Hawk before Hannah and Hawk after. I bobbed my head, unable to speak as my sisters hugged me one last time and wandered off back into the zoo.

I sat there, trying to regain my composure, thinking about Hannah and the shitty life she'd condemned herself to out of guilt or some misplaced sense of penance. There were too many things written into that article to be coincidence—too many inside jokes only she and I would know. The article was written like a love letter to the zoo, but I knew it was also the most beautiful, raw apology I had ever read.

Maybe I was too afraid to ever go after her. Maybe I'd live the rest of my life with this gaping hole in my heart because I was too stubborn to forgive her. Maybe I'd never again feel like the best version of myself—the man she so easily drew out of me.

I heard the click of nails on concrete long before glancing up and finding an elderly cocker spaniel trotting up the driveway, backlit by the sunrise.

Walter.

He was probably looking for Hannah. He probably missed her as much as I did. His face looked extra sallow and forlorn, like he'd aged a whole year in the time she'd been gone, or maybe I was just projecting that onto him.

He wandered right up to me, tail waggling as he sniffed around as if searching for her, as if she should be here, right by my side. I stooped and picked him up and he let me, melting into my lap as I patted his head.

"I miss her too, bud." I hugged him tighter as emotions clogged my throat again. "Nothing feels right without her."

Whale hello there

Chapter Fifty-Eight

Hannah

Mom frowned down at the extra-large coffee in my hand, the cup holder decorated in jack-o-lanterns and autumnal leaves. "It's not even September and you're already turning into a pumpkin spice addict?"

"There's a cool, new witchy-themed café around the corner." I shrugged my shoulders up to my ears and pretended to shiver. "Besides, there was a chill in the air yesterday."

"It's seventy-six degrees outside," Mom said flatly.

"And yet you're wearing a turtleneck," I pointed out.

"It's my lucky exhibit-opening turtleneck." Mom held her hand to her chest in mock offense. "You know that. It's tradition."

I shook my head as I laughed at her. Behind her, the wall

was covered in a giant drop cloth, hiding the mural she'd been commissioned to paint for the local animal shelter.

"Nice of you to dress up, by the way," Mom said, eyeing my black daisy-print overalls and tie-dyed pink T-shirt.

"I didn't realize it was like an *opening*, opening," I said. "It's a not-for-profit animal shelter. I didn't think it'd be so glitzy. Who knew they had this kind of money?"

I eyed the guests mingling, eating finger food, and sipping on cocktails served by waiters in black bow ties.

"One of the board members is apparently quite wealthy," Mom said, leaning in conspiratorially to whisper to me. "She sent her *butler* here with her dog to represent her. Look."

I glanced over my shoulder to see none other than Alfred standing stiffly by the bar, grimacing at the middle-aged shelter volunteers trying to flirt with him. He wore gloves that I was almost certain were to hide his bandaged fingers. My eyes dropped from where he held a leash for the sleeping dog at his feet.

"Walter!" I shouted so loudly that the entire room paused to stare at me.

I didn't care though. Not as I ran over and dropped to my knees to hug him. Walter turned into an excited puppy the moment he saw me. The elderly gentleman tip-tapped across the tiled floor, wiggling into my arms.

Tears sprung to my eyes. "I missed you, buddy," I crooned as he presented me his rump for scratches. "Look at you, handsome! You look so good."

Alfred cleared his throat, and I glanced up at him, bleary-eyed. "It's nice to see you too, Alfie."

He didn't smile back but he also didn't correct me, which was pretty much his version of giving me a hug.

"How have you all been?"

"Still closing down the house since the Holloways' departure back to the city," he said.

"You going to be a city dog again?" I said in a baby voice to Walter.

"He will stay on the island this year," Alfred corrected me. "He's become too much of a handful in his old age for apartment living. He'd attack half the staff."

My heart dropped. "But who will look after him?"

"Well," Alfred said with a slight frown. "We were planning on paying the new groundskeeper to let him out and make sure he's fed each day."

"No!" I cried. "He deserves someone to be there with him."

Alfred eyed me. "You are the only person fit for the job," he said.

"I can't go back." I wiped my tears on my shoulder as I continued to give Walter a good belly scratch. "It's really complicated, and I just . . . can't."

Alfred clasped his hands together and let out a frustrated sigh. "The offer to resume your stay and the pay that comes with it still stands, by the way."

I gaped at him for a second. It was a good offer to live in a fancy house rent-free and take care of a sweet—albeit a bit snappy—elderly spaniel. I half debated whether I could pull off just hiding in the cottage and never being seen by any of the Lachlan siblings, but we all knew I was the least subtle person ever. I would definitely be caught on my Diet Coke and Funyuns runs to the grocery store—not everyone could live on beef tartare. Also, I was pretty sure the island population dwindled down to a couple dozen people in the winter, so it was not like I could hide in the crowd at the Salty Dog.

Instead of taking my silence as rejection, Alfred took it as me bargaining. "Fine," he gritted out, straightening his tie. "I will double your weekly stipend, final offer."

I opened my mouth to tell him a definitive no when a deep, rasping voice behind me said, "She accepts."

I knew that voice.

I froze for a moment, afraid to turn around and be wrong. But when I stood, cheeks already streaked in happy tears from seeing Walter, I came face-to-face with Hawk Simon Lachlan. He wore a black T-shirt and blue jeans, and it was so strange seeing him out of his usual uniform. He looked good—really good—and my heart did a little flip-flop when his cheeks dimpled.

"I . . . accept his offer?" I asked him, my brows shooting up.

Alfred wisely backed out of the conversation, leaving Walter's leash hooked on the door handle behind me. My sweet spaniel wasn't going anywhere now that he saw me anyway.

Hawk rubbed the back of his neck. "I mean . . . if you want to say yes," he said. "I think I would like that."

"You would?"

He nodded and blew out a long breath. "That article you wrote . . ."

"It was the least I could do," I said with a shake of my head. "After everything I did. I quit my job at the *Gazette*, just so you know, not that that makes any of this better. I just thought that—" Hawk reached out and grabbed my hand, silencing my word vomit. My eyes got all misty again as I choked out, "I'm so sorry I hurt you."

Hawk lifted his thumb and wiped away my tears. "I forgive you, haze." The nickname made more tears fall. I didn't know how badly I needed to hear that until he said it—

like this tight fist in the center of my chest finally eased its grip.

He forgave me.

All I could do was let out a blubbering, "Thank you."

"Hey." Hawk lifted my chin with his thumb so I'd meet his eyes. "I made something for you."

My brows knit together as he fished into his back pocket and placed something in my hand—a bumper sticker. I flipped it over to read the bold writing: "Hawk and Hannah's Jeep."

On one side was the same cartoon hawk as the bumper sticker I'd made for him, but on the other, next to my name, was a pink-haired mermaid.

I laughed through my tears, and Hawk swiped each one away. Flipping the sticker over and over in my hands, I couldn't bring myself to speak for a long time. Hawk just stood there, holding that space for me to let the emotions sweep through, somehow steadier in the presence of my tears than he'd ever been before. I wondered if he'd had a reckoning with his own emotions in the time we were apart.

Finally, I sniffed and whispered, "God, I missed you."

"I missed you too, more than I was willing to admit." He swept his thumb across my cheek. "I'm sorry it took me so long."

"I never expected you would forgive me." I could barely make out his beautiful face through my watery eyes. "I never meant to hurt you."

Hawk bent down and brushed a featherlight kiss to my mouth, telling me everything that was too delicate for words. I leaned into him, deepening our kiss, and he smiled against my mouth as he wrapped his arms around me. Fireworks exploded through me, flickering with the memory of every past kiss and of the hope for every future one.

"You want to come back to Prickle Island, haze?" Hawk asked, his voice soothing as he slid his hands up and down my arms. "Go on a proper date, maybe? Possibly one that doesn't involve animal urine?"

"I know a really great place for stargazing." I chuckled, flipping the bumper sticker over in my hands.

"Is that a yes?" I nodded, and Walter barked. "I think Walter would like that too," Hawk added with a laugh.

"Are you sure?" I asked. I couldn't believe he was really saying this. "I want nothing more than to start over, but . . ."

Hawk bent down and kissed me again, the sweet softness of it sending skitters of lightning through my body. His hand bracketed my jaw, his other arm swooping around and pulling me against his broad chest.

I said it before I could second-guess myself. "I love you," I murmured against his mouth. "I love you so damn much, Hawk Lachlan."

He smiled against my lips. "I love you too, haze." He pulled away and took my hand again. "Come on, introduce me to your mom. I want to meet the matriarch of the Murphy clan."

HAWK'S JEEP

Chapter Fifty-Nine

A few years later . . .

Hawk

I patted my pocket for what felt like the hundredth time as I walked double-speed up the hill. It was early evening, the sky already starting to darken as the crisp air blew through the zoo. A local school group had come to visit us in the morning, delighting in the fact they had the whole zoo to themselves. They carved pumpkins for all of the animals and had a science project competition of who could make enrichment that would keep the meerkats engaged for the longest. The team who hid mealworms in forage boxes won, of course.

"It's not going to evaporate." Finch chuckled, shaking her head at me. "You already know she's going to say yes."

"Oh god." I groaned, wiping a stray pumpkin seed and a thready bit of raw orange goo off my shorts. "I should go change first."

"She's not going to notice a pumpkin stain," Finch said. "And if we leave the decorations any longer, they'll probably blow away in the wind."

"It just needs to be perfect," I muttered.

"Perfect is overrated," Finch said. "You know Hananza will take happy, messy, and real over picture-perfect any day."

I sighed. It was true. Not one day together between Hannah and I could be classified as "picture-perfect," but we strung those days together into a perfectly and wonderfully chaotic life. I wouldn't have it any other way.

Every morning, I was excited to wake up to her, and every day I rediscovered the wonder of this place through Hannah's eyes. The person I was before felt so foreign to me now—so closed off from the world, too proud to let anyone help him, too afraid. But Hannah made me brave. Each day, I liked more and more who I was becoming because of who we were *together*.

Smiling to myself, I thought of all her many antics. How she grew from anxious apprentice to confident zookeeper. How she brought new ideas to the zoo much like her best friend, Dove. I never thought anyone could fit so seamlessly into our wild family, but Hannah made it look easy.

My hand nervously tapped my pocket again as we got up to the Jeep—*our Jeep*—and the treehouse playground above it. My siblings had helped me decorate it—stringing up Christmas lights and fake candles. Real candles surrounded by autumn leaves would've been a fire hazard from hell, and while Hannah's chaos brought me a lot of joy, I could just imagine her tripping over them and setting the whole place on fire.

We reached the Jeep, my breath steaming and whorling through the cold air.

Finch's wind-chapped cheeks dimpled as she clapped me on the back. "It's going to be great, bro, don't stress."

I pulled out the ring again and inspected it—a cushion-cut diamond on a pearl-studded silver band. "It's going to be great," I echoed, reassuring myself as I rehearsed my speech over and over in my head.

I was just about to put the ring back when Hannah popped through the gap in the bamboo hedges and asked, "What's going to be great?"

Finch and I jolted as the radio scratched with Crane's voice saying, "The Eagle is flying the nest."

Finch rolled her eyes and grabbed her radio. "No shit, Sherlock," she snapped. "The Eagle is already here. You and Heron were supposed to be keeping an eye on the Eagle and giving us a fucking heads-up!"

Another radio beeped and Mom's voice said, "No swearing over the radio." She paused for a beat before adding, "What did she say? Please tell me you took photos?"

I cringed, looking at Hannah, who just stared at me wide-eyed, her mouth in a perfect O. Walter barked from the little dog stroller that Hannah used to walk him around the zoo. At this point, the old man had lived double the average life expectancy for a cocker spaniel, and I thought he might be too stubborn to ever die. He was still feisty as ever, making our cottage at the zoo the perfect home for him. We could handle wild animals after all.

I looked from the ring still in my grasp to Hannah's shocked—and maybe slightly horrified—face. My stomach plummeted. Oh god, what if she said no?

Whale hello there
TICKLE ISLAND ZOO
Shop

Chapter Sixty

Hannah

I gasped, pointing at the ring in Hawk's hand. "What is that?"

"Haze," he said calmly, giving me a soft smile as he took a step toward me like I was a spooked giraffe.

"Oh god, don't do it in front of me," Finch said, fleeing back through the copse of trees but then stopping just on the other side so she was still in earshot.

"Please tell me that is not a crazy expensive ring, Hawk Simon Lachlan," I said, holding my hands up to my mouth. "How much did that thing cost? Too much. Look at it, it's huge!"

It was only then that I noticed the lights strung up along the Jeep, the candles dotting the space, the beautiful carpet of autumn leaves that someone must've raked up from the rain-forest walkthrough to blanket the normally bare ground in a layer of orange and gold. One pumpkin even sat on the hood of the Jeep with a wedding ring carved into the side of it, and I had a sneaking suspicion that was Dove's doing. It made sense now why she wouldn't show me her carving during our art project with the school.

Holy Halloween. Was he going to propose? Right now? On today of all days? The photo on my phone burned a hole in my shorts as I gaped at Hawk, who smiled at my bewilderment.

He was going to propose!

That would explain why Crane and Heron kept popping up from the shrubbery as Walter and I took our evening walk around the zoo.

Hawk shook his head with a nervous laugh. "You're angry at me because the ring is too big, aren't you?"

"I'm serious!" I bounced up and down, unable to hide the megawatt smile on my face. Was I laughing or crying? I didn't know. *He was proposing!* I wanted to skip around. Was skipping an appropriate response to a proposal? Probably not. *Dammit, Hannah! Focus!* "If it's more than five hundred dollars, I'm going to be so mad at you. We could use that money for the animals. Think of the marmosets! We could buy them a new water fountain!"

Hawk only smirked back at me. "I promise you, the marmosets can still get a new water fountain."

I narrowed my eyes and pointed a finger at him. "That money goes to the zoo," I insisted again.

"And if it's a family heirloom?"

"Oh, well . . ." I shifted my weight, bouncing between nerves and excitement. "That would be okay. I guess."

I loved the way Hawk looked at me like my chaos was adorable, like he loved everything that I was. "Good," he said simply.

A voice from beyond the trees called, "Say something more romantic than 'good,' for fuck's sake, Hawk—"

"Finch!" Hawk shouted.

"Okay, fine! I'm taking my girl into town anyway," she called. "See you tomorrow."

"Have fun," Hawk said, waving his hands, trying to shoo her away.

"Make good choices," I called.

"Just what I needed, another sister," Finch muttered sarcastically.

"You love it," I sang back.

"Welcome to the family, Hannah!" Finch shouted, her voice farther away now.

Hawk turned back to me and shook out his hands. His nerves were adorable. "Okay, I nearly threw up on the way over here. So let me say my speech before I pass out," he said, getting down on one knee.

Even though I knew it was coming, my eyes still welled. The sight of him down on one knee, holding up that beautiful, impractical diamond at me had the tears threatening to spill.

"Hannah Rebecca Murphy," he said, taking a deep breath, his throat bobbing. "These last few years have been the happiest of my life. You came crashing into all of our lives, both literally and figuratively"—we both chuckled as I wiped tears from my eyes—"and nothing has ever been the same. I thought it would ease over time, this feeling like my heart's exploding out of my chest every time you smile. But every day, I fall more and more madly in love with you. I can't imagine my life without you. I want to wake up every day to your smile and your demands for coffee."

He laughed softly then continued, "I want to watch thousands more sunrises with you. I want us to help each other dust off the cobwebs of all the years of memories we've shared. Let's grow a family together, grow old together." He scrunched his nose as his eyes misted, and that just made my tears pour faster. I loved when he was overcome with emotion, loved that he allowed himself to feel everything so much more deeply than before. "I want to dedicate every day of my life to being worthy of your brilliance and your warmth and your love. Will you marry me?"

I had to sniff several times before I could get out the word, "Yes."

Hawk leapt up and wrapped me in his arms, swinging me off my feet as he buried his face in my neck. We held each other through tears and laughter for several seconds before he finally set me down and kissed me deeply.

"That was a really good speech," I said, clearing my throat and trying to regain composure as he slid the beautiful ring onto my finger. It was a gorgeous diamond and pearl ring that wiggled over my knuckle and perfectly hugged my ring finger. "The best speech ever, actually."

"Yeah?" He smiled and kissed me again. "Whew," he added with relief. "I'm glad you liked it."

"I particularly liked the part about growing a family," I said, smirking at him. "Especially now."

Hawk pulled back to give me a questioning stare. "What does that mean?"

"I guess you're not the only one with a surprise today," I said, my eyes getting watery again. *Damn these hormones!* I was blubbery on a normal day, but I was hopeless now.

I'd been racking my brain over the course of the day to come up with some elaborate plan to tell him, but I knew the second I saw him, I'd spill the news. I couldn't keep secrets from him, especially not this one. Luckily, unbeknownst to me, Hawk had been avoiding me for a surprise of his own.

I pulled out my phone and opened it to a photo of a positive pregnancy test I'd taken that morning.

Hawk's chest heaved. "You're pregnant?" His face flushed as he wiped tears from his eyes, shock and disbelief on his face. I nodded, and he cupped my cheeks and pulled me into another fierce kiss. Our lips barely met as neither of us could contain our smiles. He dropped his forehead to mine and scrunched his eyes closed. I soothed a hand down his back and kissed him again.

"Are you happy?" I murmured against his warm, tear-stained lips.

"Really happy," he said. He shook his head as if he couldn't believe it. "We're going to have a baby," he whispered, still shocked. Then his expression morphed into a bright, beaming smile. "We're going to have a baby! There's going to be a mini you running around this place." I laughed at that. He squeezed me tighter and kissed me again. "What have I gotten myself into?"

I slung my arms around his neck, lifting up on my tiptoes to brush a soft kiss on his mouth. "You work with lions and tigers and bears for a living. Afraid you can't handle a little version of me?"

"The most dangerous animal in the zoo—a toddler." He grinned, kissing me one last time before dropping his chin to the top of my head.

"I love you, Hannah, fiancée, mother of my child, love of my life," he murmured.

"I love you too," I whispered back. "With every single piece of my heart."

The radio crackled from nearby, and Wren's voice came over it. "Okay, they're still hugging, so I think she said yes."

Hawk and I looked up at the same time and saw Wren standing in the treehouse above us, a camera with a giant zoom lens in her hand.

"Some privacy, please?" Hawk asked with a chuckle.

"You'll be happy when you have these gorgeous photos to look back on," she replied with a grin. "Congratulations, by the way."

Hawk waved his youngest sister off with a laugh.

The gibbons sang their evening love song as the sun set over the park. I tucked my head into Hawk's shoulder and a steadiness settled over me. I'd always needed to jump from place to place to get any excitement in my life. Now, all of the excitement came to me. I felt more firmly planted than ever before. Hawk's warm breath whispered into my hair, and I knew once again that I was exactly where I wanted to be, with the exact person who fit me like my very own puzzle piece.

I grabbed Hawk's radio and spoke into it. "I said yes."

The radio whizzed with cheers and hoots of congratulations.

"Can you all come up to the Jeep, please?" I said, looking at Hawk with a smile. "We have one more thing to tell you."

Crane's voice came over the radio. "Heron, if she's pregnant, you owe me twenty bucks."

I shook my head. "What have I gotten myself into?" I echoed.

"You love it." Hawk laughed. "Welcome to the family, haze."

THE END

Want to read Hawk and Hannah's wedding and get all the latest Zoo news? Scan the QR code on the next page!

SIGN UP
FOR ZOO
NEWS

ALSO BY

Ali K. Mulford Books:

The Prickle Island Zoo Series:

She's a Keeper

Easy Tiger

Party Animal

Maple Hollow Series:

Pumpkin Spice & Poltergeist

A.K. Mulford Series:

The Five Crowns of Okrith

The Okrith Novellas

The Golden Court Trilogy

Acknowledgments

To all of the real life people and animals who made it into this story! Since I was a kid, I always wanted to either work with animals or write books. I've loved having this opportunity to bridge the world between my two great passions!

Thank you to all of my amazing readers for coming on this new adventure with me. I am so humbled by your support and all the ways you champion my books out in the world!

Thank you so much to all of my Patrons! I love writing new stories, commissioning spicy art, and getting to connect with you on Patreon! A very special thank you to Val, Lindsay, Samantha, Bri, Divya, Kat, Stacy, JeNaya, Lauren, Alyssa, Lauren, Myth, Audrey, Mandy, Leigh, Jaime, Kelly, Hannah, Sarah, Amy, Marissa, Ciara, Linda, and Virginia!

Thank you to Sara Kingsley from Adore Editing and Norma from Norma's Nook Editing

Thank you to Enni from Yummy Book Covers for designing the gorgeous covers for this series

Thank you to Holly Dunn for designing the Zoo Map

To my PAs, Treece and Hannah, thank you for helping me launch this new pen name and keeping Team Mulford going! I love working with you!

To my book wifey and publishing bestie, Kate, thank you for formatting this book, designing the gorgeous interiors to this book, and running the Zoo Gift Shop!

About the Author

Ali K. Mulford (also known by their bestselling fantasy pen name **A.K. Mulford**) is a rom-com author and former wildlife biologist who swapped rehabilitating monkeys for writing novels. A US and NZ citizen, Mulford now lives in Australia rearing two human primates, writing lovable characters, and making ridiculous TikToks (@akmulfordauthor).

www.akmulford.com

www.ingramcontent.com/pod-product-compliance
Lightning Source LLC
Chambersburg PA
CBHW050953210726
48287CB00004B/1211